Prais‹

Winner 2013 Golden Crown Li...   ...on

Winner 2013 Moonbeam Children's Book Award ... ion—
Mature Issues

Finalist 2013 Lambda Literary Award

Huffington Post's 21 Best Transgender and Gender Nonconforming Books for
Kids

"It's rare to read a novel that's involving, tender, thought-provoking and
informative. Rachel Gold does all this in 'Being Emily.'"

-*Twin Cities Pioneer Press*

"Rachel Gold has crafted an extraordinarily poignant novel in 'Being Emily.'"

-*Lambda Literary Review*

"[Being Emily] feels incredibly honest, and there are moments of joy, anger,
and sorrow, laced together in a way that will make you cry and laugh along
with the characters. It doesn't shy away from the hardship but it also doesn't
make the claim that *this hard stuff is all a trans person's life is ever*."

-*YA Pride*

"...it's a wonderful read for any teen (or anyone else) dealing with gender
issues or the question of nonconformity ... [Gold] does a fabulous job of
explaining what it means to know in your heart that something's not right,
that the body you were born with doesn't match the true person inside."

-Ellen Krug, *Lavender Magazine*

"Certainly, this book is going to be a fantastic resource for teens and youth
who find themselves in Emily's shoes. However, a book like *Being Emily* is also
an excellent place to start for cisgendered adults who want to be allies to the
trans community, or even people who are uncomfortable with the subject."

-*Twin Cities Daily Planet*

"Being Emily is a wonderful, valuable and very contemporary book that I
believe will change minds and save lives. I was very much affected by the story,
which feels piercingly real in all its details."

-Katherine V. Forrest, author, editor and
Lesbian Literature Trailblazer Award winner

being emily

rachel gold

BELLA
BOOKS
2018

Bella Books, Inc.
P.O. Box 10543
Tallahassee, FL 32302

Printed in the United States of America on acid-free paper.

First Bella Books Edition 2018

Editor: Katherine V. Forrest
Cover design: Kristin Smith
Photograph credit: Sergey Smolyaninov
Cover Designer: Judith Fellows
ISBN: 978-1-59493-598-5

This edition has been augmented with substantial additional text and contains editorial changes from the original.

Other Bella Books by Rachel Gold

Just Girls
My Year Zero
Nico & Tucker

About the Author

Raised on world mythology, fantasy novels, comic books and magic, Rachel is well suited for her careers in marketing and writing. She is the author of multiple queer and trans young adult novels, including *Just Girls*, *My Year Zero*, and *Nico & Tucker*. She has a B.A. in English and Religious Studies from Macalester College and an MFA in Writing from Hamline University, St. Paul, MN.

Rachel also spent a decade as a reporter in the LGBTQ community where she learned many of her most important lessons about being a person from the trans community. In addition, she's an all-around geek and avid gamer, and teaches a writing class for teens that is itself a game.

For more information visit: www.rachelgold.com

Acknowledgments

Deep gratitude goes to Stephanie Burt for making this edit fun and helping in more ways than I can name. A huge thank you to Katherine V. Forrest for editing this book twice and pushing for the new edition to be as good as possible! Also to Elyse Pine, MD, and Troy R Weber-Brown, MS, LMF, whose expertise has been so helpful and whose friendship I value.

Many thanks to the college and university professors who have taught this book in their classes, and particularly to those who invited me to speak to your classes or shared feedback, especially Lisa Hager, Laina Villeneuve and Brandy T. Wilson, PhD. And thank you to Cheryl A. Head for helping me bring more diversity to this edition.

I'm very grateful to the many members of the trans community who were generous with their time, stories, and love. Especially my aunties Kate Bornstein and Rachel Pollack: growing up would've been much harder without you. Also much love to my former roommate Scott, Debbie Davis of the Gender Education Center, and the members of GenderPeace, especially Elise Heise.

I also want to thank my family members who gave me emotional, editorial, and material support: my parents and brother, my grandmom Claire and my great-aunt Rhoda. I am blessed to have a family that's even more excited about the 2018 edition than they were about the first edition!

Thank you to my amazing former coworkers for edits on the first edition: Wendy Nemitz, Dawn Wagenaar, Liz Kuntz, Christine Nelson, Kathy Zappa and Sara Bracewell. I'm also grateful to the members of my very long-running *World of Warcraft* guild who don't care what gender I play, and who put up with me missing raids to finish the first edition edits—and to the many gamers who have created LGBTQ-friendly places in game.

A huge thank you to my amazing set of last-minute readers for the final round of edits the first time and my repeat readers: Jeni Mullins, Nathalie Isis Crowley and my dear friend Alia, who holds the record for reading the most drafts.

And of course I give my gratitude and love to a certain someone who kept bringing me soup while I worked: this would not have been possible without you.

For Elise Heise and all the Emilys in the world—past, present and future—we need you.

INTRODUCTION

This is the book.

I'll start again. There isn't just one book that explained me to myself—there never has been, and my gender, my embodiment, are far from the whole of me. Also, Emily is in high school. I was already a grown-up when I came out, to myself and to my loved ones, not just as someone who had feelings about gender, who once thought they might be trans, but who well and truly was.

And yet. This is the book: the book where I saw the part of myself, for real, full-on, that I had only seen in profile, or in half-light, for so long. This is the book that said to me, in fiction, what I had waited to hear, and strained to hear, and sought and not quite found, in other books, and in real life: *yes, you're a girl.* Or: *yep, you're supposed to be a girl.* Or: *Okay, you wished you could be a girl, consistently, for most of your life; you resented, and wanted to alter, whatever marked you as a guy; you're already a girl in some ways, and you can be a woman in the others, if you want. You're not alone. You won't lose everything. It's not too late. Some people—people you are going to want to meet—already understand.*

Maybe you know somebody who needs that story too. Maybe they're just like Emily, or not like Emily; maybe they're 12, or 18, or 68. Maybe you are that somebody. Or maybe you're looking for a good story about some teens who *aren't* like you. Rachel Gold has now told a few pretty great stories about teens and people not long out of their teens. This is the one that comes first.

Like all Gold's novels, *Being Emily* shows us trans and queer young people trying to live with one another, and maybe to undermine patriarchy together, finding and building better lives. More than the others, though (with the partial exception of *Nico & Tucker*), Gold's first published novel clearly and centrally belongs to the genre of the what-to-do YA, the information-bearing, instructional, linearly plotted novel that shows readers what we might do and how to get help if we see ourselves, or our friends, in its characters.

When the first edition of this book appeared in 2012, that kind of instruction was not only achingly needed (it still is) but—especially for younger readers—shockingly hard to find.

Being Emily is far from the first book—or first YA book—with trans girl characters, but it appears to be the first novel in English (it's surely the first YA novel) with a trans girl's voice at its center, the first one you could give a trans girl and feel good about the idea that she'll see herself in it. (As I did; as I do.) Earlier novels made trans characters into magical helpers, or obstacles, or problems, or (at best) grown-ups who had already learned to inhabit particular urban queer subcultures. Emily is none of those things: she's a problem for other people, but in the way that all of us can be problems for friends or families. She is not A Problem, but a person who seeks love and makes decisions herself.

That's in part because we see through Emily's eyes. Teachers warn beginning writers not to start with their narrator before a mirror since that's a clichéd way to show us a narrator's face. But Emily looks in the mirror and sees…nothing: "I refused to look at myself." There's only "the version of me that didn't really exist," the male version named Chris. It's a joke, and more than a joke, about how we see ourselves—or try to see ourselves—in stories, as well as a point about what trans people (in this case, trans girls) weren't seeing, and need to see.

Three chapters later she does see herself. In her locked bedroom, through the clothes she's chosen rather than the body that she has been given, Emily "slowly became visible." By that point we know we are **inside a novel made so that trans girls can see ourselves**: and it gets better. I reread Chapter Four this year (that's the one with the duffel bag) in a coffee shop with Grimes's "Flesh without Blood" blasting out of the ceiling monitors: I had to try hard not to get up and dance.

Emily also sees herself in roles created by works of art, works that she can share with other characters. When Emily-as-Chris and Claire are "flopped out on her bed together reading a poem and talking about it, I forgot that I had to play a boy and got to be a person for a while." That's why she has to come out, but also why she doesn't want to come out: "I couldn't risk losing that." I've been there too.

What's better than poetry, if you need a body other than the body that the world has insisted you have? Role-playing games, of course: Emily is a reader, she saw herself first in the Oz books, but she's also, deeply, a gamer. Gameworlds allow her "to step into a world fully female." Gameworlds, too, are spaces we can inhabit "where you yourself are never quite yourself/And did not want nor have to be," to quote the great cisgender (non-trans) poet Wallace Stevens. Gameworlds are like ours, but not; novels are like our life, but not quite our life; we can escape into them, or learn from the analogies we find in them, and if they are good enough, we can do both.

Being Emily can let you do both. It can also show you what it's like to change your mind about what's possible. Claire tells Emily (whom she knows as Chris), "It's not like you can turn into a girl or anything." Maybe this Claire doesn't know; or forgot, that trans people exist, which is plausible for a bright high school junior in exurban Minnesota in 2008. The Claire of 2018 might say the same words, but mean something else. Maybe: "it's not like *you* can turn into a girl." Trans people might already exist, for her, but elsewhere, as exotic grown-ups, on TV.

And it's important to know what Claire knows. For every reader who sees herself in Emily, there is at least one who sees their own picture in Claire (possibly because their Emily gave them the novel). *Being Emily* says to the Claires, and also to the dads, that we know they are trying; that they are not bad people because they can't do everything Emily wants, make every recommended adjustment, at once. "Could she ever stop thinking of him as 'him,' she wondered?" Maybe she could, but not without forgiving herself for having to try, and for sometimes getting it wrong. As for the sexy parts of their connection, Claire doesn't know if she wants to stay with Emily; she doesn't know what she wants. And that's okay.

Nor does she know what God wants. People who insist, because they've been hurt by religion, that religion as such is hurtful or homophobic or transphobic or exclusionary or useless, are almost as wrong as people who call all bicycles evil because they were hit by a bike. That said, there are a lot of bad bicyclists: a lot of us have been hurt by what living humans think that long-dead humans, and the God or gods that they worshipped, enjoin or forbid. Claire doesn't just model how a cisgender friend, or lover, accepts coming out as trans (gradually, patiently, with time off for herself); she models faith. "Her work was to have faith, and not be a blaming jerk like Job's friends."

Most novels have characters who behave like readers. Emily is one, and Claire is another: she has to learn to read Emily correctly, almost as cisgender readers learn to read—and learn about trans people from—*Being Emily*. Natalie, however, is more like an author: she already knows what many readers will learn; she invites the reader-figures on a journey, and her invitations drive parts of the plot. She's there to help answer—but cannot, on her own, answer—the questions we ask. Now that I know who I am, and have some idea where I might be going, will my loved ones come along? Will I be physically safe? How will I know? Can I trust the professionals who say they have my interests at heart? "What's it like taking the hormones?"

The general answer to all of those questions is: unless you try, you'll never know. And Emily—with help—learns how she can try. She tries to become herself, which means that she tries to be seen as herself, not only in her own eyes but also in the eyes of others. If you don't care how you're seen in the eyes of others—if you're resigned to a life where nobody sees the real you—maybe you need to find other others. Maybe you need to find your Natalie: someone who has been a few steps ahead, or shown others a way.

If you are an Emily, unless you are very unlucky, coming out as trans will let you make new friends, and the pretransition friends (and colleagues and maybe lovers) who stick with you—your Claires—may take a while to learn that you won't abandon them, that you can (and you will) run out of hours in the day, but you will not run out of love. The Claires of this life have done a lot for the Emilys, especially early in the coming-out process. If you are an Emily, remember to give your Claire their own space and time for self-discovery, hours or days or months when he or she or they can be the protagonist and you can be the ally. That's a novel I'd like to read too.

But I'm me—I'm an Emily; I cried all over a Kindle screen when I realized how thoroughly I am an Emily—and thank God, or thank the gods, or thank the forces of chance, or the good fortune that comes from Minnesota, because exactly when I needed them I found sentences like this one: "It was like sitting in a dark room for months and then suddenly having the sun fall through an open window." That's not about hormones, or winning a legal battle, or making irrevocable decisions; it's about how it feels when somebody else sees you as girl for the very first time. (It's important enough that Gold nearly repeats the scene: I, too, was surprised when I learned how good it felt when a store clerk called me "Miss.")

Part of growing up is learning how much other people are like you; part of coming out (as anything, really, but especially as trans) is realizing how most other people are not. "There had been so many years of pretense that I guess I didn't realize how different it made me to always be pretending": that's in Emily's teen voice, but it's a sentiment that fits the lived experience of many adults.

That good fit makes for one reason so many older readers stay with, or return to, or discover, YA. The rules and conventions of YA fiction have evolved to fit the experience of coming out, of becoming yourself, at whatever age. Those rules and conventions also make YA, in general, antitragic—its endings can be inconclusive or clear, but they are rarely grim tableaux of characters resigned to the way things are. (Could things have worked out worse for a real-life Emily than they do in the novel? Of course they could—but we have newspaper stories for that.) It's also a genre that finds it easy to fold in concise and practical instructions: how to handle therapists, what to expect when you first buy makeup, "things you can do before your parents know." Reading this novel is, itself, one of the things you can do before your parents know.

There are other things you might be doing, things many parents would rather not know; Emily and Claire have a deeply loyal, realistically and sometimes uncomfortably sexualized, romance that looks just right to me. "It was easier to be sexual without the constant reminder that my body wasn't right." They're also gamers: games, role-playing, fiction, "often felt more real than my real life." That feeling may, or may not, go away. (For more on the merits of gaming, and more on trans and queer sexuality, consider Gold's later novels, especially *Nico & Tucker* and *My Year Zero*.)

I have been describing the reactions, ideas and feelings that I had while reading Gold's first novel for the first time, and, also, the way I felt while rereading it. There's another feeling I had *after* reading it: it's the feeling the great literary critic Eve Sedgwick described in her essay "How to Bring Your Kids Up Gay," which is—despite the title—possibly the first really thoughtful treatment of trans or potentially trans kids and teens in the academic literary world.

It may seem a bit dated; bear with me. Sedgwick's 1991 essay addressed the now-bizarre, distressing, not-quite-there attitude many psychologists and psychiatrists took, in the late 1970s and 1980s, towards gender-divergent kids: they wanted to show that gay male adults were okay (when earlier psychiatry called gay men sick), without seeming to encourage gayness. Those psychologists and psychiatrists therefore decided that masculine adult gay men were healthy, while femme-acting men and boys (some of whom were no doubt trans)—well, they were the real problem; they, or we, were sick, and needed a cure. (In other words, *Being Emily*'s Dr. Webber.)

These unprofessional adult professionals were not only (as we would now say) erasing trans people; they were saying, tacitly, that they wanted "the dignified treatment of already-gay people" (Sedgwick's words), but that they did not want there to be any more. Against this kind of nonsense, Sedgwick (writing in 1991!) described "many people's felt desire or need that there be gay people in the immediate world." (Later she might have said "queer people.") Sedgwick, and her favorite authors, did not simply want us treated justly; she wanted and needed us to exist.

And that—for the first time, though not the last, in YA; for one of the first times in all of American fiction—is the way that all of Rachel Gold's novels, starting with this one, treat trans and gender-divergent people, especially young people. We are not a problem, or a conundrum, or a failure that somebody needs to fix, or a population (like stray pets) our parents and teachers are obligated to protect, now that we (alas) exist: we are one of the reasons that the world is good. If the world we inherit doesn't recognize that, we'll fix it or build a better one. And fiction—especially fiction written for young readers—has to be one of the tools we can use.

Most parts of *Being Emily* address the feelings that come up when you come out, and the feelings (including Hulk-like anger) that come up when you are not permitted to be who you are. Other parts address particular arguments we can have with ourselves, or arguments that we might encounter from others (who are, sometimes, just concern-trolling), against coming out. *Is coming out, or transitioning, selfish?* No more so than any other life choice that isn't entirely self-sacrifice. *Why do you care how other people see you, whether and where you get to wear a dress, whether your breasts will ever be real?* Because it's terrible to go through the day or the year with the feeling your body is wrong; because most of us learn to see ourselves by thinking about how other people will see us; because that kind of feedback loop, powered by our brains' mirror neurons, won't go away. *Is it consumerist to go to a mall and drop cash on makeup?* Is it consumerist to buy—or, really, to want—anything at all?

Emily knows what she wants; she just doesn't know how to get it, or what it will cost, or how long it is likely to take. It's okay if you, yourself, are not yet sure. It's also okay—and you can still learn, or see yourself, in Emily's discoveries—if who you are and what you want does not fit into any familiar boxes. Some trans people (me, for example) are binary: we are women, even though the world said we were men, or the other way around—the world put us in the wrong box. Some of us are deeply nonbinary: neither box fits, and both of them hurt. Some of us know we're trans (we've been in the wrong box) but aren't sure what kind of trans (what box or set of boxes might be right): we have to move between the boxes, try out various places to stand, climb up, jump around, and see. (If you're genderfluid, no one box will do: I know people who feel very male on a given day, very female on the next—they have friends who understand how they feel, too.)

There's now a short stack of books—including some joyful books—about all those kinds of motion and labels and boxes. *Being Emily* names a few of them, and Gold has written a few more. I'd now add the novels of April Daniels, the essays of S. Bear Bergman, and a whole box-within-the-box of poetry, by Cat Fitzpatrick, Cam Awkward-Rich, Trace Peterson, TC Tolbert, and many others. There are even anthologies and magazines devoted to trans poetry, like Peterson and Tolbert's ample *Troubling the Line* and H. Melt's great new *Subject to Change*. All of these writers might help you, too, get out of the wrong boxes, or imagine the right ones.

Gender, moreover, is only one set of boxes, one category around which we organize, not just sexual, but social life. We live, all of us, in other boxes too, affinity groups or institutional categories created by things like taste (science fiction, or science fiction conventions), age (11th grade or senior citizens), race, ethnicity, profession, future profession, locale. In categorizing people, we place them in groups; we try to see who belongs together, and we hope we can feel we belong. "How could I make my way in the world," Emily asks, "if I couldn't stand up for myself?" But no one should have to learn to stand up on their own; we find our people, real people and fictional characters, along with our organizations and our safe physical spaces and our games and our alternate worlds that help us with the real one.

Being Emily, as much as any one book of prose, has been that help. It also moved me to tears—before I started hormones. (Now scrambled eggs, stoplights, and bad jokes about superheroes also move me to tears: that's what it's like being on hormones—and it feels marvelous.) Someday this novel may feel like a historical document, a moving story about how a girl and her allies confronted antagonists that no longer exist. Until that day it's going to be a source of hope and possibility, as well as a source of practical advice—and, in the very best possible sense, it is likely to make lots of other girls cry.

Stephanie Burt
Belmont and Cambridge, Mass./ Harvard University
December 2017

CHAPTER ONE

.

The noise of the alarm cut through the peaceful darkness of sleep like wind heralding a winter storm. I reached over to smack the snooze button and hit the bedside table. I'd been up half the night so I'd moved the alarm to my dresser to prevent snooze abuse. Once I'd lurched across the room to stop the grating sound, I was upright and might as well shower and get it over with.

I refused to look at myself in the bathroom mirror. During those first foggy minutes of morning I could keep being the person I'd seen blurrily during the late, dark hours when I was alone and safe. I wanted to be myself for a little while longer.

Under the hot stream of water I kept my eyes closed. It felt like I was washing someone else's body. Even after sixteen years I had moments where I couldn't understand how I got here or how such a mistake could've be made. I knew what I was, and this tall, angular body was not that.

As I scrubbed, I flip-flopped on my decision to talk to my best friend and sort of girlfriend. "Sort of " because Claire was dating the version of me that didn't really exist. I liked her enough that I felt bad about deceiving her, maybe more than anyone else, and I guess that's one reason why I decided to tell her first. I'd tried to tell two other friends, years ago, but one stopped talking to me and the other laughed so hard I said I'd been kidding. Maybe I should've stopped trying to tell anyone, but the truth welled up in me so thickly I couldn't hold it back much longer.

Like every other morning that winter, it was dark outside when I woke up and the window barely hinted at light when I got out of the shower. Time to confront the dozens of outfits that I could wear but didn't want to. Worn down by years of dressing up as a boy, I'd pared my clothing options down to three basic outfits: jeans and T-shirt, jeans and sweater, jeans and button-down shirt (for days when I was supposed to look dressy).

But what do you wear to tell your girlfriend that the boy she's dating is really a girl inside? Grandma Em had sent me a cashmere sweater two Christmases ago that I hoped would give me some courage. I loved the softness of it, even if the olive color wasn't one I'd pick for myself; it made my skin look gray. I put it on, ran my fingers through my hair and went down to get cereal.

Dad leaned against the wall by the door, pulling on his massive, thickly lined boots. Barely taller than me, but inches of muscle wider, Dad's dense body was wrapped in a gray flannel-lined shirt and heavy, brown Carhartt jacket. Dad was a Carhartt junky and wore their work pants in olive or tan every day, even when he wasn't on a job. He owned four of their fifteen-pocket vests: two in "moss" and two in "shadow."

"Lookin' good, Chris," he said. "Swim meet?"

"Last of the season," I told him. "Claire's coming."

His eyes went unreadable. I wasn't sure if he liked her or not, but I think he was glad I had a girlfriend this year. He nodded, waved and slipped out into the snow.

In our house, the kitchen is to the left of the front door when you're coming in, and to the right is the living room, which turns into a den at the back of the house. The kitchen opens into an eating nook, big enough for a table of four. The house used to be a three-bedroom until Dad and his buddies built the addition over the garage that's my bedroom. That gave him and Mom one bedroom for paperwork and crafts.

On my way to the kitchen table I grabbed milk and cereal and mumbled a "good morning" to Mom, who stood at the counter assembling sandwiches. Her turquoise skirt suit was the wrong color for her skin and gave her a pale, tired sheen. Or maybe she was tired.

At the table, I poured milk into a bowl and then dumped a few cups of Cheerios on top. I don't know why people pour milk over cereal, that makes it get soggy so much more quickly than if you put the milk on the bottom. Mom finished making our lunches and set the two bags on the table as my nine-year-old brother, Mikey, blew into the room. His short brown hair stuck out in all directions, not that he cared. He grabbed a bowl, snatched the milk from in front of me, and poured it over his heap of cereal until the whole mass threatened to spill over the side.

Mom tried to fix his hair while he ate and managed to get the worst bits to lie down. "I'll probably be working late today," she told us. "But your dad will be home."

"I'm going to Claire's after the meet," I said.

"Dad's not cooking . . . is he?" Mikey asked.

Mom smiled. "No, there's lasagna in the fridge. Chris, what time are you coming home?"

"Eightish," I told her.

"You make sure you get your homework done, okay? I don't want you playing computer games all night or whatever it is that takes up all your time."

"Yeah."

"Is Claire's mother going to be there?" she asked.

Claire is the only child of a divorced mother, which worries my parents for reasons I could not begin to imagine. I think they assume that Claire and I spend every spare moment we're alone at her house having sex and smoking pot while selling illegal weapons via the Internet.

"Yeah," I told her, though it was a lie. Claire's mom usually got home around six or seven at night. "She gets home around five." As I said it, my stomach tightened. So much of my life was a lie, I hated to add to that pile of deception. But I'd hate life more if I didn't have the relative freedom of being at Claire's house.

I finished my cereal and looked pointedly at the clock on the microwave. "Gotta run." I grabbed the lunch bag and stuffed it in my backpack, kissed Mom's cheek, and made for the front entryway.

Winter in Minnesota is its own creature. Like a wild animal, you have to treat it with respect, which includes wearing a down coat and huge boots from November through March. I toed the line on those items because I refused to wear a hat if the temperature was above zero. With a little bit of gel, my dark brown hair held its natural curl, which I loved. Thanks to the popularity of Orlando Bloom and the long hairstyles in the *Pirates of the Caribbean* movies, I'd persuaded Dad that it was okay for me to keep it a few inches long, even touching my collar in the back. A hat inevitably crushed the cute little curls, and so the hat spent most of winter on the closet shelf.

I looped a scarf around my neck twice and tucked the ends down into my jacket. Then I threw my backpack over my shoulder and pushed out into the wind.

February is bleak the whole month. The days are short and cold, the nights long and frigid, the snow is feet deep and the wind has a razor's edge. I'd turned sixteen last spring and Dad insisted on getting me a car. His passion in life is restoring classic cars. He offered me a Mustang, which I managed to dodge by pointing out a '56 Chrysler 300B in bad shape that we could restore together. Granted I had to spend the summer working on a car with my dad while he called me "son" every five minutes, but on the bright side, I got to drive a tri-toned, candy apple red, classy, chromed-out car, rather than a dirt-ball, I-watch-pro-wrestling mobile.

The car definitely helped my reputation around school as a cool kid, and Claire reminded me weekly how lucky I was. I was a good-sized kid for my age, a little above average for the guys in my class and much too above average for the girls, while Claire described herself as "a runt." She's five-feet-four and skinny. I tried to tell her that if she'd stop dyeing her hair goth-black she might have better social standing, but she accused me of not understanding girls. Girls, she explained, are mean. If it wasn't her hair that stood out, the rest of the girls would find another reason to harass her.

"I'm an outcast," she said. "They're like wolves; they can smell it on me."

My car was an ice block when I started it, and I sat in the driveway for five minutes, freezing my butt off while it warmed up. I could've gone back in the house, but Mom would try to have a conversation with me about school or Claire. She and Mikey would be out in a few minutes so she could drop him at the elementary school on her way to work. She's the secretary for a financial planning office. Most days she works from nine to three, but once or twice a week they keep her later.

When the car had warmed up enough, I pulled out of the driveway and pointed it toward school. Like a well-trained horse, it knew the way and drove itself while I listened to the radio. In Liberty we get four stations, two from the Cities and two Christian stations. That meant my choices were "Top 50" and "Hip Hop/Dance." I chose the latter.

Liberty-Mayer High School served parts of three counties west of the Twin Cities and had about five hundred students in a long, low, tan brick building. Being in outstate Minnesota we had about twelve students of color and the classes were, for the most part, equally colorless. I pulled into the student lot and slogged across three hundred feet of trampled snow to the front doors. A blast of hot air hit and made me peel off the scarf as I headed for my locker.

A couple of the guys on the swim team shouted greetings and I yelled back with the automated voice program that takes over as soon as I get to school. I hardly have to think about it anymore. My larynx is programmed with all the appropriate responses, and I don't even pay attention. It's like I wrote all the code years ago and now my brain just reads it:

/run: greet teammate
1. speak: "Hey man, how's it going?"
2. joke about: a) sports, b) cars, c) weather, d) class
3. make inarticulate sound of agreement
4. run line 2 again
5. make gesture: a) grin, b) shrug, c) playful hit
6. repeat 3–5 until bell rings

My mornings are drab. I start with science, a scheduling glitch that is an offense against all night owls, and then go to American history. Between history and study hall I usually pass Claire in the hall and she tucks a note into my pocket.

That day the note said: "Hey boo, are we on after the meet? Mom's working late. I'll see you after school." One tiny piece of notebook paper and my heart started racing again.

Sitting in the library for study hall, I tried to concentrate on schoolwork, but I had to figure out how to talk to Claire. I had plenty of "friends" from the guys on swim team to various kids I had class with, but Claire was the only person I felt excited to see on a regular basis. With the other kids it was too hard to keep up the pretense of being Chris all the time. My life could be worse, and if I lost my relationship with Claire, it would be. I didn't know how much worse I could handle, but if I didn't talk to someone soon there wouldn't be any of me left at all.

Claire breezily described herself as bisexual and she was the weirdest person other than me that I knew. But she'd never had a relationship with a girl…well, other than me, but I didn't really count because I looked like a boy to everyone. What if she didn't like girls as much as she thought she did? What if she stopped liking me?

I stared at the distant gray sky outside the library window. What was the worst that could happen? She could dump me and tell everyone at school and my parents. Then I'd either have to lie and say I made it all up as a joke, or run away.

I had to do this right.

There was no way I could use the library computers to research anything to help me come out. I'm sure the school monitored our computer use, and some other kid would probably walk by. All I needed was for one of the swim team guys to see COMING OUT AS TRANSGENDER in huge letters over my shoulder.

Opening my math book, I made my eyes focus on the hardest problems. That distracted me until the bell, and then math class itself kept me occupied until lunch. Unfortunately, Claire pulled fourth period lunch this year and I had fifth, so I sat with the swim guys or did homework at the table.

After lunch the tiredness from being up half the night caught up with me. Could I sleep through my sixth-period psych elective? The teacher was cool, but we'd been talking about schizophrenia for most of the week and I was over it. I leaned back in my chair, preparing for an eyes-open doze, when Mr. Cooper wrote two alarming words on the board: "Sex" and "Gender."

"Can anyone tell me the difference between these two?" he asked.

Mr. Cooper was a tall man with messy red-brown hair that my dad would call much too long, even though it only covered his ears and the back of his neck. He had super pale Irish coloring and a case of ruddy windburn on his cheeks, so I couldn't tell if this subject was making him blush as much as it made me. He stood with his hands clasped behind his back, his small gut pushed out, and shifted his weight from left to right and back again. But his eyes swept over the class calmly.

I could answer his question, but no way was I opening my mouth. A football kid in the front row volunteered, "Sex is what you do, gender is who you're doing it with."

Laughter all around.

Jessica, the blond girl who sat next to me and I think had a crush on me, rolled her eyes. "What a jerk," she whispered.

"For the next two weeks we're going to study different aspects of sex and gender," Mr. Cooper said. "I'm going to hand out permission slips you need to fill out in case any of your parents don't want you to hear about sex, as if that will stop you. We'll be talking about normal and abnormal sexuality, and we'll have speakers coming from OutFront Minnesota, an organization for lesbian, gay, bisexual, transgender, and queer equality."

I contemplated putting my head down on my desk and crying, but that would probably give me away as being the wrong gender. I pushed the permission slip into the front of my psych book. I'd forge the signature in study hall tomorrow. That was one conversation I didn't want to encourage with my folks.

Mr. Cooper spent the rest of the hour explaining how sex often referred to a person's physiological characteristics, while gender pointed to the psychological, cultural and learned aspects. I could have taught the class. Instead I sat very still and felt like someone had wrapped one hand around my heart and with the other hand crushed my throat.

CHAPTER TWO

English saved me. I had a chance to recover while Ms. Judson lectured on nineteenth-century British writers. Claire met me outside the classroom door afterward and gave me a quick hug and a kiss on the cheek. She was in the black knit sweater with textured lines down the arms that I liked.

I must have held her too close because she peered at me searchingly and asked, "You okay?"

"Long day," I evaded.

"I'll see you at the meet," Claire said, pulling her backpack strap up higher on her shoulder. "I'm driving over with the yearbook staff so we can have our meeting on the way."

Despite her protests about being unpopular, Claire was on the yearbook committee, in the drama club and in a poetry workshop that I sometimes attended. She said she got in the habit of extracurriculars in junior high when her mom wouldn't let her come home early and now she was hooked.

Liberty-Mayer High School didn't have an indoor pool, so we swam at the city pool after school most days until 5:30 or

6:00 p.m. It was a great way to avoid being stuck at home with my family. I'd get home in time for dinner, eat, and then go up to my room for homework until bedtime.

Tonight was the last of the boys' swim team's regular competitions, and our last chance to qualify for sectionals. I wasn't the only one on the team convinced that we didn't stand a chance. We competed against a lot of bigger high schools with their own pools and a larger student base to draw from. Plus our team wasn't particularly competitive, which was another reason I stayed on it. Our coach always emphasized beating our own personal times over beating another team, though that may have been a tactic to keep us from getting too depressed over our competitive futility.

I didn't mind being in the boys' locker room any more than I minded using the boys' restroom at school. I could robot through it. At least the locker room didn't have the same level of disgusting graffiti as the boys' restroom. I don't know why guys are so obsessed with their junk that they have to draw it all over the stalls. I lucked out in terms of not being embarrassed because I'm not attracted to guys, so the only awkward part in the locker room was changing into my swim trunks. I turned into my locker and did it quickly.

Our team trunks resembled black biker shorts with the school symbol on the front of the right thigh and our colors up the sides. After pulling them on I shoved my clothes into the locker. Then I turned and smacked my shin into the low bench between the rows of lockers.

"Shit!"

Ramon turned around a few lockers up and shook his head. "Again, Hesse?"

I had a reputation for knocking into things or tripping over my own feet just about every practice session. I did it at home too. Downside of being a robot. My shins, knees and feet always had two or three bruises on them.

"It's for luck," I told him. "Part of the ritual."

He laughed. A junior, Ramon was in the running for team captain next year and already swayed decisions about the team.

He took a liking to me last year when I said I'd swim the 500 freestyle. It was the event no one else on the team ever wanted to swim and he'd been stuck with it. He had curly black hair, inches longer than mine. Add his deep tan skin, big masculine chin and the best muscles on the team, and at least a dozen girls at school had crushes on him, according to Claire.

I put on my swim cap and rested my goggles up on my forehead. Then I wrapped the big towel with our school emblem on it around my shoulders like a shawl and followed Ramon out to the pool.

Unlike football where most of the team is on the field, the swim team spent most of each meet sitting by the pool stretching and bullshitting. There were twenty guys on the team but at most we had four competing at a time. Those of us out of the water only fell silent during the races. Each guy swam two to four events. I only swam two: one leg of a relay and then the 500.

The 500-meter freestyle was the longest solo swim of the meet—more than double any other. Ten laps in the pool covers about a third of a mile. I actually liked it, but the guys never believed me when I said that. Of all the events, it was the one where pure muscle strength was less important than pacing, endurance, breath control and strategy. I had to manage how fast I swam the first six laps so that I had the right energy available for the last four.

It was also the most boring event of the meet. Watching guys flash through the water racing against each other for up to two minutes is exciting—watching that same thing for about five minutes really loses its thrill.

Our relay came early in the meet, and then Ramon and I sat on the side of the pool and stretched. The 500 was always one of the last events, which gave me time to recover before I swam again.

"How's it going?" he asked and jerked his chin toward where Claire sat in the bleachers.

In her black goth clothes she looked like an inkblot on a bright painting. Three colorfully dressed girls from the yearbook committee sat with her in the middle of a larger, spread out grouping of family members, friends and girlfriends of the team. Shrugging, I rubbed my big toe around one of the tiny octagonal tiles that covered the floor.

"Do you like it?" he asked.

I examined his face but couldn't read his half smile. Ramon got around, we all knew that, but he wasn't one of those guys who bragged about it. At least not more than usual. I knew he'd had sex with two girls already this year, so he couldn't be asking how I liked sex with Claire, could he?

"What?" I asked.

"Being with the same girl that long," he said. "You've been together like, half a year?"

"Just over," I told him. We'd passed the seven-month mark two weeks ago, but I didn't want it to seem like I paid too much attention to that. He waited for me to say more. I had to split my mind into two halves—one half held all possible real answers to his question and the other half pretended to be Ramon and scanned the answers to find the acceptable ones.

/error scan: boy test

for each answer string (item in list)

if item sounds like girl—discard

else—echo item

1. test "I feel at home with her"

2. discard—sentimental

3. test "I don't have to do as much work"

4. echo

5. test "I like the emotional intimacy"

6. discard—major boy fail

7. test "she's a sure thing"

8. echo

"It's easy," I said. "I mean, I know what she likes so I don't have to work at it. And she's a sure thing." Guilt lurched through my gut. My relationship with Claire was so much more than that. With her I felt more myself than I did with anyone. Sometimes when we were flopped out on her bed together reading a poem and talking about it, I forgot that I had to play a boy and got to be a person for a while.

That's what made me think I could be a girl with her.

But I couldn't tell her. I couldn't risk losing what I already had.

"You don't get bored?" Ramon asked. "Or look at the prettier girls?"

"Pretty girls are a lot of work," I said.

"Ha!"

They called the 500 and I got up, leaving my towel next to him. When I started on the team, Ramon was swimming the 500 and he told me the trick to it: have two songs cued up in your head. The first song has a good steady pace and the second song is a little faster.

I didn't have a waterproof MP3 player, but I listened to my songs whenever I did strength training. When I hit the water, I started Beyoncé's "Irreplaceable" in my mind. The upbeat R&B rhythm of the song gave me a moderately fast pace.

The problem was I *really* wanted tell Claire. How bad could it be? No, that was a terrible question to ask because it could be awful if I misjudged and she told everyone and stopped speaking to me. What if I was replaceable to her? I couldn't tell her.

By the start of lap five I was trailing badly. Obsessing while swimming was a terrible strategy. I switched to my second song early. "Girlfriend" by Avril Lavigne.

That is what I wanted—to be Claire's girlfriend.

Hitting the second to last lap, my lungs burned and a dull fire ran along my arms and legs. In the water, feeling my whole body didn't bother me. The soft pressure reassured me of my reality. The water didn't judge. I pushed hard into the pain.

Fifteen seconds behind first place. Not bad. The coach slapped me on the back as I climbed out of the pool.

"Good swim, Hesse, you really picked it up. That's your best meet time."

"Thanks."

I stumbled back over to Ramon, sat against the bleachers, and tried to catch my breath. My time wasn't good enough to go to sectionals. Even the guy in first wasn't going to do well against the stronger teams from the Cities. But the time was good for me and all the effort had cleared my mind.

I had to tell Claire.

* * *

"Go chill at my place, I'll be there in less than an hour," Claire told me when the meet was over. I was glad she didn't drive with me because I didn't know how I'd manage small talk when I had something so important to say.

Unbeknownst to any of our parents, Claire had given me a duplicate key to her house for days when her extracurricular activities went longer than my swim practice. Her house was on the other side of town from mine, all of a mile-and-a-half apart, but she thought it would be silly to have me go home for an hour and then meet her at her place, so she'd copied her key.

Her house was nothing like mine. First of all, it was tiny and in the well-to-do part of town that bordered on our one lake, and therefore more expensive than my family's larger house. Secondly, it was obsessively neat. At our house, Mikey or Dad always left junk around in the living room and kitchen, and Mom complained periodically and instituted weekend cleaning times, but it was never finished and tidy. Claire's house looked like a furniture showroom. Even the bookcases were designed more as works of art than functional pieces; each shelf held a few books and then some small statue or knickknack or a picture turned at an angle for effect.

Her mom worked at a flooring and countertop store, helping people pick out expensive tile and granite for their fancy houses. This house had simple wood floors, but the kitchen did boast the yummiest counters I'd ever seen: black stone flecked with reflective bits of other colors. Claire's mom made a good living and still got money from Claire's dad, who lived in St. Louis, so Claire rarely wanted for anything. She didn't have a car, true, but she did have her own TV in her bedroom and a Mac G5 desktop with a blazing-fast Internet connection and a monthly online game subscription to *World of Warcraft*. She let me have three of her character slots. I logged on and fired up my level 85 mage, Amalia.

Sometimes these online games got tedious for all the monsters a character had to kill to get to a new level, but that was more than made up for by the great gear I could buy and make, and the cool spells I could cast. Claire didn't have the patience to play magic-users, but they were my favorite. I admit, the fact that they always wore robes figured into that preference.

When I logged into the game and selected Amalia on the character screen, I turned her 360 degrees to admire how awesome she looked. She always had beautiful hair. Sometimes I got it styled in one of the game's barbershops, but right then it was flowing free all down her back. Her robes hung gracefully around her figure in violet and gray hues with gold tracery. I pushed the button to enter the game as her and got to step into a world fully female.

While I moved her around the city, I felt what it was like to be in her body. Some of the characters in the city were other players like me, but the computer created all the shopkeepers and city guards. They called me "m'lady" and simple as it was, that made me grin.

I was shopping for a new mage's robe when I heard the key in the door. "Hi honey, I'm home," Claire yelled from the entryway. I immediately started sweating while my skin went cold. That didn't seem fair. My body should have picked one or the other, but instead I ended up a damp popsicle.

I heard the thomp of her boots coming off. Claire had three pairs of thick, black boots that she rotated through in the winter. Each pair made her at least two inches taller, but when she appeared in her bedroom doorway she was her usual petite self. Today she wore a bunch of silvery bracelets around her right wrist and a silver cross hanging down the front of her sweater. Her entire wardrobe was black. She once told me she started it when other girls teased her about trying to be fashionable in the eighth grade. Not only could she avoid those taunts, but this style let her get away with wearing an ornate cross and no one knew if she was serious or not.

She was very serious about her own brand of radical Christianity. From time to time she came up with surprisingly contextual Bible quotes. The one she liked to give people who hassled her about her all-black, heavy eyeliner look was: "Do not let your adorning be external—the braiding of hair and the putting on of gold jewelry, or the clothing you wear—but let your adorning be the hidden person of the heart with the imperishable beauty of a gentle and quiet spirit, which in God's sight is very precious." That shut people up fast and was pretty fun to watch.

I gestured toward the computer screen. "Amalia's got a new robe," I said, trying to sound normal while my tongue stuck to the roof of my mouth. "Plus 120 Intel."

"Sweet, and it shows off her cleavage. She's hot," Claire said, trying to trip me out, like I'd care. Wow, was I about to test her true coolness factor. With a silent prayer, I logged out of the game.

She put her arms around my shoulders from behind and kissed the side of my face. "Mom's not coming home for a few hours," she said quietly, running one hand across my chest.

Our relationship had been getting more sexual over the last few months, and I had the distinct impression that Claire liked it a lot more than I did. To be fair, I'd like it a lot better if I had the right equipment. We hadn't gone "all the way," but at this point we'd done a lot of other things, some working better than others since I had trouble connecting with my body. She'd been sexual with a couple of other people and said I was the least selfish guy she'd ever met, which I suppose was a compliment.

Claire spun my desk chair around to face her and sat down on my lap. It would've been a lot easier to let her talk me into fooling around, but I had to have this conversation with her and if I waited, I was only going to feel worse.

"Can we talk about something?" I asked.

She ruffled my hair with her fingers. "Whatever pops up," she quipped.

I don't know what expression I had on my face, but I suspect it was an echo of the crushing feeling in my chest because her eyes opened all the way and she stood up. "What's wrong?" she asked. "What happened?"

"Sit down," I said, which was stupid because her eyes got even wider.

She perched on the edge of the bed across from where I sat. "Are you sick?"

"No," I said quickly.

"There's someone else?" Those bright golden-green eyes narrowed.

"No."

"You're gay," she declared, leaning back on her hands and kicking my shin lightly. "I knew it. Of all the luck."

"No. Claire, let me talk."

She sighed and flopped all the way back on her elbows. Claire had this fantastic mass of black hair that spilled down her back. I loved playing with it. Unfortunately, what she didn't know was that half the time I was thinking about what it would be like to have hair like that. She complained about it a lot: how long it took to dry, how hard it was to keep it from frizzing out, what a pain it was to dye it goth-black when her natural color was a mousy brown, but she never made a move to cut it off. Lying back on the bed with her hair spread out behind her, she looked like a pixie with small bones and big eyes. I offered another quick prayer to anyone who was listening that she could understand what I was going to tell her. My brain kept coming up with things to say, but my mouth wouldn't cooperate because everything sounded so idiotic.

"You're sure you're not gay?" she asked while I struggled. "I mean, it's okay if you are, though I'll be upset 'cause I like fooling around with you."

"I like girls," I said through my constricted throat.

"And me in particular?" she asked. "Did you screw around on me?"

"No, again no, give me a minute." I couldn't breathe, but now that I'd gone this far, I had to keep going.

"Chris, you're kind of creeping me out here," she said, but then stared up at the ceiling. "I'm shutting up."

Time stretched into an infinite plane. I thought about running, standing up and going for the car, driving until I got to Minneapolis and never coming back. Then I considered telling her I was gay after all, but I'd lose her and gain nothing. It wasn't too late, I told myself, just jump her, she'll eventually forget the whole thing. But she wouldn't. Claire was not only smart, but she remembered entire conversations weeks after they happened. You could not get anything by her.

Claire sat up straight again and opened her mouth. I didn't want to have to bat down another false guess.

"I'm a girl," I blurted. It wasn't the elegant explanation I'd intended, but I had to start somewhere. As soon as I said it, I blushed and couldn't look her in the eye, so I stared at the left side of her jaw.

Claire cocked her head and blinked at me, her eyebrows drawing close to each other. Her mouth opened and closed and opened again.

"What?" she said with a sideways shake of her head.

The iron fist in my throat eased now that I'd started. "Ever since I was a kid I've known I was a girl," I said. "But I got stuck with this body. I thought God made a mistake, and I kept waiting for Him to fix it." I ran my hands down the front of my chest. "This isn't who I am."

Her face was white enough that I worried she was going to faint, but she reached toward me and laid one hand alongside my cheek. Then she traced her thumb down the line of my nose and across my lips. She put her fingertips between my collarbones and ran them down to my sternum.

"How?" she asked.

I didn't know if she was asking how I knew or how I planned to fix it, but I wanted to answer that first question, so I did.

"When I was about seven, Grandma Em sent me a set of books for Christmas," I began.

I told her how the set included *The Wonderful Wizard of Oz*, *The Marvelous Land of Oz*, and especially *Ozma of Oz*. The first book was cool, Mom rented the movie and we watched it, but the second and third were a revelation. In them a young boy,

Tip, escapes a wicked witch and goes off on an adventure to find the missing Princess Ozma. At the end of *The Marvelous Land of Oz* it's revealed that Tip *is* Ozma—that the princess had been bewitched into a boy's body and now would be restored to her rightful self.

I told Claire how the first time I read that scene an electric shock traveled from the hair at the very top of my head down to the soles of my feet. In the scene, Glinda asked the witch, "What did you do with the girl?"

And the witch said, "I enchanted her...I transformed her—into—into a boy!"

At first Tip protests but Glinda says very gently, "But you were born a girl, and also a Princess; so you must resume your proper form, that you may become Queen of Emerald City."

Claire listened, mouth half open, as I said how I'd read the scene over and over again. How I'd searched everywhere in my life for the magic to turn me back into my rightful self. I knew I was born a girl, and I wanted so badly to resume my proper form as Ozma had. Claire closed her mouth and her eyes turned down at the corners.

"How old were you again?" she asked.

"Seven or eight," I said. "But I knew I was a girl before that. In kindergarten, I kept lining up with the girls when it was time to come in from recess and the teacher would make me go over and get in line with the boys. Before I was five it didn't really matter if you were a boy or a girl, but as soon as we started getting divided up, I knew I should be with the girls."

"So what...what happened next?" she asked.

"I tried harder to be a boy," I said. "I thought maybe I'd just missed something, that maybe everyone has to work at it, so I had Dad teach me about cars, and I went out for the swim team, and I hung out with guys and did what they did. And after about six years of that I started to think that I'd become a very good fake."

"But you're one of the sweetest guys I know," she said. "I always thought you might be gay. You're so..." She trailed off.

"What?"

"...different from the other guys," she finished. "I mean, there's the cars and the swimming and stuff, and you look like a really cute guy, and your parts work—" She gestured at my crotch, causing me to reflexively cross my legs. "But you don't talk like a guy. At least not when we're alone."

"Talk like a guy?" I asked.

"I don't know how to describe it, but it's different. The only time you really talk like a guy is when you're mad, otherwise it's a little like talking to my girlfriends." She pressed the heel of one hand to her temple. "I think my brain is scrambling."

She stood up from the bed and moved into the open part of her room, between bed and closet. I watched her gaze travel up and down my body a few times.

"It doesn't make any sense," she said, shaking her head. "I don't understand how you can be that way."

"There are some good websites that explain it," I said and wrote a few on the pad of paper by her computer.

"How are you going to be able to live like that?" she asked.

"What?"

"It's not like you can turn into a girl or anything."

Her voice sounded distant and she was still standing across the room, away from me. How upset was she? Was she in shock or was she taking this relatively well? I couldn't afford to let myself hope and so my answer came out harsher than I intended. "I can get a sex change," I said, the words hanging in the air like icicles.

"You're kind of tall for a girl."

I stood up. "I should probably go." I wanted her to contradict me and tell me to stay. I needed to know she was going to be okay with this revelation.

"Yeah," she said. "I'll see you at school tomorrow."

My heart clenched. I went into the living room and put on my boots and coat. She followed and watched me.

"Does this mean we're going to split up?" I asked before I could stop myself.

Claire's face was still paler than usual and at first she only stared, as if I hadn't been speaking in English. "What?" she asked.

"Are we going to split up?"

"Chris, don't ask me that. I don't know." She sounded angry, each word bitten short.

"Well tell me when you make up your mind," I said and stepped through the door into the freezing air.

By the time I'd started the car and driven halfway to my house I wanted to turn around and take that back, but I was afraid I'd find her still standing in the living room and staring after me in shock.

When I got home I had no appetite, so I told Mom I didn't feel well and I was going to bed early. Up in my room I set my alarm for four a.m. and then lay down and stared at the ceiling. The conversation with Claire played over again in my head until I finally fell asleep.

CHAPTER THREE

Claire

After she did the dinner dishes, Claire wandered around the house twice before settling into her room. She sat at her desk, fingertips tracing the website addresses Chris had written in her notebook. *Chris thinks he's a girl*, sounded in her brain like a gong that rang and echoed and rang again. *Chris thinks he's a girl*. How should she feel about that? How *did* she feel? When he'd told her, she'd been angry, and then sad for herself. But as he talked about it, he'd looked so relieved that all her own feelings kept turning into guilt.

Most of the time he was so sad or angry or under a dark cloud, and this afternoon as he talked to her, his eyes lit up from deep within. For a moment, telling the story about Ozma, he'd relaxed in a way she'd never seen before. She couldn't begrudge him those feelings, but the whole situation was so awfully bizarre.

Could she ever stop thinking of him as "him," she wondered? The idea made her brain ache and tilt sickeningly sideways, until she put one hand on either side of her face to try to hold her mind still. There had to be answers. Chris had left her these website addresses for a reason. If her Mom saw, she'd wonder why Claire was reading those sites, but she'd already visited gay, lesbian and bi teen sites, and Mom would never suspect Chris was…whatever Chris was. Plus Claire could say it was for a school project or something.

Her mom knocked on her door, waited for Claire to say "Yeah?" and opened it.

"Want to watch *CSI?*" she asked.

Her mom had dyed her light brown hair to a dark blond and it still seemed weird to Claire. Maybe her own black-dyed hair seemed as strange to her mom. Beyond their clashing hair colors, they looked too much alike: round faces, slight dimples, hazel eyes.

Claire forced a smile. "I've got a lot of homework."

With a resigned nod, her mom went back into the living room. She must've been feeling lonely again. Mom's last boyfriend had been a dud and they'd split up before the holidays.

Claire called up the websites and read until her eyes burned and all the tiny muscles around them ached. When she squeezed her eyes shut, her eyeballs wanted to drop backward into her skull.

First, it turned out that genetics weren't the final word on whether a baby was a boy or a girl. Based on two weeks of sex ed in junior high, Claire had thought everyone with XX chromosomes became a woman, and XY meant you were a man. But because of the way hormones, genes and other factors combined, babies with XX genes could turn out male or somewhere in between, and the same was true for XY. Some people were even born with both XX *and* XY chromosomes, or XXY, XYY, or in very rare cases, XXYY.

Plus people didn't begin as boys or girls. In the womb, all bodies started out very similar and then moved toward boy or girl or combined characteristics from both. Sex and gender were so complicated that no one had yet pinpointed why some people were transgender and others weren't.

Transgender. That was the word Chris had written at the

top of the page of website addresses. "Trans" from the root for "across, over, beyond." Meaning Chris thought he could cross from one gender to another. Could he?

Claire had been staring at web pages for so long that the words danced on the screen. Rubbing her eyes, she minimized her browser and logged into *World of Warcraft*.

From the login screen, her character gazed back at her: a human paladin with very black hair and light brown skin. When the *Burning Crusade* expansion came out a year ago, she'd tried making paladins of the newly available races: aliens and elves. The alien females resembled tall women with big boobs and bigger butts, and the skinny elves appeared breakable. Claire had gone back to her trusty human.

Chris had created a statuesque alien, female priest. Claire remembered teasing him, saying, "You just want to look at her butt and boobs."

And Chris had replied, "Sure," in that distant, uncommitted tone he used most of the time.

"Do you wish I looked like that?" she'd asked.

"You are kind of short," he'd said, flashing her a thin smile because all the aliens were seven feet tall or more.

He'd changed the topic quickly after that and Claire had spent weeks studying the other girls in school, worrying that he wanted someone with more curves, with a bigger chest.

But maybe he didn't want to be with someone who looked like that. Maybe he wanted to look like that?

She selected his priest, Thalia. Despite her considerable chest and the fact that there were dozens of skimpy outfit choices for the alien women, Chris had dressed her in a demure robe.

He hadn't made her so he could stare at her boobs. He'd made her to imagine himself like that.

Claire switched to staring at Chris's main character, Amalia the mage. She'd never realized how much Amalia resembled Chris, with curly brown hair and brown eyes, thin lips and a cute, narrow nose. This was how Chris saw himself? How did he know how he was supposed to be?

She went back to her web pages, to the studies she'd found about transgender people, searching for ones about trans women. That's what Chris would be, because he wanted to be, or was, a woman.

Two studies performed on the brains of transgender and nontransgender people had found that an area in the brain of trans women was the same size as that area in the brains of the women in the study who weren't transgender. In men the area was bigger.

Other studies about gender found differences in brain structures and even the way parts of the brain were linked together. In some, trans women's brains looked just like other women and in some trans women had distinct brain structures—but Claire didn't find any that said that trans women had brains like men.

Was it possible that Chris had been born with a girl's brain but his body developed male? All this time he'd been perceiving himself as a girl when everyone else naturally assumed he was a guy. How weird would that feel?

Claire put her fingers to her temples and rubbed her sore head. Maybe she could find out how weird it felt. She logged back into *World of Warcraft* and clicked the "new character" button to make a human male version of herself. But she kept getting distracted by picking hair or a face that looked attractive to her, rather than like her. No facial hair because that seemed like it would itch, black hair, pale skin. She named him "Klahr."

He appeared in the human start zone, picked up a quest and went to kill some marauding wolves. She'd played as a male character before, but always a nonhuman and she didn't think of the character as being her: more like being in a really great Halloween costume. She tried to think of Klahr as her, but his clunky run and the top-heavy way he swung his mace felt off-balance. Plus he had no waist at all. He was a total brick.

She couldn't imagine having to play him all the time. What if she was only allowed one character and that was it? What if she had to go around in that brick-like body all the time? It would be time to find a better game.

She deleted him.

She went into the kitchen and refilled her glass. Her mom had gone to bed hours ago. The ruddy clock figures on the microwave read: 2:13.

To bed soon, just not yet.

More searching, more numbers and studies. Being transgender was not as rare as she first thought. In the US about 0.6 percent of people identified as transgender. And some surveys said if you included all gender nonconforming people, that number went above 1 percent, more than one in every hundred people. That meant there were millions of people like Chris in the world.

But she didn't want Chris to be a woman. She liked him as Chris, maybe a Chris who wasn't sad as he was now, but still the guy she knew. It made her feel sick to think about any guy turning into a woman, let alone her boyfriend. There were men and there were women and you couldn't go from one to the other.

It seemed unnatural. But when she'd started to wonder if she was attracted to girls as well as boys, she'd heard plenty from people who found that unnatural. To her it only made sense to like whomever she liked and not bother about what gender they were. Was it any different with Chris?

Sure it is, the back of her mind said. *We're talking about changing his whole body. Guys don't just turn into girls, the world isn't set up that way.*

Claire couldn't even understand how it was done medically and wasn't sure she wanted to know. In the articles online, there were references to surgery and often multiple surgeries. How could it be right to change like that if it involved all that medical intervention? Didn't that point to the unnatural craziness of it all? Who needed to take a perfectly good working body and turn it into something else?

And even more importantly, why would God create a world in which women could be born as men and vice versa?

She turned off the computer and sat on her bed. "God?" she asked in a whisper. "What were you thinking? Why would you make people transgender?"

She talked to God a lot and sometimes God answered—or maybe God always answered and at times she was too boneheaded to figure it out. She'd been raised Lutheran, like just about everyone in these parts, but her relationship with God came from her earliest memories of Sunday school when she remembered Jesus as the kindest, wisest man in the whole world. At times she could feel Him near her.

She regularly went to church, but she didn't always feel God there. More often she skipped the service and attended an open Bible study held afterward. She didn't believe in a literal interpretation of the Bible, but she did believe it was a divinely inspired text and a way to engage in a relationship with God. Maybe it was because she loved words in all their forms that it was easiest for her to feel God's presence when she read the Bible or even in the words of poets and writers.

Pulling her worn Bible off the shelf by her bed, she let it open where it wanted. Her eyes fell to a verse toward the end of the Book of Job after Job loses his family and his health and all his money. He cries out to God for a reason for all the bad things that have happened to him.

"Where were you when I laid the foundation of the earth?" God asks Job. "Tell me, if you have understanding. Who determined its measurements—surely you know!"

What was that supposed to mean? What had the Bible study leader said when they studied Job? In the end of the story, Job actually gets to speak to God—and if she remembered right, that was the last time God spoke directly to a human being before the birth of Jesus. That was huge! The whole Book of Job was about testing the depth of Job's faith, just as this situation with Chris tested her faith in God's design. Job got to hear God answer his questions and came out of the situation with renewed faith, even if it wasn't the answer he expected or wanted.

While Job suffered, his friends blamed all his misfortunes on him and acted like huge jerks to him. That was the other lesson Claire remembered learning about this book: Job was a story about compassion.

God was telling her that some hard things that happened to people were beyond her understanding. What God made for the joy of creation, that was God's work, and if that included men who turned into women and women who turned into men, who was she to argue? Was she there when God created the world? No. Did she help to determine its measurements? No.

Her work was to have faith and not be a blaming jerk like Job's friends. No matter how upset she felt, Chris didn't deserve to have her take it out on him.

In the next verses, God asked Job if he knew what the foundation of the earth was laid upon, "or who laid its cornerstone when the morning stars sang together and all the sons of God shouted for joy?"

She loved that image of the world being created and the sons of God shouting for joy. The world was made for joy. Did that include transgender people? She didn't understand how it could, but maybe she didn't have to. Plenty of people in the world were going to be awful to Chris if he kept going down this path, and she didn't need to be one of them.

But Chris also asked if this meant they were going to split up. Not being a jerk to him was one thing but being his girlfriend was a lot more than that and she didn't know if she could. If he started to change his body like that, would she still be attracted to him?

She had so much to learn and think about and maybe mourn…

CHAPTER FOUR

The small, quiet alarm beside my pillow chirped once and was silent, but that was enough to wake me. I wanted to run over to Claire's house and ask her again if she was going to split up with me, but it was four a.m.

Avoiding the creaky part in the middle of my bedroom floor, I slid the bolt on my door to the locked position. I'd installed the sliding bolt last summer and Dad let me keep it. He realized that I could only lock it when I was inside the room and contented himself in knowing he and Mom could still search for drugs, or whatever they looked for, when I wasn't home. He probably thought I'd put it on so I could masturbate without Mom walking in on me. Dad thinks like that. I wasn't going to argue as long as I had some measure of safety for what I really wanted to do.

When I'd come in from school that afternoon, I'd carried my backpack up to my room, along with a nondescript black nylon gym bag. No one paid any attention to it, of course, which was the point. I'd thought all this through to the nth degree, and the bag was not only beneath notice but the luggage tag had Claire's name and address on it.

At least up until I'd come out to her the day before, Claire wouldn't have minded me using her name to throw my parents off the track of a secret; she was pretty sneaky herself and had taught me a few tricks about hiding files on my computer. Luckily I had the kind of parents who hardly knew how to turn the thing on, unlike Claire's mom, who had probably installed two kinds of cybersnoop software to protect her one precious daughter from sexual predators online. Claire came over and used my computer whenever she had something "of a delicate nature" that she needed to research, and paid me back in tips about how to keep my parents in the dark.

The duffel bag had her name on it because inside it was a pair of girls' jeans, a long skirt, two sweaters, a cute hat, underpants and two bras. None of them were anywhere near Claire's size. But if my parents looked in the bag, they would never consider any possibility beyond the obvious explanation that the outfits belonged to Claire. Plus they had no idea that she hated hats.

I unzipped the bag and paused to listen. Silence. More silence. Chirping bugs outside, neighbor's dog barking, the distant sound of a car and the rapid thud of my pounding heart.

I shucked my pajamas. The next few minutes were the best and worst of my whole day: the worst because I felt like such a freak, and the best because I slowly became visible. I went from being a charcoal outline of a person to being a flesh and blood human being, my skin filled from the inside out as I arrived into my body and my life.

I put on the underpants and the skirt. Because of the competitive swimming, I had an excuse to shave my arms and legs—plus swimming got Dad off my back about doing something I could letter in—but mostly it was the smooth skin of the swimmers that caught my attention. If they'd told me before my sophomore year that they shaved for meets, I'd have been swimming my whole school career.

I put on the bra and hooked it, filling the cups with cotton balls, because they were easy to have around, and I found it impossible to actually stuff a bra with socks the way girls did in books. Then I pulled on the short-sleeved sweater with the scalloped neck that was my favorite and set the hat on my head, tilted back.

The inside of my closet door had a mirror that I could easily avoid in the mornings, but now I opened it and looked at myself in the darkness. Subtle light from the moon filtered in through my unshaded windows and mixed with the light of my computer monitor. I preferred that to the bright overhead light that would reveal too many of the rough details of my face. In this dreamy light I felt whole.

When you're a little kid, you don't really think about what you are; you just are. Some of my happiest times were when I was four and five. We lived in a different town then, across the street from a blond girl named Heather whose mom would bring her over to play with me in the basement all afternoon. Heather's mom often marveled that I was such a quiet kid, so thoughtful, and that I played so gently with her daughter. It seemed natural to me. We'd sit in the middle of the basement playroom that my dad had set up, and she'd show me her dolls. We'd dress them up in the other dolls' clothes and drive them around in the cars I'd gotten for my birthdays or build them houses out of the empty boxes Dad brought home for me to play in.

"Isn't he such a sweet boy," Heather's mom said one afternoon. "He's made a house for the dolls." I didn't know who she was talking about, but I started to feel that something bad had happened and I didn't know what it was.

I ran into the laundry room and hid until Heather and her mom had gone. From then on, I was on the lookout, trying to figure out what had happened to make Heather's mom talk about me like I was a boy.

When I went to first grade, the problem started to become clear to me. The teacher wanted the girls to line up on one side of the door and the boys to line up on the other side. I lined up with the girls and she told me to get in the other line.

"I'm not a boy!" I told her.

She knelt down and took me by the shoulders. "Are you afraid of the other boys?" she asked. "Did they do something to you?"

"No," I said. "I'm a girl."

She laughed, right in my face, her breath dark and earthy. "You're funny," she said. "You're playing a game with me, aren't you? You're pretending to be a girl today, but I know you're a boy. Do you know how I know?"

I shook my head.

"Because of your name, Christopher. That's a boy's name, so you get in line with the other boys."

I got into line with the boys. She had said one thing I understood: "pretending." Something had gone wrong with the world and I had to pretend to be a boy until I could figure out how to fix it. I knew how to pretend.

When Mom came to pick me up, I asked if I could have another name. At six, I thought that maybe if I changed my name I could be a girl.

"Why don't you like your name?" she asked.

"It's a boy's name," I said.

"Yes," she said, obviously not getting it. "It's a good name for a boy. Your grandfather was named Christopher."

"I want a girl's name," I said.

She stopped the car and looked at me. She stared at me for so long that another car started honking behind us. Then she let out a long breath.

"Sometimes," she said. "Sometimes Chris is also a girl's name. It can be short for Christine."

I beamed. I don't know what prompted my mom to say that, but it was one of the best things she'd ever said to me. The teacher was wrong; I did have a girl's name. I was going to be all right. Ever since then I've heard my name as "Chris, short for Christine."

Of course it turned out the name wasn't the core issue, and Mom didn't stop Dad from giving me a good whipping when he found me in her dresses a couple of years later.

My body is the problem. It's hard to tell people that you're a girl when everything physical screams "guy." Even in the semidarkness, my reflection in the mirror had these broad shoulders and no waist. I've got thin lips, but so does my mom, and my eyebrows look like Cro-Magnon man. They'd look better if I could pluck them, but I'm not too old to get a good whipping from Dad, so I leave them shaggy. I can still see his face, the grim set of his lips and how quiet his voice sounded as he told me, when I was eight, to take off the dress while he pulled his belt free from its loops. I think we both felt ashamed afterward, but for very different reasons. I never wanted to be the kind of kid my Dad would have to whip, so I retreated into my dreams and stayed away from girls' clothes until this year when I was sure I could wear them in secret.

I turned away from the mirror and went to my computer. It was a 2004 iMac that I'd gotten off eBay for a few hundred bucks a year and a half ago. Although slow, it still had some life in it, and anyway it only connected to the Internet at a blazing 56K. I wanted high-speed access, but Mom and Dad wouldn't pay for it, and I didn't want to spend that much of the money I made helping Dad with his cars just to get online.

There were a few good online communities for trans girls, but my favorite was called GenderPeace. I'd found it last fall and had been hanging around on it for about six months. Members participated from all over the world. They gave great advice and talked about their lives. I spent a few months lurking and reading the public posts until I decided to create a free account and become a member. I had to sign in each time rather than being logged in automatically, because I erased any evidence of my having been there when I logged off for the night, in case Mom and Dad suddenly figured out computers. I assumed I could never be too paranoid.

My user name was "EmilyCH" for Emily Christine Hesse. I thought I'd keep Christine in honor of my Mom's cool moment and the choice they made to name me in the first place, and I got Emily partly from my Grandma Em and, I confess, a little from Emily Dickinson.

A couple days ago, a new thread had caught my eye, especially a post from a girl whose online name was "Bratalie." In her profile it turned out her name was Natalie and she had already transitioned and was going to high school as a girl in Minneapolis, an hour's drive from me. First I had a gut-wrenching pang of jealousy. To be able to go to school as a girl, how amazing! But then I wanted to know all about it. I'd sent her a quick note saying I was in Liberty, Minnesota, still living in drab (dressed resembling a boy), and asking what it was like for her to go to school as herself.

When I logged in that night, I saw that I had private mail from her.

"Hi Emily," she wrote. "We're neighbors! Liberty is out in the boonies, though, how do you survive? You should come into the City! We could have lunch!" She included her cell phone number in the closing, along with more exclamation points.

Between my excitement about Natalie, and the growing dread in my stomach about seeing Claire at school, I couldn't go back to sleep. I stayed up posting on the GP board for a while and then doing my homework. I couldn't explain it, but homework was easier to do in my girl clothes. Like I'd been concentrating on holding the shape of my body in my mind, but now I could relax and focus on school.

Twenty minutes before my other, loud alarm was due to ring, I erased the evidence of my web surfing, undressed, put my clothes back in the decoy duffel bag and dropped it casually at the foot of the bed so it would look like I didn't care about it. Then I crawled under the covers and waited for the alarm to ring while I searched for stars through the unshaded window. I only found a few points of light in the murky, dark gray sky.

"You look awful," Mom said when I appeared for breakfast in my jeans and sweater number two.

"Yeah," I agreed. I didn't want to attribute it to Claire or she'd think we'd had a fight and possibly ask why. "I might be getting a cold."

She touched my forehead. "You feel fine, but bundle up." She turned back to the sandwiches she was making. "Chris, I've been meaning to talk to you about seeing a doctor for your moods."

"What?"

"You're so unhappy all the time. I want you to go talk to someone professional and have them help you."

I tried to figure out if I was supposed to fight about this or not. It really depended on the doctor whether it would be worthwhile. I settled for indifference, which always worked when I didn't know what to do. "Sure, Mom," I said.

"Good, because you have an appointment today after school. I want you to meet me here at three forty-five and we'll go over together."

Okay, that was my cue to get mad, which wasn't hard since I already felt like crying. She'd messed with my schedule without asking, that was a clear violation. "What? You made an appointment without even asking? Mom, what the hell!"

She closed a paper bag with a sharp snap and glared. "Chris, watch your language, young man!"

That shut me up, but not for the reason she thought. I hated being called "young man" even more than "son." I took a deep breath. "You didn't even ask me."

"I'm your mother," she said. "Sometimes I can do things just because they're good for you."

I shrugged. On five hours of sleep for many nights running, I didn't have the energy to keep fighting. "Fine."

"Don't be late."

I stood up and automatically kissed her cheek though at that point I was honestly pissed.

Halfway to school, I realized I'd forgotten my lunch and would have to eat a dry hockey puck, or whatever the cafeteria was serving.

A doctor? Some psychiatrist or psychologist, when what I needed was an endocrinologist to put me on the right hormones. I felt a miserable disconnect between my body, which wanted very badly to punch something, and my heart, which wanted to cry. My eyes burned but didn't tear up, which was for the best if I didn't want to get my ass kicked by the football guys.

When I rounded the corner of the main hall, I saw Claire standing at my locker with her back to me. Momentum carried me toward her for a few more steps and then I stopped. If she dumped me now, I would fall apart.

She turned and saw me, pushed through the two dozen students between us, while I stood frozen in place. She was wearing her favorite black sweater, the one with a cobweb design stitched around the elbows, and a long, black skirt over her boots. Despite her backpack, she held a blue-covered notebook to her chest.

"Are you okay?" she asked. "Your face is all misery or exhaustion. I can't tell."

"I'm sorry about last night," I told her.

"Sorry for telling me?"

"For my stupid question about us being together."

"Is that why you're upset?" she asked.

All I saw in her face was confusion, and what I wanted was certainty that she wasn't going to break up with me. I didn't have the guts to ask again if we were still together.

"That and Mom wants me to go to a shrink," I told her almost inaudibly.

"That could be good."

Her fingers worked around the edge of her notebook, pushing ragged edges of paper back among the pages. She stared down at the notebook, not at me.

The bell rang, warning us that we only had a minute to flee to class.

"Hang in there," she said.

I tried to smile, but failed pretty badly. She hadn't said we were together. Was she trying to let me down gently?

CHAPTER FIVE

I stumbled through the day on autopilot.
/run: please teacher
1. raise hand
2. give correct answer
3. repeat once per class
/run: lunch with the guys
1. pick one parent—complain
2. mention sports
3. mention car
4. joke about girls
5. nod
6. nod
7. nod
8. grunt
9. nod

While that covered me externally, I tried to puzzle out how
Claire felt from our brief conversation. She hadn't said one way

or the other if we were going out or how she was dealing with everything I'd told her. Was she freaking out and hiding it, or was she supportive? Did she want to break up with me and not know what to say?

In psych class we learned how embryos developed in the womb. That was a good distraction though I had to keep my eyes half-closed in mock boredom and remember to groan when the guys did. Mr. Cooper gave a lightly updated version of the classic story. He did say that in the first weeks of gestation, embryos are all the same. But then in his version once the hormones started, everyone fit neatly into a female or male configuration.

I couldn't blame him for not wanting to get into the full spectrum of diversity in human bodies, not with this lot. But I wished he'd said the part where although the sex of the body was kicked off at around eight weeks, the parts of the brain that determined gender identity didn't start coming together until months later. So gestating babies could have one hormonal environment for their bodies and a different one when their brains started working on gender identity.

Even as the fetus developed physically, it wasn't as clear-cut as simple male and female. Mr. Cooper didn't talk about it, but a small percentage of babies were born with ambiguous genitals or genitals that didn't match their genes or their internal sex organs. In the past doctors picked which one they thought the baby should be, but recently some had started letting the kids grow up and say for themselves what gender they were, which made sense to me. I wished I'd had a chance to tell a doctor that I was a girl and have them work that out for me.

By the end of class I needed to talk to someone who would understand how I felt. I hightailed it for the door the minute it ended. The school lobby was a mess of sound, but I went for the pay phone anyway. I had no cell phone for the same reason I had no high-speed Internet: cha-ching. I crammed a bunch of quarters into the phone.

On the third ring, someone answered.

"Natalie?" I asked.

"Who's this?" she asked and my heart fluttered because she had a girl's voice, a little throaty, but clearly feminine.

"I'm from GP," I said neutrally. "You sent me your number last night. I'm the one in Liberty." I was hyperaware of every word I used because there were about a hundred students who could overhear me if they wanted. Of course none of them were listening, but I couldn't be too careful.

"Emily?" she asked.

"Um, yeah, I'm at school. No cell phone."

"Oh, you can't talk, got it. Do you have a car? You want to meet this weekend?"

"Totally," I said, biting the inside of my cheek to keep from grinning.

"Saturday afternoon? Do you know where Southdale is?"

I wanted to say so much to her, but I could tell I was forgetting how to look like a guy. I'd leaned into the phone, cradled it to my ear, a suppressed grin twisting my mouth into a weird smirk. I blanked my face, rocked back on my heels, pushed my voice flatter and said, "I can figure it out."

"Great, meet me at two in the lobby of the theaters. What do you look like?"

"Orlando Bloom," I said. "Only taller and a lot less cute. And my hair's lighter. You?"

She was laughing at my description. "I'm tall with red-brown hair. I'll wear a black skirt and black boots and carry a flower or something."

"Hey, can I bring my girlfriend if she wants to come?"

"The one you just came out to? Your post was awesome! Of course, that would be great. She sounds fantastic! See you on Saturday!" Natalie talked with as many exclamation points as she used in her forum posts.

"Cool," I said and hung up. Then I glanced at the clock hanging over the big double doors of the school and bolted for my car. I drove it cold, groaning and complaining all the way, and skidded up to my house at three forty-five on the nose.

Mom came out of the front door as I pulled up. I slammed my car door and crossed the icy front lawn, hands jammed deep in my pockets. She was in gray slacks from work with her eyes made up and little earrings glinting in the amber sunlight.

"You're pushing it, kid," Mom said as she locked the front door behind her and gave me a shove toward her car.

"Sorry, school's crowded when it lets out, you know. I don't have a clear shot home."

"No lip," she said. "Get in."

We drove in silence to a low office complex.

On the second floor was a uniformly beige waiting room where we waited. Mom filled out a bunch of forms and then a man came out of an office and shook her hand. He was almost handsome, with short black hair that grayed in that dignified way over his ears, and steel-colored eyes. Two elements messed up his good looks: his thick brow ridge, like seriously caveman thick, and how his smile looked like someone had pushed the sides of his mouth up with their fingers and he was trying hard to hold the shape.

"I'm Doctor Dean Webber," he said. "Thanks for bringing Chris in to see me."

He shook Mom's hand and then mine. His hand was strong and dry, but really smooth and I slipped out of it mid-shake.

"Thank you for fitting us into the schedule," Mom said.

He nodded to her. "I'll have him back to you in an hour."

Dr. Webber showed me into his office. It was big enough for a long couch, a couple of comfy chairs, a few folding chairs, a clunky coffee table and a big, dark wood desk. Brown colors dominated the room. I sat down on the side of the couch away from the desk. He took the wingback chair across from me.

"Hi, Chris," he said, as if we hadn't just met in the lobby. "Your mother tells me you're not very happy."

I shrugged. He hadn't done much to sway me one way or the other to liking him or disliking him, but I erred on the side of caution.

"If I'm going to help you, you have to tell me what's going on with you. It's not unusual for boys your age to struggle with anger and sometimes depression. Your mother is worried about you, and I'd like us to have productive visits here. What you say to me is confidential."

Right, I thought, *my ass*. I had the distinct impression that it was confidential as long as it fit within his expectations. There was no way I was going to tell him the truth and trust him not to talk to my parents.

"I don't know what to say," I told him.

"Why don't we start with a small test," he suggested.

He handed me a form on a clipboard with the same depression questions that were on tests like this all over the Internet. Did I have a loss of appetite? Was I having trouble sleeping? Did I think about suicide? I answered it, putting in some positives and fudging the other answers toward the middle.

When I gave it back to him, he read it for a few minutes, nodding. "What about anger?" he asked. "Do you have a lot of anger?"

Yeah, I wanted to tell him, *but it's because of all the fucking testosterone that my mutant gonads are shooting into my bloodstream.*

"I suppose," I said. "I don't yell and stuff, but I can get pretty mad."

"What makes you angry?" he asked.

"My brother's a pest. Some of my teachers are pretty stupid." Oh, and did I mention that I'm stuck in the wrong body 24/7 and people keep treating me like someone I'm not?

"What about your father?"

His question cut through my thinking. Why did he want to know about Dad?

"Dad's okay," I said, picking at the round border at the edge of the couch arm. "He's a regular dad, you know. He's not home a lot these days, now that he has the building job."

"Has he ever hit you?" he asked.

Now I was on to him. He thought I was all depressed and pissed off because I was abused and sublimating my anger at my father. I debated whether it would work to use the word "sublimating" out loud to him, but then he'd probably say I was transferring my anger at my father on to him. I'd read plenty of psychology books while trying to figure out what was wrong with me.

"No, not really. He whipped me a few times when I was misbehaving, when I was a kid, but like a spanking, nothing major," I told him, all of which was true. It's important when hiding something big to tell as many small, distracting truths as possible.

Dr. Webber rubbed his chin, which would have come across as very distinguished except his face was too square and smooth to pull it off without looking self-mocking. "And what were you doing to misbehave?"

Wearing a dress, I thought. "I was going through my parents' stuff," I answered. "I was eight, and I was curious. I think he had his porn stash in there or something." I went on spinning a story that was as close to the truth as possible without revealing any dangerous details.

I went into my mom's closet a lot as a kid. I loved the way her clothes felt. I'd rub her dresses against my cheeks and sometimes I'd fall asleep in there. My parents thought it was cute. I guess they figured I was comforted by her smell, or the close darkness of the closet, both of which were true, but what I loved most was dreaming of the day when I'd grow up and get to wear clothes like that.

I knew what kind of woman I would be. I'd be a lot like my grandma Em who made her own clothes and devoured memoirs of powerful women—last time I'd visited her, she'd been reading Nawal El Saadawi. And I'd be a little like my mom, the way she knew the birthdays and tastes of all the people at her office and always took them gifts or food.

That afternoon when I was eight, Mom and Dad were out and the babysitter was watching TV. I figured I'd try on Mom's dresses, in practice for that far-off day when they'd be mine. In my kid's logic I'd already given up on changing my name as a way to change sex, but I still figured that when we grew up, Mikey would get all of Dad's stuff and I'd get all of Mom's stuff. When I got to wear her clothes for real, I'd become the woman I was supposed to be.

Dad caught me in one of Mom's summer dresses and that was the end of that fantasy. I stayed out of the closet from then on, but not because of the punishment. What really scared me was the way Dad stayed quiet the whole time. The few other times he'd spanked me in the past, he'd talked through the whole thing, telling me what I did wrong and how he was sorry to have to spank me but it was for my own good and so on. This time he didn't say a word, and I knew I'd done something so awful he couldn't talk about it.

And I knew I shouldn't talk about it now either. I told Dr. Webber that I'd been making a real mess in their bedroom and didn't mention dresses. He nodded and made understanding sounds and notes on his clipboard. I kept an eye on the clock and kept talking.

I was trying to draw these stories out as long as possible and fill up the hour. I told him about another time Dad gave me a spanking for stealing some of his tools and burying them out back of the house. Actually the tools were mine. Dad gave me a toolbox for my tenth birthday and I was trying to get rid of it, but that story sounded close enough. Dr. Webber kept asking for more details about how I felt, what I remembered Dad saying. I paused as long as I could before answering, pretending to scour my memory for details about each question. The minutes ticked by.

At the end of the hour, Dr. Webber shook my hand and said we'd see each other again next week.

I got into the car with Mom and stared out the window, trying not to feel like I'd been kicked in the gut. Saturday, I told myself, would make it all worthwhile.

"How did it go?" Mom asked.

"Fine, I guess. Hey, can I take Claire to the city on Saturday for a movie?"

I planned to go whether or not Claire would come with me, but saying that I wanted to take Claire made the trip sound less suspicious. If Claire didn't want to come, she'd probably cover for me. Or if she wasn't talking to me, at least she wouldn't be around for my mom to ask how she liked the movie.

"At night?" Mom asked.

"No, a matinee. We'll be back by eight."

"All right," she said.

I let out the breath I'd been holding. One more day of school and then the blessed weekend would be here and Minneapolis and Natalie. I really wanted Claire to come with me.

CHAPTER SIX

Claire

Claire paced across the living room and into her bedroom and back to the living room again. She tried to stop. Then she paced again. Chris had gone to the shrink today, and she needed to know how it went. Was there some psychological way to fix Chris's problem? If so, she hoped he'd listen to it. Chris could be stubborn when he made up his mind on something, but that was surprisingly rare.

When the phone on the end table rang, it was Chris's number on caller ID. She darted into her bedroom and answered the phone by her bed.

"How was Dr. No?" she asked, recasting the psychologist as the villain from the first James Bond movie.

Chris's laugh had a sharp edge. "As well as you'd expect."

"How's that?"

"Lousy. He's no good. There's no way he's going to help." His voice was a low monotone.

"Come on, you don't know until you try," she suggested. She hoped her disappointment didn't show in her voice. But life would be so much simpler if this was something Chris could solve in therapy.

"He just wanted me to talk about how angry I am and if Dad ever beat me. He thinks I'm an abused kid with a bunch of pent-up rage."

"You are kind of angry," Claire ventured. He didn't show it often, but there were times she felt Chris's body vibrate with tightly held frustration.

"Yeah," he said. "But now you know why."

"True." She sighed.

Could she get her mom to send her to a therapist? Maybe Claire could find one who did know what to do about a teen who thought they were transgender. Even having someone to talk to confidentially felt like a good idea, but then she'd have to talk about her own life too and her feelings about her father leaving and all of that. She didn't want to go digging around in there until it was time to write her memoir.

"Hey." Chris's voice brightened. "Want to go to a movie in Minneapolis on Saturday?"

"Why not go to one out here?" Claire loved going into the Cities for any reason, but she didn't want to show her excitement too soon. Since she was always the one pushing for a field trip, the fact that Chris brought it up meant that he had something planned. She wanted to know what that was before she got her hopes up.

"We're meeting a friend. From my support group online," he said.

"A real transgender person?"

"Claire!"

"What?" She tried to sound innocent, despite being embarrassed by her own outburst. As far as she knew, she'd never met a transgender person before—well, other than Chris—and she was curious.

"That's kind of…reductive," Chris said. "We're more than a label, you know, and I think Natalie would rather be called a girl."

"Oh, yeah, sorry." Claire paused and wondered if she should apologize more, or if that was enough. "Okay, movie on Saturday."

They hung up and she stared at the phone as if it was going to ring again and answer all the questions chasing each other around her brain.

Chris talked about everything so naturally: feeling like a girl, meeting a transgender girl in the Cities, but it felt alien to Claire and vaguely disgusting. Every time she tried to imagine Chris with long hair and breasts, it seemed so wrong.

While Claire had been on the phone in her room, her mom had settled on the living room couch and put on the TV. Claire dropped onto the couch next to her. She'd learned long ago that if she maintained a certain amount of Mom-time every week, she could get away with just about anything. Her mom acted younger than Chris's parents, even though she was a bit older. Often Claire felt that she had more of a big sister than a parent. That had bugged her in junior high when life was tougher and she'd wanted a parent she could go to for help, but now she loved that she had way more freedom than other kids at her school.

"I'm going to the city with Chris on Saturday," she said.

Muting the volume from the TV, Mom asked, "Are you having sex with him?"

"Whoa, where'd that come from? No," she protested.

"Honestly, Claire, I want you to tell me if you are."

For a moment she wondered what would happen if she said "Mom, he thinks he's a girl" but Chris would kill her.

"No, Mom, we're not having sex. We fool around and stuff, but I don't want to get pregnant or anything, that would be a real mess. Besides, I might turn out to be a lesbian."

Mom rolled her eyes and put the TV volume back on. "I swear, Claire, you make this stuff up to torment me."

"I thought that was my job," Claire replied automatically. Her mom had no idea what a person could be tormented with.

Claire wanted to be supportive of Chris, but she couldn't shake the nagging concern that he wasn't right, that all this stuff about being transgender was wrong.

"Oh, I've seen this one before," Mom said as she switched the channel from *Law & Order* to *Law & Order: SVU*.

Either of them could turn on the TV at any time and there would be some *Law & Order* show on. Mom could go for months sitting on the couch every evening watching crime shows. Then without warning she'd decide she was ready to date again and be out almost every night of the week socializing with the women from work and trying to meet a decent man. Claire's money was on that happening in April this year.

Although the crime shows followed the same pattern, it felt more comforting than boring. The contents of the stories were sensational enough that Claire could always watch one, plus it counted as bonding time with her mom. She settled back on the couch, glad to have something to take her mind off Chris.

Twenty minutes into the episode, one of the suspects was revealed to be a transgender woman. A bolt of electricity zinged through Claire. She peered upward and asked God silently, *Are you hinting?* Seemingly random coincidences were usually the divine trying to get her attention.

Of course the story was overblown, with the character having accidentally killed a man to protect herself and then being sent to men's prison where she was severely beaten. At the end of the episode, she was wheeled into the emergency room, beaten to a bloody mess and covered in bruises.

What was God trying to tell her? That there were enough people in the world who wanted to beat up Chris that she didn't need to be one of them? Or that the path he'd chosen was a dangerous one and he shouldn't take it?

How many transgender characters had she seen on TV? This wasn't the first time she'd seen one on a crime show, but they were always the victims or prostitutes, never the cops or pathologists or lawyers. And yet in her online research she'd seen transgender women with cool jobs: scientists, doctors, engineers, clergy, company owners, poets, writers.

She wanted to warn Chris away from this path, make sure he knew how dangerous it could be, but then she'd be just like those crime shows. He didn't need her to cast him as a victim.

This was like the one time she'd tried to seriously come out to her mom. She'd said, "I think I'm bisexual."

Just that and her mom had gone on, at length, with variations of, "Oh honey, that's such a hard life, are you sure that's what you want? Maybe this is a phase. You still like men. I just don't want to see you get hurt."

She'd repeated herself a few times that week. Claire got the feeling that it wasn't about her mom's concern for her. Otherwise why not try to keep her from much more dangerous pursuits, like driving a car? Instead this was the only acceptable way for her mom to say she didn't want Claire to be bi. After all, what would the neighbors think?

And the result had been that Claire had stopped talking to her mom about it, pulled away and made jokes, waiting to see if it would ever really be a safe topic.

Was she about to do the same to Chris? Was she on the edge of making it so he wouldn't talk to her about one of the most important parts of his life?

Just because she didn't like the idea of him being transgender, because she wasn't comfortable with it, that wasn't his fault. He shouldn't have to carry the burden of her freaking out.

The trans woman in the TV episode had to deal with the reactions of everyone around her until they nearly killed her. That was like what God had been saying with the Book of Job: don't be a jerk. Don't let your reactions and your fear drive you to hurt someone you care about.

She'd already started to pull away from Chris because of her fear. A piece of her solid world fell away when he said he was a woman. The belief that men were men and women were women was a foundational part of her world—until it was gone and she found herself teetering at the edge of the unknown.

Underneath her initial disgust, and all that questioning and discomfort lay simple fear. Well, she could handle fear.

She went into her bedroom and pulled out her journal. She spent so much time on the computer she knew her mom would look for a journal there, so she kept hers in physical form and hid it among her books.

She opened it to a clean page and wrote out her fears:

What if Chris goes through all of this and he's wrong but he can never go back again?

What if I can't be attracted to him through this and we split up?

What if the rest of the school finds out?

What if tonight was a warning and God doesn't accept transgender people?

If I keep loving Chris, what am I?

CHAPTER SEVEN

Though I loved Dad, I often avoided him because the older I got, the more likely he was to clap me on the shoulder and start a sentence with "Son." Anything that started that way wasn't going to end well. Nevertheless, he caught up with me on Friday morning, clapped me on the shoulder of sweater number three and said, "Son, I've got something you're going to like."

"What, Dad?" I asked, feeling like a poorly cast character in *Leave It to Beaver.*

"It's a beauty," he said, which meant either a car or truck. "A 1976 Ford Bronco. The seller's driving it out from the Cities Saturday morning. I thought you'd work on it with me."

Okay, guilty confession, I do think cars are cool. I'm willing to give that up if it prevents my entry into the world of official girlhood, but for the time being it's saved my butt with my Dad more often than I can count.

"Sweet," I said, letting some actual emotion into my voice. "I'm taking Claire to the city at one, but I'm around all morning."

He beamed and smacked my shoulder a couple more times, then sauntered off to work. When he had work, my dad was a happy man. The few times he'd been out of work were miserable for all of us.

I grabbed two slices of bread and hightailed it out the door before Mom could appear and grill me about Dr. No again. I cruised through the school day, buoyed up by the thought of Saturday afternoon. Claire and I missed each other in the halls. This was the time of year she started to get busy with all the clubs so I didn't worry about it more than the low level background freaking out about whether or not we were still dating. At least she'd said yes to the movie. She wouldn't have done that if she didn't want to see me anymore, right?

I ran aground abruptly in psych class. Mr. Cooper handed out our assignments. The guys booed, and I forgot to join in because my mouth was hanging open. My heart threatened to leap up my throat in a mixture of excitement and panic. The assignment said, "Pretend you wake up tomorrow morning the opposite sex. Write a four hundred word essay about your experiences."

"Gross," the guy in front of me said.

"Neanderthal," Jessica shot back to him. She turned to me and batted her eyelashes. "You wouldn't be a jerk about being a girl, would you?"

/run: emergency avoidance procedure

System Failure

I stared at her blankly. "Uh," I said.

"If I were a guy, I'd show some of the guys around here how to dress," she said, clinching the fact that she'd make a terrible guy.

"Yeah," I said. "Funny." There was no emotion in my voice and I could hear that it was missing, but I couldn't do a thing about it.

"It's not bad being a girl," she said, putting her hand on my forearm. She was flirting, of all things.

"Sure." I stood up as the bell rang.

"Jeez," she said. "You guys are all alike. You're afraid of anything the least bit feminine."

"Sure," I repeated and bolted from the room. The walls were a blur closing in around my head.

An assignment to pretend we were the other sex. Who comes up with something like that?

How was I supposed to write this? My body faded rapidly from a solid to an invisible membrane so thin that if anything brushed against me I'd split open. I would have to write about waking up as a girl for the assignment even though every morning, for those few minutes between waking and having to move, I got to be a girl completely, with no stupid physiology to contradict me.

I had to get out of the school building without looking like I had to get out. I forced my feet to move, slow and steady, past my locker, past the lobby, into the biting cold, my car, the key in the ignition. Wait for it to warm up. Forget English class.

Up until I was about nine or ten years old, I held out hope that I would grow up to be a woman, even though the evidence was mounting against that idea. When the other girls started to speculate about what it would be like to get their periods, I imagined that a period was the end of childhood, like the end of a sentence, and after that I'd get the right body parts. I was old enough to have given up on a magical solution, but somehow I convinced myself that my problem would be sorted out through puberty, that I would start to grow breasts and that thing between my legs would recede and I would become like the other girls.

It didn't help that my best friend at the time, Jessie, started growing breasts just before her tenth birthday. For years we'd both been flat-chested and then a few weeks before her birthday she snuck me into her room to show me the tiny bumps her breasts had become. We'd been comparing bodies on and off for a couple years, ever since she'd talked me into peeing in the woods with her on a park outing with our families.

"I want my breasts to start growing too," I told her. She gaped at me like I wasn't a real person. I slammed out of her bedroom and didn't talk to her for weeks.

I thought about that incident a year later when I woke up to find that my nipples ached and felt swollen. For days I floated on clouds. I was going to show her and everyone. But the happy feeling dissipated. I didn't grow breasts. Instead I grew two inches in the space of a summer, my shoulders widened, and I started sprouting hair on my chest.

From school, I drove over to Claire's. I couldn't go home. Dad and Mikey would be home soon. I couldn't let myself cry with them in the house. And I needed to know where I stood with Claire.

As I got out of the car I realized I'd left my coat at school. Fumbling the key into her front door, I pushed into the house shaking with cold. I planned to have a little cry and then wash my face and wait for her to come home so we could talk, but that planning part of my brain wasn't running the show.

I walked through the living room and into her room feeling like someone was crushing my chest, like I'd gone underwater and couldn't get to the surface. My eyes swung from side to side looking for anything that would stop this feeling. Without thinking about it, I opened her closet door and curled myself into the bottom. Ever since I was a kid hiding in my mom's closet, I've found comfort in dark, enclosed places. The small part of my mind that was still thinking told me I was being an idiot, a baby, a wuss, a fool and a dozen other sneers.

I leaned against the back wall of the little space and finally managed to cry a few of the thousand tears I'd been saving up from the past months. Wiping my face, I glared at my hands. My freakishly huge hands. I hated them. I hated this stupid body. Whose bright idea was it to make me a boy? Was it so hard to put a girl together? Did they just run out of girl bodies that day? Did I do something miserable in a past life?

"Chris?" Claire called from the living room. Then closer and more tentative, "Chrissy?"

God bless her.

I cracked the door and crawled out to see her staring down at me with wide eyes. Not because I was in her closet—she'd found me sitting in my own closet a few months ago when I got a C- for a whole semester of slogging through history—but because she'd never seen me cry before.

"Sorry," I managed, hating my deep voice.

She knelt on the carpet and grabbed my hands. "What happened?"

"Weird stuff," I said. I cleared my throat and wiped a hand across my face again, managing to smear snot across the back of it. "Tissue?"

She grabbed a box off her desk and handed it to me. "You look terrible."

"Cooper gave us this crazy assignment, to pretend we wake up tomorrow the other sex."

She laughed. "Oh, that's rich."

"And then this girl in my class was...she was joking about it, but I couldn't deal because I just—" My voice broke and tears started again. "I want to be a girl so bad. Am I completely messed up?"

Claire put an arm around my shoulders and dragged me to her chest. After all the times she'd curled into me, it felt so weird to lean my monstrously huge body against her, but it was also wonderful to feel held.

"You're okay," she said. "You just have a girl brain in a boy's body. Which I think makes me a lesbian trapped in a straight girl's body or, you know, bi."

I laughed and she laughed, and then I cried some more. When I finally sat up and blew my nose, I felt a lot more peaceful. Then I noticed that Claire looked worse than me. Her eyes were bloodshot and creased with tiredness.

"Were you up all night?" I asked.

"Pretty much. I fell asleep for about an hour in the middle."

"Of what?"

She pushed up from the floor and I stood with her. Her bed was made, like usual, but with big wrinkles in the middle of the dark gray comforter and four books open on it.

"Binge reading," she said with a grin. "Come on, make me a sandwich."

We went into the kitchen together. Claire was a much better cook than me, but I had one specialty dish: the grilled cheese sandwich. I think it only tasted better when I made it because she didn't have to do any work, but she insisted I had a special knack.

"When's your mom coming home?" I asked.

"Late," Claire said. "She has a date and he's picking her up from work."

I wrapped the kitchen apron around my waist and tied it. Claire sat on one of the two stools set up by the edge of the counter so people could talk to the cook. I put a big pan on to warm and pulled the bread, cheese and butter out of the fridge. The butter was the key ingredient. I believe that like popcorn, grilled cheese is a fancy butter-delivery system.

"I've been freaking out," Claire said. "And I might freak out more, okay? But I think I'm good for now."

I took in a long breath. She wouldn't have asked me to make sandwiches or called me "Chrissy" if she was going to throw me out, right?

"What does that mean?" I asked.

"Did you know that the Bible actually talks about transgender people?" she replied.

The breath I'd taken didn't seem to want to come out now. "Um," I managed.

If she was going to get all right-wing Christian on me, I'd leave mid-sandwich. Claire had this kind of weird system of religious belief that I didn't understand. My parents took me and Mikey to church every now and then, but we didn't make a fuss about it. Claire's family had taken her to church a lot when she was young and she'd loved it. When she hit her teenage years, she started reading *The Gnostic Gospels* and getting into the early Christians and the formation of the Bible and all that. Then she read the mystics, which included St. John of the Cross and his cloud of unknowing, which she was always going on about. At least with the cloud of unknowing, she never expected to me to know anything about it.

I had no idea what the Christian mystics thought about being trans.

"There's this bit in Isaiah," she said and hopped off the stool.

I turned the pan down because I wasn't going to start cooking the sandwiches yet, in case I had to run for it.

Claire came out with her Bible and read: "For thus says the Lord: 'To the eunuchs who keep my Sabbaths, who choose the things that please me and hold fast my covenant, I will give in my house and within my walls a monument and a name better than sons and daughters; I will give them an everlasting name that shall not be cut off.'"

"Are you calling me a eunuch? Really?" I put down the spatula and started to untie the apron.

"No!" she said. "Just listen to me for a minute because this is really cool."

I stopped untying the apron string and folded my arms. The frying pan was getting too hot even at the lower burner setting, but I didn't care.

"Back when the Bible was written, the Romans didn't have a word for transgender. But their word 'eunuch' included multiple categories of people. Only one of those is what we mean by 'eunuch' today. And one of the other categories includes people who chose not to procreate, and men who dressed and acted like women. It *includes* transgender people."

"You stayed up all night reading about this?"

She put the Bible on the edge of the counter and sat back on the stool. Pressing her hands together between her knees, she stared down at them.

"I was really afraid," she said. "I'm still afraid, kind of. I read bunches of stuff, about the brain studies and how there's a lot of trans people. Way more than I thought. But, you know, nothing's more important to me than having a loving relationship with God, and I know people twist the Bible to say all kinds of crazy stuff. It's not like I'm a literalist, but I think that the Bible is a valid way for God to communicate with us. So when I read that about the translation of 'eunuch' and that passage in Isaiah— and there are others too, but that's the best one—I got it."

I put the sandwiches into the pan and listened to them sizzle. "Good," I told her.

"It's not like I was looking for God's permission, like He's some kind of angry parent," she said. "The words just cut through my confusion and showed me what was already in my heart."

I had to ask. "Is dating me in your heart?"

Claire tipped her face up toward me, eyes shining. "Yes," she said.

I grinned into the pan and flipped the sandwiches. "And you're never going to call me a eunuch again?" I asked, even though her point about the quote and the translation was awesome.

She threw a dishtowel at me. It bounced off my shoulder and I tried to catch it on my thigh as it fell, but instead smacked my knee into the oven handle. I hopped on one foot for a second, holding the knee up, but it didn't hurt that badly and the sandwiches were about to burn.

I slid the sandwiches onto plates, then bent down to get the towel. Claire hopped off the stool and pulled the towel out of my hand, dropping it back onto the floor. She put her palms on either side of my face so she could pull me down to kiss her.

When the kiss was over, she smiled up at me and said, "Besides, I've always wanted to give lesbianism a real go."

I rolled my eyes at her and picked up the sandwich plates. "Couch?"

"There's a *Law & Order: Criminal Intent* on the DVR. Let's do it."

CHAPTER EIGHT

I slept for about eleven hours, which I'm certain shored up Mom's hypothesis that I was depressed, but to me it felt great. Then I spent about a year in the shower letting the water run over me. I shaved my arms and legs again, even though the swim season was over. If anyone asked I'd tell them that the new hair itched and it was easier to keep it shaved. I would not mention that I loved the feel of smooth legs under my jeans.

Mom was cleaning up the kitchen when I made it downstairs. Mikey lay across the living room floor watching TV. He wasn't old enough to skip cartoons yet. I hoped that lasted another year because I enjoyed my Saturday mornings without him flying around the house like a pinball.

"How do you feel?" she asked.

"Great," I said.

I poured a glass of milk and grabbed two of the cinnamon rolls she'd made. Mom seemed trapped between being a career woman and being a stay-at-home mom. Either one would be great, but she wavered back and forth between the two, telling us to make our own dinner one night and then taking over the cooking for the next three or four days.

"I've been up too late studying," I added around a bite of cinnamon, sugar and dough.

"Is school hard?" she asked, fishing for problems.

"Nah, I just want to do good for college aps." Which was trueish. I had no intention of going to college near Liberty and I knew Mom and Dad couldn't afford to send me anywhere fancy.

"Chris!" Dad yelled from the garage door. "Chris, come see this!"

I flashed Mom a grin and grabbed my old jacket from the closet, wishing I hadn't left the good one at school.

Some fool had driven a junker of an old Bronco the fifty-odd miles from the Cities, his girlfriend following in her dilapidated Chevy. The Bronco was in terrible shape and looked about ready to drop parts into the street.

Dad and the scruffy man who'd driven it in walked around it, looked under the hood, and then exchanged information and money. I was supposed to be in that circle with them, admiring the car and haggling over its value, but I didn't feel like it. I smelled the guy from where I stood, a thick mix of burnt rubber and acrid sweat. And his lanky brown hair hadn't been washed in about a week.

In the rusty Chevy, his girlfriend smoked a cigarette, blowing long streams of light gray smoke through a one-inch opening at the top of her window, leaving enough smoke inside the car to make it hazy. I couldn't see her face, only her dishwater blond hair pulled back in a ponytail. What did she like about her boyfriend? Did she like the way he smelled and those skinny legs inside his faded jeans?

Dad motioned me over. "This is my son Chris," he said. "He's going to work on it with me."

"Chris," the man said. "You'll make your dad proud."

"Sure," I replied, beginning to feel like that was the only useful word in my vocabulary.

Then he was gone in the smoky car with his girlfriend and Dad drove the Bronco into our oversized garage. We may not have had the biggest house on the block, but we definitely had the biggest garage. Ironic, since I always had to park at the curb to make room for the cars Dad fixed up. The garage was two spaces wide and a little over two deep and had enough heaters to keep it at least in the fifties during the worst of winter. Dad had installed four spotlights and there were times when the garage seemed brighter and warmer than the house.

Despite the fact that I was one hundred percent clean, I capitulated and helped Dad with the car. I had the feeling I was going to need a good stash of parental brownie points in the near future, so I pushed up my sleeves and got to work.

At noon I cut out, had a quick lunch, showered again, put on my second favorite sweater and went to pick up Claire. She slipped into the warm car and gave me a kiss on the cheek.

"Claire, what do you like about having a boyfriend?" I asked.

"I don't know," she said. "I mean, I'm not dating you because you're a guy. I like you because you're funny and smart and a total geek. And sure, I like that you're tall and strong and all that."

"But what is it about guys that girls like?"

"I think strength, for sure, and guys tend to be easier than girls, you know, less complicated...well, except for you. Guys make girls feel safe," she said and pushed on my shoulder with the palm of her hand. "I wonder if I'm going to miss that," she added quietly.

"I'll always be tall," I offered.

"Who's this Natalie?" she asked.

"She's from a forum online, a support site. She knows me by my girl name 'Emily.' Is that going to be weird?"

"Girl name?"

"I'll change my name legally when I can," I said. It was hard to remember that Claire didn't know that much about being transgender, despite her long nights of study on the subject. She could sound so cool with it one moment and then completely clueless the next.

"To Emily?" she asked.

"Emily Christine Hesse."

Because I was driving, I couldn't see the full expression on her face when I said my name, but I stole and peek and caught her nodding.

"Is that why your mage in game is Amalia?" she asked.

"Someone already took the name Emily, and anyway, I like the game to be a little different from reality. But yes, I wanted a name that was like Emily."

She turned half sideways in her seat to look at me more fully. "I played a male character for a few months," she said. "Like a year ago when I was really into player-versus-player combat. It felt like people listened to me more in the game when I was a seven-foot-tall guy. But that always felt more like wearing a costume to me. I thought you played girl characters so you could look at their butts."

I laughed. That was what other guys in our guild said who played female characters. I was often surprised at how many of the female characters in the game turned out to be played by men in real life. I had no idea how many were trans or gay or really did prefer looking at a female character on the screen while they played.

"I love that there's at least one world where I can show up and female," I told Claire. "It feels like magic to me."

"Like the *Wizard of Oz*," she said.

"Yes!"

After a few quiet minutes, Claire asked, "Am I supposed to call you Emily?"

"If no one's around, I'd like that."

"Huh," she said and went silent again.

We drove past snowy fields and trees decked in white and more and more houses until we came into the western suburbs of the Cities. Southdale was in Edina, a suburb and not Minneapolis proper, but close enough that my parents didn't make a distinction. Anytime I wanted to go to the Cities, they figured I was trying to score drugs or drink or something. Of course, Dad did a lot of drinking when he was a kid, so he didn't exactly disapprove.

This was one of those funny times when it worked out that people saw me as a guy. Mom and Dad didn't worry about me, like Claire's mom did about her, that I was going to get kidnapped or raped or sold into slavery. It must've been the crime shows they watched, because Claire's mom could fret for days about something catastrophic happening to her daughter but she never seemed to worry about where Claire actually was on any given day.

I pulled into Southdale and ended up driving around the mall twice before figuring out how to get into the parking lot in front of the theater.

"Man, don't you wish we lived closer," Claire said. She paused and grinned, "And by 'man,' I mean 'person' of course."

I smacked her shoulder. "Goof. Come on."

The theater had sixteen screens and a cavernous lobby filled with what seemed like two hundred people. I was scanning the crowd, saying to myself "black skirt, boots, flower" when Claire grabbed my hand and dragged me over toward a girl. I thought Claire was going to ask for directions. Then I realized the girl was wearing a black skirt and boots, and carrying a dyed-purple carnation.

I couldn't stop beaming. She grinned back at me.

"Natalie," she said holding out her hand.

I took it, wondering at how soft it felt. "Emily," I said, introducing myself for the first time out loud. "But you should probably call me Chris. This is Claire."

"Hey," Claire said.

I looked Natalie up and down. She looked like a girl. She was a girl. She looked great. She wasn't quite as tall as my six feet, but she was a lot taller than Claire. Of course everyone was taller than Claire, even in her boots. Natalie had shoulder-length dark brown hair with red highlights and big, dark eyes that she emphasized with makeup.

"Come on," she said, taking my right hand and Claire's left. She pulled us away from the theater and down the mall to California Pizza Kitchen.

I tried to stop staring, but I kept watching Natalie out of the corner of my eye. She walked gracefully and if her hips were narrow and her shoulders broad and solid, they weren't more so than some of the members of the girls' swim team at my school.

Natalie was so lucky to already be on hormones at seventeen. She could expect her body to pad her hips over the next few years. Her pelvic bones would always be narrow, but now her body knew that fat was supposed to go to the hips. We had to be the only two girls in the whole mall who wanted fatter hips.

At the restaurant, I took a chair across from her and Claire sat next to me. We ordered pizza to share, and the waiter called Natalie "miss" without a second thought. In addition to the long, styled hair and the pretty makeup, Natalie wore a tight-fitting tan sweater that made her breasts obvious. She looked like a solid B-cup to me, and I wanted to ask her if that was all from hormones or if she was augmenting with a padded bra.

If I looked hard, I could see how Natalie's chin was thicker than most girls, but the dark copper and brown hair falling around her face masked the effect and drew my eye away. She already had great lips, not the thin lips I'd been stuck with, and her makeup on them was a very subtle pale pink. Her cheeks fell in the mid-range; I had a little surge of guilty optimism because my cheeks weren't as wide as hers and hers didn't read male because her eyes dominated that part of her face.

I had obsessed night after night over any pictures I found online of women who had transitioned. I scoured them for signs of maleness and tried to prove to myself that it was possible that I could someday live a normal life as a woman. But two-dimensional photos and even videos were nothing like the experience of sitting across from a girl who'd had to deal with a body like mine! I wanted to touch her to make sure she was solid and not just a dream.

I had so many questions that I couldn't figure out where to start, so Claire took over.

"Look, tell me if I'm being rude at any point here, okay? We're the country mice, you know, and I think we have a lot of questions," Claire said, glancing at me. I nodded and she went on. "Can we ask 'em?"

"Sure," Natalie said.

Even that one word had a slight breathiness and lilt to it, putting it firmly on the feminine side of the line. Her voice wasn't high-pitched, but my English teacher's voice was a smokier, deeper woman's voice than Natalie's.

"Start with 'I was born a boy' and tell the whole story," Claire said.

Natalie gave a short huff of a laugh. "Well, it was the usual. You'll start hearing this a lot if you hang around us types. And, so you know, I wasn't born a boy. I was assigned male at birth; that's how to say it so you don't erase gender diversity."

"Oh I read about that. Because people get born all sorts of ways and then dumped into either the boy or girl bucket based on what the doctor thinks they see," Claire said. "But what do you call yourself? Is 'transsexual' gauche?"

"It's not great, at least in the sense that it objectifies us and narrows us to that one thing. And transsexual is a very clinical term. My whole life isn't about my gender identity, you know. I prefer to be called a girl."

"But then how do you talk about it?" Claire asked.

"Some people say transgender or trans girl, trans woman. And some people still say transsexual. If it's necessary I guess I like trans girl, but otherwise, girl."

"That's cool, thanks. Go on with the story?"

"When I was young I played with other girls, and I got upset when my sister got dresses for her birthday and I didn't. I played with her dolls, and by the time I was about six I wouldn't play with boys. Mom and Dad took me to two psychologists and one of them was smart and said not to push me about my gender, just to make sure I had lots of all kinds of toys and watch how I developed. I told Mom I was a girl a few different times. She tried to explain that I was a boy, but I wouldn't believe her. When puberty hit, I started getting more and more upset. I mean really confused and sad and depressed. Some days I wouldn't get out of bed at all unless my mom made me. We went back to the psychologist, and Mom explained that I could choose to have a girl's body if that's what I really, really wanted."

Natalie paused, watching the server bring our pizzas. He set them out and checked to see if we needed anything else. I think Claire was almost as eager for Natalie to go on as I was.

"I've read all your posts," Natalie told me. "And you sound like me, like you knew since you were a kid. But, Claire, it's not the same for everyone. People come out at different ages in different ways. I have a friend who says it wasn't that she felt she was a girl, but when she looked to the future, she saw the woman she could become. There are a lot of different ways to know you're trans."

"Wait, she didn't feel like a girl, but she wanted to be one?" Claire asked.

"I guess some people think it's so impossible that they don't feel it in themselves," Natalie told her. "But they dream of a future where they're a woman, or they have to see other people before they realize, 'I'm like that; I want that.' Or they have a lot of identities to work out as a kid and the trans one gets shoved to the back."

"When did *you* start being a girl all the time?" Claire asked.

Natalie pulled a slice of pizza onto her plate and said, "They put me on hormones a couple years ago and then we moved here a year and a half ago so I could go to school as a girl. It's been going super well. This summer I get my last surgery and then we're all done."

"What surgery?" Claire asked.

Natalie raised an eyebrow and pointed under the table toward her lap.

Claire stood up. "Okay, I'm going to the bathroom," she said. "I don't want to know this part. Back in a bit."

Natalie watched Claire weave between the tables, then turned to me. "She'll be okay," she said, though I think she was trying to reassure both of us.

"Yeah. So, wow, that's really cool about your parents. What's it like taking the hormones?"

"It's great. I don't feel so angry all the time, and it's easier to cry when I'm upset, and all my hair got finer and softer and my skin."

She moved her hand toward me and I touched the soft skin across the back of it. "It didn't used to be like that?" I asked.

"No, not that soft. It was like yours." She ran her fingertips down my forearm. "You shave your arms?"

"Swimmer," I said. "It's a good excuse to shave just about everything."

She laughed. "That's smart."

"Are you scared about the surgery?"

"A little," she admitted. "I want it to go really well."

Claire came out of the bathroom and regarded us warily. I waved her back to the table. "We're done talking about that part," I said.

She forced a smile. "So, do you like boys or girls or both?" she asked Natalie.

"Boys," Natalie answered. "But there are all kinds of sexual orientations in the trans community. I think sometimes it's harder for trans girls who like boys to figure it out, because we can think we're gay. But then if you like girls it's hard because you're going to end up a lesbian and some therapists don't like to recommend a sex change that's going to make another lesbian. They think if you like girls you should just try to be a boy. And for trans girls who are bi, mostly they have to hide that from therapists and doctors until after they transition, which is its own kind of yuck because you're hiding one part of yourself so another part can get seen."

I'd finished one slice of pizza and Claire had about nibbled hers to death. I stole her crust so she could eat another and I'd have something to fiddle with. I'd already had lunch before the drive and anyway, I was too curious to be hungry.

"Were you always this pretty?" Claire asked. "I mean, were you a really pretty boy?"

Natalie cocked one eyebrow at Claire. "I was never a boy," she said. Claire blushed, but Natalie went on talking. "I look like my baby pictures. When I hit puberty, I started looking like a guy. You might not recognize a picture of me if you didn't know."

"Your makeup is amazing," I said because it was true, but also to give Claire a moment to recover.

"Years of practice," Natalie replied, flashing me a grin.

"I'm sorry," Claire started, but Natalie waved a hand to stop her.

"You're going to slip up, it's natural. You've been really cool to Emily, and I know your heart's in the right place, so don't worry about it. Do you want to catch a movie? *Cloverfield* is starting in about twenty minutes."

"Oh I totally want to see that," Claire said and I agreed.

Natalie paid for the pizza, though I tried to protest, and we were off. I watched her walk and smiled more. Sure her hips were narrow, but she looked great. There might be hope for me after all—the faint flickering glimmer of hope that lay on the far side of having to talk to my parents. Could I get on hormones without their permission? A bitter taste flooded my mouth. The answer was as close as Natalie walking two steps in front of me and still impossibly far away.

CHAPTER NINE

Claire

Even with previews blaring from the big screen, the cool darkness of the theater was a relief. Claire didn't want it to bother her, but there was something about the way Natalie sounded so cavalier about surgeries and sex changes. There were only a few things in her life that Claire hadn't gotten around to questioning, but sex and how bodies were made was one of them.

And she liked Chris's body. He was a cute guy. Except for the girl-brain part. He looked great in sweaters because of his swimmer's shoulders, and she loved the feel of his hard chest and strong arms. Now he wanted to go and change everything. Was he going to grow breasts and have long hair and paint his nails? Wouldn't he just look like her boyfriend in drag?

Probably not, she had to admit, after looking at Natalie for most of lunch. She might not know all the details, but she could see that the medical stuff they did to Natalie had worked. She had kind of a big jaw, but no bigger than a few of the girls at school. Claire knew plenty of girls who were taller than Natalie, and a few who were taller than Chris.

When she and Chris started going out last summer, she always assumed he would dump her someday for a prettier girl, not that he would want to *become* a prettier girl. The thought made her giggle and she put her hands over her mouth.

They'd met in a two-day poetry workshop offered by a visiting teacher from the Cities over a weekend. After the first day, Chris told her he liked what she wrote, and how could she resist him after that? Besides, they liked a lot of the same things: music, computers, games, books, each other, and Chris even admitted to talking to God from time to time, but not in some weird superreligious way, which Claire thought was an adorable footnote to add to every other good quality about him. They'd been dating almost eight months. Chris was already her best friend and she felt like she'd known him most of her life—only to find she didn't know him that well at all.

She felt jealous of Natalie. Not that Chris was going to run off with her, just that she so clearly had what he needed right now.

And then there was that dizzy feeling, like the seat was going to fall out from under her at any moment. Men didn't turn into women, and yet here in the theater, two seats away, was a girl who had been born a boy, or assigned male at birth, however she was supposed to say that. And, if Claire understood correctly, had at least one very boy part on her still. She couldn't help but think about it. What would it be like to go to school and have to hide that? Natalie couldn't change in the locker room, that was for sure. What happened if someone found out? She didn't know about Minneapolis, but out in Liberty lesser infractions than that sent people to the hospital. Some of the Neanderthals at school still thought it was sporting to "roll fags."

Off balance as she felt, a strong wave of protectiveness welled up in her. Chris had stepped in and stopped other kids at school from calling her "death freak" or worse for wearing all black. Dating him improved her social standing immensely, which meant almost no taunting anymore and occasionally an invite to a cool party. Not that she cared about those and she'd lose all of that if anyone found out about this transgender stuff, but he'd lose a lot more. No matter what happened, she wouldn't let any harm come to Chris if she could stop it.

When the movie ended, Claire could barely have said what it was about. They had another hour to play with before they had to drive back and assure their parents that the big city hadn't corrupted them.

"Come on," Natalie said. "Let's go shopping. What've you got for girl clothes?"

Chris blinked a couple times, glanced at Claire and then said, "Two sweaters, a pair of jeans and a skirt."

"What?" Claire asked before she could stop herself. "You have girl clothes? Do your parents know?"

His cheeks reddened as he admitted, "They're in a duffel in my car with your name on it."

She laughed. "Oh. Cute. They're like ten sizes too big."

"They'll never notice."

"No pants?" Natalie cut in. "You need a good pair of dress pants. Come on."

She pulled them into Banana Republic and in a matter of minutes collected an armful of pants. Then she dragged the three of them into the women's largest dressing room stall. "I need my boyfriend's opinion," she told the startled attendant and shut the door firmly, pushing the pants at Chris. "Brown first," she whispered.

Claire sat on the chair in the dressing room and watched with amazement. Natalie had plastered herself across the door and after a moment's pause, Chris pulled off his jeans and stepped into the pants, turning away to tuck himself so he'd fit into girls' pants. Claire forced herself not to look at Natalie and wonder what she did with her... *Don't think of that*, she told herself.

It wasn't the fit of the pants Claire saw when she turned from Natalie back to Chris, it was Chris's face. As the pants were zipped and buttoned and he turned to show them off, his face lightened. Most of the time his eyes were dark, haunted, and looked as if he was staring out of them from far away inside himself. Now they sparkled. It was like sitting in a dark room for months and then suddenly having the sun fall through an open window.

"Wow," she said.

"Do they look good?" Natalie asked because Chris couldn't voice the question. If the attendant was lurking outside, they needed it to sound like Natalie was showing off the pants, not Chris.

Claire stood up and touched this bright, glowing person's cheek. "You look really happy," she said almost in a whisper. "I never saw how very sad you look all the time. I thought that was how you looked, but this...this is you, happy."

From inside Chris, Emily smiled, eyes bright with joy.

"I think I should get these pants," Natalie said loudly enough for the attendant to hear and winked.

Chris tried on the next pair, while Natalie quietly told Claire, "My mom said something similar when I started going to school like this. She said she'd been so worried about me and suddenly I was full of confidence and optimism. I told her I'd always been like that, I'd just spent so much energy fighting against that other thing that I had nothing left over."

None of the other pairs of pants worked as well as that first chocolate brown pair. When Chris was back in jeans, Natalie took the brown pants and went to the register. As they left the store, Chris offered to pay her back but she insisted it was a gift.

They said goodbye in the theater lobby with hugs all around. Claire tried not to pay attention to Natalie's breasts during the hug, but she couldn't help it. They felt very real, and she smelled like clover and oranges. It felt like hugging any other girl.

All the way back to Liberty, Claire watched Chris's face. It was like the sun coming out from behind clouds. She wanted to find a more unusual metaphor, but none came to mind. She just knew she'd never seen anything like it in her life. The closest was her mom the year after Dad left. She'd turned dark for a while, but that was because she literally never opened the window shades. And then slowly, day-by-day, she went from being shadowed back to the life-giving colors Claire remembered. Even that wasn't as dramatic a change as she'd seen in Chris.

Up to that point, Emily had been a faint idea. Something strange that Chris wanted and maybe Claire could support him because she cared about him. But in the dressing room and now on the drive back, Claire saw distantly, like spotting a friend across a crowded cafeteria, the presence of a scared, happy, shy, proud girl. She seemed to be inside Chris and yet so much more vibrant, bright and alive.

"You look good happy," she said.

"Is it that obvious?"

"More than obvious."

She kissed Chris in the car and held tight to that newly alien, newly bright body for a few minutes. Then she trooped back through the snow to her living room where Mom was watching TV as usual.

"How was the city?" Mom asked as she paused the episode of *Bones* that she'd recorded. She wore her around-the-house blue terry-cloth pants and jacket.

"Great. Really fun." Claire dropped onto the couch. "We went to a big mall for pizza and a movie. What about your day? I thought you had a dinner date tonight."

"Are you trying to get me out of the house?"

Claire laughed. "If I wanted to see more of Chris, I'd have him sneak in the window," she said.

"You're kidding, right? I hope you're kidding."

"Mom. Really."

"My date turned out to be a typical Aquarius," Mom said with a sigh.

"I told you those air signs are trouble for you."

Mom shook her head but she was smiling. She hit play and they watched to the next commercial. While her mom was fast-forwarding through it, Claire asked, "What are you doing tomorrow?"

"Cleaning and I hope you are too, why?"

"Can we go shopping for nonblack makeup? I think it's time for me to learn how to wear it."

Her mom grinned. She'd been trying even harder to get Claire interested in cosmetics for the last year, since the lesbian jokes had started.

"Sure, honey."

Claire smiled and settled back into the couch. If her mom knew what she was really going to use the cosmetics for it would probably fry her brain, but let her be happy about it instead. Everyone deserved to be happy.

CHAPTER TEN

Saturday night I watched a stupid kids' movie with Mikey, but I wasn't really watching. I took the opportunity of sitting on the couch to replay the afternoon with Natalie and Claire over and over. I fell asleep later still thinking about Claire saying I looked happy. I hadn't known it was that obvious, but I did change that afternoon. "Change" wasn't the right word. That would mean I'd become something else. I'd relaxed into myself. I could let other people see me.

There had been so many years of pretense; I hadn't realized how different it made me to always be pretending. The trappings of boyhood were wrapped around me in layers, like wearing all my winter clothes, one sweater on top of another and then the jacket and scarf, in the middle of summer. Everyone was so used to seeing me as a mummy, they didn't know I could be any other way.

I'd learned to disconnect my ears and mouth from the rest of me so that I could hear all those words "son," "boy," "he/him" without them taking a chunk out of my soul every time. But what did that make me?

I wanted to live a real life. If magic didn't turn me into a real girl, the way I'd wanted as a kid, there were other ways. Natalie had done it. Now she went to school every day like I did, but she got to be fully herself. I fell asleep wondering what that would be like.

In the morning, still in the T-shirt and boxers I slept in, I silently locked my door and then sat down at the computer to start my next phase of research. I'd seen a lot of these sites in the last few years as I was figuring things out, but now I researched in earnest, read deeply and made cryptic notes in my science notebook. One site had a list called "Things you can do before your parents know." A few of those I was already doing, like working hard in school, saving money and researching my options. I already had my name picked out, but I hadn't started working on my voice.

This summer would be the perfect time to practice my voice. I'd download a few tracks to my iPod and rename them as exercises from a drama class I took last year. The iPod was another device my parents had no idea how to use, but even if they did snoop, they'd see the names and never give it a second thought. Then I could take it with me and practice in my car when I was alone.

The list also said I should take care of my skin, though there was no way with Dad and Mikey in the house that that was going to happen. They'd spot an exfoliant in the "men's bathroom" in a hot second. Mom had long ago taken over the master bathroom as her sanctuary and I could sometimes sneak in there, but not often enough. Maybe Claire would let me keep some skin products at her house.

Next I had to figure out how to get hormones. Mom was too young to start menopause, so I wasn't going to be able to sneak any estrogen replacement therapy from her, assuming she'd even use it. I laughed. How many teenage kids sat around thinking about their mom's menopause? It was possible to illegally order hormones from an overseas pharmacy. But first there was that whole illegal issue, and I'd seen other girls on the forums say there were no quality and safety checks. So I could spend a bunch of money only to get pills that didn't work or made me sick.

I couldn't waste money now. In addition to surgery, I'd need electrolysis or laser hair removal. I needed to make a lot more money.

Okay, that was the plan. This summer I would work on my voice and skin, while making as much money as humanly possible. The tip sheet also said it would be good to talk to a therapist, but I still thought Dr. Webber was not my guy. I'd try some hints in the next session because you never know. Speaking of hints, I wondered what my parents were doing today. Maybe I could start to see if Mom was at all receptive to the idea of having a daughter.

I unlocked my door, showered and threw on a weekend outfit: jeans, T-shirt, sweatshirt. Mom was in the living room reading the Sunday paper, and I heard clattering sounds from the garage.

"You're finally up," Mom said, talking across the hall to me while I poured a bowl of cereal.

I glanced at the clock. It was almost eleven. "Yeah, I guess I'm catching up on my sleep."

"Do you really have that much homework?" she asked.

I took my bowl of cereal into the living room and sat on the other end of the couch from her, stretching my huge feet out on the coffee table. In Claire's house, no one ever rested their feet on the coffee table, but here it was impossible to keep Dad from doing it, and generally if Dad did it, Mikey and I could get away with it.

I shrugged while I swallowed a few bites. "It's not that much," I said. "I do some extra stuff, you know, for college and that. And sometimes I get interested in something and stay up."

She rested the paper on her lap with a wistful smile. "I used to stay up half the night reading when I was your age." That only enforced my belief that Mom was a lot smarter than she let on. She never went to college because she got pregnant in the last year of high school and married my dad. Sometimes I joked that she and I could go to college together, but she ignored that.

I think she'd given up. At best she said she'd take some classes after she retired.

It was easy to forget how young my mom was. In another year, I'd be the same age she was when she'd had me. She actually looked youngest when she dressed up for work and blew her hair dry so that it feathered back in waves from her face. When she wasn't bustling around the house with her hair rough and her face scrunched in a look of disapproval, she was prettier than Claire's mom.

"Mom, do you ever wish you had a daughter?"

She folded closed the section of the paper she'd been reading and picked up the next section. "Sometimes," she said. "I thought about getting pregnant again after Mikey. I love both of you, you know that right?"

"Sure, yeah. But it would be nice if you had a kid who was a girl, right?"

I must've had a look because she asked, "What are you worried about? I know you're not as masculine as your father, but you've become a wonderful young man."

"It's not that. I'm not worried about not being masculine," I said.

I'd put too much dismissive tone on "masculine." Mom's face hardened and she straightened up, folding shut the section of newspaper she'd opened.

"Chris, I know your father and I don't take you to church every weekend, but we are good Christians and we don't support alternative lifestyles. You do understand that, don't you? If you have questions, you should talk to the doctor about that and get help."

My heart shriveled into a small, dark mass and then crumbled. If she was going to freak like that at the idea that I could be gay, there was no way I was getting anywhere with the "I'm really a girl" conversation.

"It's fine, Mom, it's not that. I like girls, really."

She smiled, though the gesture looked forced.

"Are Dad and Mikey in the garage?" I asked, standing up. She nodded and opened the paper again. I put my bowl in the sink, washing the uneaten cereal down the drain. "I'm going to go bang on the car with them. Yell if Claire calls."

"Okay," she said.

I thought that would be the end of it, but it wasn't. You know what they say about adding insult to injury? Well, that came later in the evening. I worked on the Bronco with Dad and Mikey most of the afternoon. Showered again. Did some homework.

Dad knocked on my door after dinner, which was weird enough. Not the knocking, but him coming to my room instead of waiting to run into me around the house or in the garage.

I glanced toward the foot of the bed to make sure that "Claire's" duffel was in my car, which it was. "Come in," I said.

He was already halfway through the door, but he shut it behind him, also unusual. He sat down on my bed. His hair was still wet from the shower, making the brown gray a shade darker. He'd put on clean carpenter pants and a different waffle pattern shirt, but had the same dark gray vest over it with its fifteen pockets filled with tools and bits of car.

"Son," he said. "Your mother told me you were asking some questions this morning."

"Yeah," I replied, voice carefully neutral while the ice of panic dripped down the inside of my ribs.

"Were you afraid to talk to me?" he asked.

I thought, *About being your daughter? Yeah*.

"Um, I guess," I managed. Could he possibly have figured it out? Or did they still think I was gay? "I'm not gay," I told him.

He smiled thinly. Strong, creased fingers took a small pair of long-nosed pliers out of his vest pocket and turned them over as he talked. "Of course you aren't. These kinds of things can happen to anyone."

Okay, he definitely had something in mind. Was he thinking what I was thinking? "So you know someone else with my... situation?" I asked. I felt like I was on some perverse game show where the loser is taken out back and shot.

"Oh yeah, some of the guys I work with. You know, it's natural to go through this."

Now I knew we were *not* on the same page. But what page was he on? "What did they do?" I asked.

"Well, you should make sure you're taking your vitamins and eating well," he said, fingers rubbing along the tips of the pliers like he was cleaning them. "And your mother thinks you're not sleeping enough. Try not to be so uptight all the time, and don't…ah…take too many solo flights, if you get my drift."

Suddenly I was in that *Star Trek* episode where Picard cannot, for the life of him, figure out what the alien captain is saying because that race speaks entirely in metaphor, and yet they're supposed to fight a monster together. Vitamins? Solo flights?

He went on. "You tell Claire it's normal, and I'm sure she'll understand."

"She's fine about it, Dad."

"That's good. If it doesn't clear up in a few weeks, you come talk to me and we'll take you to a real doctor." He paused, jaw set, looking from the pliers to me. "It still works some, right?"

I stared at him blankly.

"You can get it up some of the time?" he asked. "And you're not having trouble peeing or anything like that?"

My face turned redder than Mars. I wanted to burst out laughing and crying. He thought I was having trouble with impotence. Good Lord!

"No, Dad," I managed, barely remembering the question he'd asked. "It's probably the late nights and stress."

He stood up and clapped his hand on my shoulder, pliers vanishing back into their pocket. "That's my boy. Don't be afraid to talk to me."

"Sure," I said, holding my breath until he was safely out of the door.

The room felt too small and closing in even further, but where could I go? It was February and I didn't want to go for a walk in ten-degree weather. No stores were open on Sunday night. I swore soundlessly for a few minutes and then put my face in my hands. I try to talk to my parents about being transgender and they think I'm impotent.

Well, I thought, *it's almost in the ballpark.* I still wanted to put my fist through the wall.

I carefully went downstairs saying to Mom, "Books are in my car" and then continued on blessedly outside into the frigid night. The icy air helped. I'd left my scarf inside and kept my jacket unzipped, standing out by my car, staring up at the sky until the tips of my fingers started to go numb.

* * *

After school on Monday, Claire had one of her bazillion clubs and Tuesday I had a short off-season swim training, so it was Wednesday before I could tell her about the bizarre conversation with Dad. She literally fell off the bed laughing.

"Impotent," she gasped from the floor. "Oh, that's rich."

"Sometimes I wish I was," I admitted.

She pushed up on her elbows, static making single strands of hair rise behind her head. "Well I don't. I like your...boy parts."

"Thanks, I think."

"Oh don't mope," she said, picking herself up. "I got you something."

"What?" I asked, hoping for a new computer game or a book.

She got a small black satchel from her closet and handed it to me. Square and moderately heavy for its size, it had a zipper around the top that I opened. Inside was liquid foundation, a compact with four shades of eye shadow, a bunch of brushes ranging from tiny to medium-sized, bronzer, an eyebrow pencil, two lipsticks and mascara. My face must've registered the confusion and sparks of fear I felt, because she sat down looking worried.

"Is it okay? I told Mom I wanted makeup, so some of it might be the wrong colors, but I can show you how to do the eyes, I think. I'm sorry, I've avoided my mom's crazy ideas of womanhood so long that I missed a few lessons in all this stuff."

I'd been afraid to believe she got this for me, but she had! I hugged her until she grumbled, "You're crushing me."

"It's the best," I told her.

She shut her bedroom door and locked it. "Here are the makeup removing wipes. Mom isn't supposed to get home for a couple hours, but if she does, I'll go distract her while you get it off, okay?"

I nodded.

"All right, hold still." She took the foundation and a triangular sponge out of the bag. "Man, this is weird."

"If you don't want to—" I started.

"Shut up," she said. "Just let me be weirded out, okay?"

Her little smile seemed real, so I let it go.

We played around for about an hour, and I turned out to be better with the eye makeup than Claire. "You are so doing my makeup for prom," she quipped after seeing herself in the mirror.

At the end of it, I looked okay. Slightly drag queenish because we overdid the eye color and Claire put the blush too low, but on the whole, very good for a first try. I was going to have to figure out some reason to pluck my eyebrows. Maybe I could audition for the school play; that would give me a good cover story.

I contemplated my face and hair in the mirror for a while, wondering where I could get a wig. Natalie would know. Then I wiped off all the makeup, using three wet wipes to make sure I got every last trace.

"Thank you," I told Claire.

I flopped down on the bed on my back and held my arms open to her. She cuddled in beside me and propped herself up on her elbow so she was looking down into my face.

"Don't mention it," she said. "Is it okay if I still think you're cuter without makeup?"

"I guess. I kind of still have a guy face."

"You should try guyliner sometime."

"What?" I asked.

"You know, when guys in the movies wear dark eyeliner and it makes their eyes look sexy."

"But—" I started.

"I know," she said. "You're not a guy. But if you ever get busted, tell them you were going for the guyliner look."

I grinned up at her and wondered if she would think it was too weird for us to kiss after I'd been wearing makeup. I didn't get to find out because we heard her mom coming in the front door and she sat up quickly on the bed. "That's your cue," she said, giving me a quick kiss. "See you tomorrow."

"Bye, Ms. Davis," I called to Claire's mom as I was heading for the door.

She turned from the counter where she'd set her purse. "Hi Chris, you don't want to stay and catch *NCIS*? There's a gothic woman in it, like Claire."

From the doorway to her room, Claire rolled her eyes at me, though we did both agree that the character of Abby on *NCIS* was awesome. The issue was her mother's attempts to be friendly. Claire thought it was bad enough that her mom was more like a sister to her. She didn't want the three of us to pal around together, even on the couch in the privacy of her own home.

"Thanks, but I've got to get working on my homework," I said and slipped into the cold air.

I drove home and checked myself in the rearview mirror one more time to make sure I had no lingering eyeliner. I felt a little stupid to be so jazzed about makeup. The guys at school would royally kick my ass if they knew. But on the other hand, I looked better than some of the girls who went crazy with makeup and huge hair. I had to figure out how to look less like a drag queen, though. If only I had a sister whose fashion magazines I could steal. I'd have to find good makeup tips from the Internet.

CHAPTER ELEVEN

Claire

Claire cleaned up the compacts, bottles and jars scattered across her bed. She'd put on light eye shadow so she could tell her mother she'd been showing her boyfriend her new makeup. Mom was delighted, but Claire was feeling more than a little freaked out as she wiped the makeup off after two hours of *NCIS*.

The first problem was that Chris looked good with makeup—and not just Zachary Quinto with eyeliner good. In part it was the way Chris's whole self brightened around girl stuff. Again Claire had that sense that she was seeing parts of him—maybe the most real parts—that he'd buried for so long. "Parts" was the wrong way to think about it, though. She'd been only seeing parts before. Now she saw a whole person.

Plus Chris's deep brown eyes got super intense with a good application of color. And he was better at putting it on than she was, which embarrassed her, though she'd spent a few years deliberately screwing up any nonblack makeup so Mom wouldn't make her wear it. When she had to wear it, it felt oppressive. She didn't think girls should have to paint themselves to be pretty.

Too bad she and Chris couldn't swap bodies. Not that she wanted to be a boy. She liked the whole girl thing, minus the übergirl activities that her mom went in for, manicures and that stuff. She liked being able to cry at movies and the feeling of being held by someone bigger than her. She really liked that part, and she and Chris hadn't done as much of it since he started talking about being Emily. Come to think of it, she'd spent more time holding him lately. Tonight was the first time in weeks she'd curled up under his arm.

"What were you thinking?" she asked in the general direction of up. "You couldn't just keep the girls in the girls' bodies? Aren't giraffes weird enough?"

She didn't get a direct reply, but she did feel a vast patience settling down on her as she often did when she asked something ridiculous.

"I guess I'm still scared," she said more calmly. "Like what if that happened to me? And what's Chris going to do? And what...what are people going to think about me because I love a freak?"

She paused. "I don't mean it like that. He's not a freak. Not much anyway. I mean not any more than half the kids at school, the Future Farmers of America and all that. I don't know what you were thinking with those kids either."

She felt smiled upon. At least God had a sense of humor. Claire reached for her Bible and let it fall open. She probably shouldn't dog the FFA kids when she consulted her Bible on a regular basis.

It opened to the Song of Solomon, Chapter Three: "On my bed by night I sought him whom my soul loves; I sought him, but found him not. I will rise now and go about the city, in the streets and in the squares; I will seek him whom my soul loves."

Her Bible study group had a guest speaker last summer who talked about how the Song of Solomon was a metaphor for the love affair between the soul and God. "Him whom my soul loves" could refer to God, Himself.

"It's another way to find You," she said, mostly to herself since God already knew. "You want us to keep discovering You, and this whole thing with Chris, it's another way to have faith in You, to see You in the world no matter how crazy it looks at first."

There was something St. John of the Cross said in a poem he wrote. She pulled the book off her bookshelf and thumbed through to the poem entitled "A Vital Truth." There was the line: "An altar is every pore and every hair on every body—confess that, dear God, confess."

That included Chris's body. People liked to think that life was so stable and easy to define, even her with her own pretensions of being holier than thou and oh so open-minded. But God's plan was so much more vast and diverse and wondrous than the small, constricting ideas humans had about the world.

What was the saying? "Men plan, God laughs."

She curled up in bed to read the whole Song of Solomon. The dialogue between two lovers was one of her favorite parts of the Bible. It echoed the longing she felt for God sometimes. She might not have any person she could talk to about the situation with Chris, but she could talk to God and as strange as it seemed, she understood that God knew what He was doing.

CHAPTER TWELVE

After the evening at Claire's house playing with makeup, I figured it was time to tackle the psych class assignment. I sat down at the computer, opened a new file and stared at it. I couldn't say any of the things that came to mind.

What would I do if I woke up tomorrow as a girl? I'd cry for joy, to start. Then I'd run around and show myself off to everyone. I'd make Mom take me shopping for all new clothes, and I'd grow my hair long. I'd probably still swim; it made me feel good and kept me in shape. The girls who swam had really nice bodies. I wonder if I'd still be this tall. If I could pick it, I'd be a few inches shorter with B-cup breasts, nothing too outrageous, and hips like Mom's, kind of solid-looking.

While I was thinking, I opened GenderPeace in my browser and sent a note to Natalie, asking where I could get hormones. I reflexively glanced over my shoulder, but my bedroom door was solidly closed. Since meeting Natalie I felt bolder, but I didn't want to get careless. Message sent, I closed that window and stared at the blank page again.

This was going to take all night. I heard Mikey coming up the stairs and yelled, "Hey, come here."

He stuck his head in my room, "What?"

As usual, his light brown hair was going in three directions. His Marvel T-shirt had a dribble of milk down one side and he was clutching a Spiderman action figure like any of us might dare try to take it from him.

"I have to do this lame thing for psych class. What would you do if you woke up tomorrow as a girl?"

"Gross," he said. "I'd stay home."

He pushed himself out of the doorway, without bothering to close my door again, and into the bathroom. Well, that was a start. I wrote:

"If I woke up as a girl, I'd stay home and play video games. If it didn't go away, I'd call the doctor. If I had to go out, I'd go to another city where no one would recognize me."

That was so stupid I had to stop writing. I went down a few lines and tried again, reversing it:

"If I woke up as a boy I'd pretend everything was normal and go to school as usual. No one would know what happened and they'd be afraid to ask me about it, so I could pretty much go through my life as usual. They would wonder what had happened and if I was okay, but they wouldn't know how to talk about it with me and I'd use that to my advantage. I would pretend it didn't matter to me what they thought, even if it did.

"Over time I'd get good at pretending, and people would forget that I'd been different. They'd go by what they saw and treat me like a boy and after a while I'd wonder if I'd really been a girl at all. I'd start to think I was supposed to be a boy, even if I felt like a girl on the inside.

"I wouldn't forget how heavy it is to act like a boy all the time, how much attention I have to spend to get it right, but I might start losing hope that things could be different. Maybe I'd stop thinking I deserved to have my own interests, my own attention, maybe I'd stop thinking I have the right to my own body. I'd let other people tell me what to wear and how to act. I'd tell myself it didn't matter that I wasn't there."

Somewhat better. I went back and changed "boy" to "girl" and vice versa. I cut the last paragraph, putting it into another document. I couldn't turn in that part, no matter how true it was, or because of how true it was.

That night I dreamed that it was Sunday morning again and I woke up with a girl's body. In the dream, I got up and showered for the longest time. No one treated me any differently, except Claire who said I looked really cute.

* * *

Thursday brought another session with Dr. No. I'd been dreading the stupid appointment all day. I didn't want to talk about my childhood or my dad, so I figured I'd bring up something I did want to know about. I dropped down on the couch and watched Dr. Webber settle into his seat, notepad in his lap. The creases in his khakis were super crisp, his button-down shirt almost without wrinkles, but no tie and the top button open, edge of a white undershirt showing, like he was trying to look as approachable and comfortable as a rigid guy in khakis and a button-down could.

He opened a tin of mints from the table next to him and put one in his mouth. When he held it out to me, I shook my head.

"What would you like to talk about today, Chris?"

"What do you know about transgender people?" I asked. I figured what the hell, I could always say I was joking, and I was sick of screwing around with this goon.

He scribbled on his notepad and then looked up. "It's a very rare condition," he said. "Do you like dressing up in women's clothing? Does it turn you on?"

Not when you put it like that, I thought. Gross. "No," I said.

"But you have concerns."

"Just curious."

"Have you ever dressed in women's clothing?" he asked, crunching his mint.

"I don't know, maybe as a kid. Did you?"

"You know what I think," he said, leaning forward in a conspiratorial way. "I think you're afraid of growing up like your father. You may have fantasies of being a woman because you think that's the only way to avoid being like him. Let's come up with some other options, okay?"

"Sure," I said. Worried this sounded like I was agreeing with him, I added, "But it's not about that. We're studying it in class. I was just asking."

I should have known he'd be able to put a bizarre spin on this, but it still caught me off guard and shut me up again. I wanted to be able to tell him I didn't have fantasies of being a woman when I grew up, but that felt too important to lie about.

"Who are some other men you can think of?" he asked. "Men you could be like when you grow up?"

Why was it a fantasy if I saw myself as a woman but it wasn't when Dr. Webber asked me to imagine growing up into a man? What counted as a fantasy? Being able to shoot fireballs like my *World of Warcraft* mage—now that was a fantasy. Getting to grow up so people saw me the way I saw myself seemed healthy and kind of awesome.

Dr. Webber watched me with his brows elevated, like "I'm waiting," and sucked his mint.

Who did I want to be like when I grew up? Natalie, I thought, or any of a dozen people I'd met on GenderPeace. Or Tammy Baldwin, the State Rep. from Wisconsin who had the guts to be an out lesbian in the US Congress; she was great. Or any woman politician or scientist, or those running big technology companies… Oh, right, those aren't men. Think.

How about Joan Roughgarden the biologist? I'd loved reading *Evolution's Rainbow* and learning about how diverse sexuality and gender could be on our planet. Maybe Mae Jemison who was the first African American woman astronaut to travel in space and she got to be on *Star Trek*. Or Dr. Ellen Ochoa, Director of the Johnson Space Center, she'd been to space four times. What about Susan Kimberly, the former St. Paul City Council member who transitioned and went right back to being in politics? Nope, being born with a "male" body and having the guts to transition to be yourself wasn't going to count for Dr. Webber's quiz.

"Mr. Cooper, my psych teacher, he's cool," I said, thinking, *crap, that assignment is due tomorrow.*

"What do you like about him?"

This was the stupidest game, but I had to go on playing it for the next forty minutes. "He's smart and educated and he usually *listens* to the students." That last part was thrown in for Dr. Webber's benefit, but he didn't seem to get the hint.

He popped another mint and again offered them to me. I shook my head.

"Good, Chris, so you'd like to be a man who is smart and educated. Do you want children?"

I shrugged. "Maybe." I glanced at the clock on the wall. What I wanted was to carry my own children… I couldn't even stand to think about it in front of this jerk. I stood up and paced across the room.

"You're afraid if you have children, you'll hurt them, aren't you?"

"Sure," I said, thinking, *You absolute dumb ass.* I didn't want to talk about having children, so I went back to brainstorming other male role models and letting him pick out the qualities of the man he thought I should grow into.

In the car with Mom on the way home I told her, "I don't want to go to Dr. Webber anymore. It's not helping."

"But you seem happier," she said.

I hadn't thought about the effect that talking to Claire and meeting Natalie had on me, and that Mom connected that positivity to me seeing the shrink. Damn. I'd have to go again. Maybe I could fake an illness next Thursday.

At home I automated my dinner table conversation.

/run: dinner with the family
1. smile
2. listen politely
3. look bored appropriate to normal teenager
4. talk about math class
5. ask Dad about the Bronco

6. smile
7. get Mikey talking about comic books
8. exit

I excused myself as soon as I could, saying I had to finish my psych paper. I pulled out a notebook and a pen and wrote so hard the tip tore through the paper in places:

"If I woke up as a girl I'd have my own kids, and I'd let them grow up to be whatever they wanted. I'd get pregnant and carry them in my own body. I'd get a period like a normal girl. I'd be able to go through labor and nurse my own babies. I'd be able to be a mother."

At that point I was crying so hard I couldn't write anymore. I tore the sheet out of the notebook and ripped it up until I couldn't make the pieces any smaller. Then I threw the notebook across the room and crawled into bed, curling up as small as possible and crying myself to sleep.

* * *

On Friday, the essay I turned in to psych class bore no resemblance to what I'd written the night before. After school, Claire told me that her mom was out on a date again and did I want to come over? I didn't know what I wanted to do. I felt like I could sleep for a week.

"Sure," I said.

"You look like crap," she told me while we were eating a pizza in front of the TV. "What happened?"

"A bunch of stuff. Stupid Dr. Webber…and I have to keep going because Mom thinks that's making me happier, and then that dumb psych assignment. What if I woke up as a girl? Geez."

"Harsh," Claire said. "You know what you need?"

"What?" I mumbled. If she wanted to make out for a while I could probably pull it off. The physical contact would do me good.

"A hot bath."

"For real?"

"Totally."

When we finished the pizza and *NCIS*, she started filling the tub and dumped in some bath salts.

"Take as long as you want," she said. "You can use my soap and loofah and stuff. I'll be gaming. Vaorlea the Mighty is close to leveling, and then I can finally get out of that stupid zone."

"This whole bath thing is so I'll leave you alone so you can game, isn't it?" I asked. It wasn't a serious question. Claire had plenty of gaming time anyway. Her mom always assumed that being alone in her bedroom meant she was reading or doing homework.

"Whatever you say, honey," she said with a wink as she closed the bathroom door behind her. She was too sweet.

I shucked my clothes and lowered myself into the steaming water. I took baths sometimes when I had the house to myself. Mom's bathroom was the only one with a tub, and I was afraid I'd give myself away if I took too many lingering baths. Plus at my house we didn't have all this cool stuff: exfoliating facial scrub, a loofah, bath salts.

I soaked for a while and then took up Claire's razor to do away with the new growth of fuzz on my arms and legs. If I could've thought of a good cover story, I might have stopped shaving my arms, but since the going belief was that I shaved everything to cut drag in the water, I had to keep it all up or let it all go. I was not going to let that hair grow back on my legs or my chest. Most of the swim team guys stopped shaving when the season ended. Okay, except for me they all did. But they left me alone about it.

All smooth, I drained out the hairy, dirty water and filled the tub again with clean, hot water. I put my head back and soaked longer. Then I tucked what Claire calls my "boy parts" down between my legs and had a good look at myself.

Yeah, I looked like a boy all right, but when I squinted I saw how I could've looked. I had good long legs and, if I kept weight off, a flat stomach. Still no waist to speak of. Claire had this cute little waist that I could almost wrap my hands around, which made me feel monstrous. I wondered if she'd trade my waist for hers.

She tapped on the door. "Hey Little Mermaid, how's it going?"

I untucked and sat up. "Come on in."

She opened the door and stuck her head in. "I wanted to warn you that we're approaching the earliest time Mom could return home if the date wasn't that interesting."

"Oh thanks." I opened the drain and let the water start to run out.

"You look cute," Claire added and closed the door again.

A few times in the past, she'd climbed into the tub with me, and I wondered why she didn't now. Probably because her mom could come home. But it worried me. She still kissed me and touched me in that slightly possessive girlfriend way when we hung out together, but she hadn't tried to initiate anything longer or more intimate.

We used to make out at least once a week and if we knew we had an evening to ourselves, go further than that. She seemed to really like kissing and wasn't that self-conscious about taking her clothes off. Often she'd end up mostly undressed and somehow I'd still have my jeans on. It was easier to be sexual without the constant reminder that my body wasn't right.

And Claire had rarely pushed me about that even though she initiated our times together. How had she explained that to herself? Had she assumed I was pathologically shy about my parts? Now that I thought about it, that was a pretty good explanation.

In the last few weeks, she hadn't really tried anything—not since that night she hopped into my lap before I came out to her. What would happen to us if she wasn't attracted to me anymore? I was already cold when I stood up from the bath and toweled off quickly. She never would have put me in the bath by myself before.

I pulled on my clothes and left the bathroom intending to ask her. She was on the couch with another episode of *NCIS* cued up and a bowl of popcorn. She patted the seat next to her and my momentum dissolved. I didn't want to have a long emotional talk about our relationship. This was comfortable.

When I sat next to her, she put the popcorn bowl in my lap and leaned against my shoulder. I gazed down at the top of her black hair and wondered, *was our relationship changing as I changed?*

* * *

The first sign of a bad week was that I got my psych paper back on Tuesday with a "C" on it and a note that said "See me." I thought about bolting for my car, but this meeting was inevitable. I waited until the end of the day, so there wouldn't be other students around in case Mr. Cooper was going to say something embarrassing.

He sat at his desk sorting papers, so I knocked on the open door. Glancing up, he ran a hand through his hair, which made it messier. Pink windburn still shone on his cheeks and two of the knuckles on his right hand were cracked from dryness. I didn't know his story, but he was clearly not from Minnesota. If I hadn't been freaked out about the paper assignment, I'd have recommended he get some Corn Huskers lotion like Dad used.

"Ah, Chris, come on in. I thought you might be avoiding me."

I stepped up to the front of the desk. "You wanted to see me."

"About your paper. I was surprised. It showed a real lack of imagination," he said. He tapped the paper in front of him with a long, blunt finger even though it wasn't mine. "That's not like you. And the end was pretty dark. Do you have a problem with women?"

"No," I said.

"But you can't imagine yourself as a woman." It was a question delivered as a statement.

I shrugged.

He picked up notepad and flipped pages filled with his blocky handwriting until he got to whatever note he'd made about my paper. He read a few sentences silently to himself.

"At the end of your paper, it sounded like you think that no one notices you. Do you struggle with low self-esteem?"

I shrugged again.

"Chris," he said. "You're one of my smarter students. You have the potential to be very good with people. If there's something bothering you or you're in some kind of trouble at home…"

"Mom has me seeing a shrink," I said. "And I've been doing better the last few weeks."

"Good, good. Now, do the paper over again and apply yourself, and let me know if there's anything else you need."

He stood up and held out his hand to shake. He was taller than me by a couple inches, which I didn't notice when I was in my seat. I thought we were the same height.

"Lotion," I told him.

"What?"

"Your knuckle is bleeding."

While he studied the back of his hand, I backed out the door. Do the paper again? He had to be kidding me. I wasn't one for cheating, but this was one assignment I was going to hand over to Claire wholesale. She'd swap me for help on her geometry homework.

If I hadn't been so rattled by the thing with Mr. Cooper on Tuesday I might have checked my psych class schedule and realized that I'd planned to skip Wednesday's class.

This was the day we had the guest speakers from an organization called OutFront Minnesota representing the LGBTQ community. As it turned out, we got one gay and one lesbian. Probably good because if we got the "T" from that acronym, I didn't know what I'd do.

Our guest speakers had guts to drive out into the boonies and talk to a bunch of high school kids about, as Mom archaically put it, "alternative lifestyles." They were also talking to a senior history class and someone's social studies class. We were right in the middle and our class was combined with a second history class, which was how another twenty students, including Claire, got crammed into our room. Like a secret agent, she winked at me and then sat down across the room and ignored me completely, earning my profound gratitude.

I already knew all sorts of stuff about being gay, lesbian or bi because a lot of the transgender resource pages I looked at were on LGBTQ sites. Plus I liked girls, which meant I was going to end up as a lesbian at some point in my life. So I settled in to listen, but practiced my deeply bored face.

Most of the kids in the class had boring questions, so the bored look wasn't hard to come by. "What do you think about the Bible's condemnation of homosexuality?" "Do you plan to have kids?" "Are you scared of getting AIDS?" "When did you know?" "How did you know?" etc.

The speakers were better than I expected. The woman worked as a marketing person for a big corporation, and the guy designed and built furniture, which I thought was neat. Thank goodness he wasn't a hairstylist. He was awfully pretty for a furniture builder, though; it might have been better if he hadn't cleaned up so well for this event. His hair was shaved on the sides, longish and curly on top, with the tips dyed a golden color, a few shades lighter than his skin. His neatly trimmed beard and round glasses made him look smart except when he grinned. He had a dorky, too-big grin, but it made me like him more anyway. He wore khakis and a button-down shirt, but no tie, and the woman wore gray slacks with a burgundy sweater that I wanted to touch to feel if it was as soft as it looked. Her blond hair fell past her shoulders. I think someone at the LGBTQ Center picked out a feminine lesbian and a butch gay man just to say: *See, we're not all stereotypes.*

I listened more intently to the questions than the answers, because of the crucial importance of knowing my classmates' various stands on queerness, and by association, gender diversity.

"Don't you wish you'd just been born a woman?" one of the girls asked the man. I braced my hands against my desk so I wouldn't lean forward.

"Not really," he said. "I have no desire to be a woman. Being attracted to men and being a woman are two very different things."

My face felt like the surface of the sun. I prayed it didn't look that red.

"I think your teacher has been talking to you about this," he said as he stood and went for a piece of chalk. He wrote "sexual orientation" across the board and below it "gender identity."

"These are two different things and they don't go together. Sexual orientation is what makes you straight or gay, lesbian, bisexual, queer. Gender identity is what has you be a man or a woman. Since I'm a man who is attracted to men, that makes me gay. If when I was born the doctor had said 'it's a boy' but I knew I was a girl, that would make me transgender." He wrote "transgender" across the bottom of the board.

I prayed to vanish in an abrupt fashion like teleportation or being hit by a meteor. I thought I wanted to know how my classmates felt, but now that it came down to it, I didn't. I'd take any random act of God to get me out of this class. At any moment I was sure every head in the room would turn and stare at me, and the only thing that kept me in my seat was knowing that if I bolted for the door it would happen that much sooner.

"What?" some hulking guy near the front asked. "What the hell is that?"

"Jason," Mr. Cooper responded in a warning tone.

"It's okay," the gay guy said. "Transphobia is one of the last remaining prejudices that many people think is acceptable. While it's becoming more mainstream to be gay and lesbian, and therefore less cool to be homophobic, a lot of people in America still react badly to transgender people—probably because of their own insecurities about sex and gender. 'Trans' is an umbrella term that includes anyone whose gender identity doesn't match what the doctor said when they were born. Some trans people are very clear that they're one gender, man or woman, while others identify as both or neither. That can be called genderqueer, genderfluid, nonbinary, agender. There are a lot of different ways for people to be."

I was in a rictus of frantic prayer: *let this end, let this end.* Across the room, Claire's hand shot up.

"Yes?" Mr. Cooper sounded relieved to have someone to call on who wasn't a football guy.

"Does it really work to put that all in one category?" Claire asked. "Is someone who feels like both a man and a woman, who has a lot of flexibility about their gender the same as, say, a man trapped in a woman's body?"

"That's a great question," the lesbian said. "There's a lot of debate going on in the LGBTQ—that's lesbian, gay, bisexual, transgender and queer—community about that. Some transgender people don't want to be associated with the larger community because they're heterosexual after transition and simply want to live a normal life."

"Whoa," said football guy Jason. "You're saying a guy can turn into a girl and live a normal life? That's fucked up."

"It is not!" Claire said too loudly.

Everyone stared at her and I could only think, *Thank you Lord that isn't me.*

Claire went on talking, still at high volume, "Transgender people are like you and me, they just have a much harder life. How would you feel if you knew you were a girl trapped in that meathead body?"

"Like a pussy," Jason said and the class cracked up. Except for me. I couldn't move.

"Quiet down!" Mr. Cooper shouted. His face was very red now beyond the wind-burned spots and all the way up to his forehead.

"That's fucked up," Jason said into the silence. He continued, "God didn't make gays, and he sure as hell didn't make men to wear dresses and want to be chicks. That's disgusting."

Mr. Cooper opened his mouth to shut Jason up, but before he could, a hurtling mass of bound paper smacked into the side of Jason's head and knocked him out of his desk. He was on his feet in a second, Claire's offending history book in his hand, lunging toward her. Three other football guys grabbed him, while the two kids closest to Claire got hold of her arms.

She looked fantastic, all that dark hair flying around her head.

"You unholy, unwashed, blaspheming, heathen bastard, you think you know the will of God! How dare you!" she was screaming, followed by a string of fairly unchristian words.

My body got up without me and walked down to her. I thought I was still sitting in my seat, shaking, but the preprogrammed part that played her boyfriend day-to-day knew what to do at a time like this.

/run: protect girlfriend
1. square shoulders and jaw
2. tell self: I am a guy!
3. repeat 2, if having feelings, go to 4
4. identify feelings
5. crush feelings into a tiny mass
6. lodge mass behind breastbone
7. repeat 2

My hand reached for Claire's shoulder. She stopped fighting and threw herself at me crying. *Well, at least one of us gets to cry,* I thought.

"Both of you, principal's office now!" Mr. Cooper shouted. He really was a lot taller than me when he stood up straight like that.

He closed his hand around Jason's arm and propelled him through the door into the hall. Claire followed, and I went with her.

CHAPTER THIRTEEN

In the hall outside the classroom, Mr. Cooper glanced at me. "You can come too," he said in a normal tone as he shifted his grip on Jason's arm and marshaled us all toward the end of the hall.

I ended up in the waiting area outside the principal's office with Jason while Mr. Cooper dragged Claire in to explain why she'd chucked her book at Jason. His eye was darkening where the corner of the book had hit it. An inch shorter than me, he was also at least an inch wider. Okay, I told myself, time for an Oscar-winning performance playing guy-to-guy conversation to make sure Claire would be okay around him and the other football lunks.

Sprawled into the seat jock-style, I looked over at him. "Man, that's gonna be a shiner."

He touched it with his fingertips. "I've had worse."

"No shit," I said. "Sorry she went apeshit on you. She gets crazy sometimes. You know, girl stuff."

"Yeah?"

"Yeah." I took a deep breath. "Look, she may be a little nutty, but she's my girl, so if you're going to take it out on someone, come find me, okay?"

"Hey, I wouldn't hit a girl anyway," he said. "I just don't want a fucking suspension. Then I might come kick your ass." He was grinning as he said it, so I grinned back. He made a fist and slammed it into my shoulder. It hurt enough that I knew I'd have a good bruise, but things could have been so much worse that I didn't care.

"We're cool," he said. "As long as you keep her the hell away from me."

I nodded, trying to figure out if I was supposed to say something else. The principal's office door opened and Claire came out while Mr. Cooper waved Jason in.

Claire kept walking out of the administrative office, so I followed her.

"I'm sorry," she said.

"What? Did you—?" My blood froze.

"No," she said. "I didn't tell them anything. Can you drive me home?"

I was going to miss English again, but I'd survive. The teacher loved me, and I'd already done the homework for this month. "Yeah, what happened?"

"I'm suspended for a week."

"Crap."

"Yeah."

I caught up to her and put an arm around her shoulders. "You gave him a black eye, you know."

She shook her head, tears welling up in her eyes again. "I'm sorry. I didn't mean to hit him in the face. I was aiming for his shoulder. I hate to hurt anyone, but he was such a jackass." Her lips quivered and she pressed them together before saying more. "I told the principal and Mr. Cooper that I have a cousin who's trans and that it's really hard on her and we're close. They might've thought I was talking about myself, wouldn't that be funny."

"Funny," I said, deadpan. "I told Jason you were PMSing and that he could beat me up if he had a problem with you."

"You did not."

"Guy's honor," I told her.

"Good Lord," she said. "We're too weird for this place. Take me home. I've got to figure out how to bribe Mom to lie about my 'cousin' if they call her."

* * *

I didn't tell my folks about Claire's suspension, but I sent Natalie a note, and posted a long description of the incident on GenderPeace. Thursday at school sucked without Claire, made worse by the recollection that I had to suffer through Dr. Webber again. I thought I'd lucked out and the appointment was going to be cancelled because his office called early in the week to move the time an hour later. I'd been waiting for another call cancelling, but it didn't come.

Maybe we could talk about his issues for once instead of mine. With as harsh as this week felt, I wasn't sure I could handle the "men I want to grow up to be" bullshit. Worst case, I'd sit in his office and cry for fifty minutes.

At the appointed time I sat with Mom in the dreaded waiting room, trying to come up with things I could say to kill an hour. I could pretend to have questions about being gay. No, safer to talk about schoolwork. Or I could bring up Claire and see if he'd give me more information about being a woman. That could be fun. Maybe I'd ask about PMS.

Mom had finished straightening all the stacks of magazines and settled down to read one. I watched the hall. At the right time, a person came toward us, but not Dr. Webber. She looked like someone's grandmother with her short gray-black hair above a wide, friendly face. Instead of walking by us, she came over to Mom and me, holding her hand out to my mom.

"Mrs. Hesse, I'm Dr. Mary Mendel. Dr. Webber has had a family emergency and I'm seeing some of his clients. Chris, would you like to talk to me today?"

"Sure," I said. I didn't care who I had to spend the time with and anyone had to be better than Dr. No. Plus there wasn't any other answer I could get away with in front of Mom.

When I stood up, Dr. Mendel came to my midchest, even shorter than Claire. I followed her into an office the same size and shape as Dr. Webber's, but much more colorful. In the corner where Dr. Webber had his desk, she had a big box of toys: stuffed animals and foam bats and funny shaped pillows. Her couch bore a red, gold and purple throw blanket that matched the colors in the abstract paintings around the room. In addition to a few mismatched chairs, her office had three beanbag chairs: green, orange and red.

"Do you see kids a lot?" I asked as I sat on the couch.

"Yes, and sometimes my adult clients like to play with the toys too." She smiled, crinkling her eyes.

Her eyes were a clear blue like the January sky when it's too cold to snow but the sun feels really warm on your skin. I liked her hair too because it was one of those I-don't-care-what-you-think short styles. It complemented her square face, but I got the impression that she'd just picked it from a list of the most low maintenance styles possible.

She lowered into a chair across from me and opened a manila file, scanning down the page. "So you've been here a few times, how's it been for you?"

"It's fine," I said. "Mom thinks it's making me happier."

She nodded, read more in the folder and then looked up at me. "You like to make the people around you happy, don't you?"

"Yeah."

"What makes you happy?"

I shrugged while I went through the long list of things I couldn't say. "I like to read, and hang out with my girlfriend Claire, she's cool. And she lets me play *World of Warcraft* on her computer, that's fun."

Dr. Mendel grinned, which made the corners of her eyes crinkle more. "What characters do you have?"

"Do you really want to know?" I asked. I didn't have the patience to bullshit about stuff I cared about. "I mean, do you know what kinds there are?"

"My grandkids taught me to play *Champions of Norrath* on their PlayStation," she explained. "Sometimes we play games as a family. I like the Cleric; isn't that funny for a therapist, so righteous?"

"Yeah," I agreed. "I've got a mage, Amalia, she's my favorite, and a Priest. Claire plays a paladin. But I like the magic-users."

"Because of the magic or the damage they can do?" she asked.

I sat up in the chair and really looked at her. She smiled back at me. She was serious, and she'd just asked me the smartest question I'd ever heard about gaming outside of the game itself.

"The magic," I said.

"I like characters that heal," she told me. "I think you can tell a lot about what's important to someone by the kinds of characters they play. What's your Priest's name?"

"Thalia. They're both girls. Do you think that's weird?"

"No," she said. "Do you?"

"I don't know."

"Really?" she asked.

I'd evaded her question and we both knew it, but what was I going to say? Should I tell her it wasn't weird for me at all and often felt more real than my real life, at least the part about being female? I was not going to sit through another hour of hearing how I wanted to grow up differently from my father.

"Yeah, I think it's weird," I said. "But a lot of guys play female characters. They have nice butts."

She touched her fingertips to her lips, watching me. "And you're like a lot of guys, are you?"

"No," I said really fast and then stopped myself.

She returned to the open folder in her hands and traced down the page with one finger.

"Last time with Dr. Webber you brought up questions about gender. Were you trying to get a rise out of him?" she asked.

"Sure," I said.

Again, she considered me for a long time without saying anything. I tried to look back at her, but I ended up picking at the seam of my jeans inside my knee.

Finally she asked, "'Sure' means 'I'm agreeing with you in order to make you happy,' doesn't it?"

I didn't know what to say, but I gave her a little nod.

"You weren't trying to be antagonistic, were you?"

She paused again and I nodded. I was so afraid and hopeful at the same time that I could feel tears pushing at the edge of my eyes. I blinked hard and let my eyes burn with the effort of not crying.

"I'm not crazy," I said.

"I don't think you are," she agreed. "We have about forty minutes left together today and if you want we can spend all of it talking about *World of Warcraft*. What do you *want* to talk about?"

I glanced up enough to point at the folder, then went back to staring at my knees. I wanted to believe we could talk about this and it would be okay but it was so dangerous. If she turned out like Dr. Webber or told Mom, I didn't have a lot of reserve left.

"Can I tell you what I'm seeing when I look at you?" she asked.

"Yes."

"You look like someone who is very tense, very guarded. You have a lot of anger and grief, and some very strong defenses. You're also sensitive, intelligent and caring. I'd like to see more of you come out." Dr. Mendel closed the folder and set it on the end table next to her. "I want you to know that anything you say in this room I will not repeat to your parents. No notes, no record, a safe place for you to talk, okay?"

I wanted to tell her but I couldn't.

After a moment of quiet, she went on. "I think if I had something that was very sensitive and I wanted help but was afraid to ask for it, that I might bring it up casually to see what response I got. If you had asked me what I thought about trans people I would tell you that I'm familiar with the standards of care detailed by the World Professional Association for Transgender Health. I do meet their guidelines for mental health professionals."

"You do?" The question jumped out of my mouth.

She nodded.

I'd read the WPATH guidelines. If she met their standards, she could help me. She could see me.

I stared at the folder she'd closed and put on the end table. Was she for real about this being a safe place? If she met the WPATH guidelines... I mean, even her just knowing that organization existed was amazing. But if she also met their guidelines that meant she could help me transition.

I had to try.

"Claire says when I'm...when I get to be a girl that I look happier." Just saying the words put a lump in my throat but lifted a huge weight off my chest. "But she and Natalie are the only two people who know. Other than you."

She smiled. "Chris—" she started, then paused. "That's not right is it? Do you have a name you call yourself?"

I didn't know if I had the guts to say it out loud in the middle of the day in the shrink's office, but my lips moved without me telling them to. "Emily," I whispered. "After my grandma."

"Emily, do you want me to transfer you into my care, so you can see me every week?"

"Totally!"

"Wonderful. Why don't you bring me up to speed on what you already know and what you hope to get from therapy?"

I filled most of our time telling her about coming out to myself and then to Claire, and meeting Natalie, spending time online, starting to make a plan to transition.

As the minute hand of the clock wandered back toward the top of the hour, she asked, "Do you want to bring Claire with you next week?"

"Yes!"

"Good, I'll see you both then. I need to talk to your mother now about transferring you into my practice. I promise I won't tell her anything about what you said here today. I'm going to tell her that I think you respond better to a woman doctor, and then I'm going to call in some favors with Webber so he won't argue. We should be all set."

"She is so going to think I have it in for Dad," I said with a groan.

"We can work on strategies for relating to your parents," Dr. Mendel assured me. "And for coming out to them. But for right now I want you to know you're safe."

"Thanks," I told her. "That's…that's *great*."

* * *

The visit with Dr. Mendel gave me enough hope to coast through the following week. Claire had had a rough time with her mom about school and ended up grounded, which meant she spent all her time in her room reading and playing *World of Warcraft*. She could only talk to me on the phone for five minutes at a time, to get updates from school, but we sent each other long emails.

Her mom had tried to cut off Internet access, but Claire protested that she needed it to research the papers she was working on. That might have been true, but it was more to research having a higher level WoW character. I wondered if someday we could get Dr. Mendel into WoW with us when I wasn't her patient anymore. We already had one grandmother in our guild; she was very sweet to everyone and always called me "honey" when we chatted.

Natalie invited me to meet her in the city on Sunday to go to a support group she attended. Off I went, with a flimsy excuse to Dad about a pair of goggles I wanted to buy for swimming that I couldn't find in Liberty. The team still had off-season workouts twice a week, though missing one wasn't as big a deal as during the season. I usually went out of habit.

I picked up Natalie from her house and we got brunch so I could catch her up on all the news, especially Dr. Mendel. Then we drove to a stocky brick community center. The inside resembled a mutated school with long corridors branching off each other, filled with thick wooden doors.

Natalie knew where she was going, so I followed. "This group is pretty random," she warned. "My shrink suggested I go once a month, sometimes I come twice. The facilitator is great. And some of the people have amazing stories."

"What do you mean random?" I asked.

"It's a general trans support group, so we get a lot of different people, ages, backgrounds."

She wasn't kidding. There were about fifteen people in the room when we walked in. Natalie introduced me to the facilitator while I got my bearings.

"Elizabeth," she said, holding out her hand.

"This is Emily," Natalie said and I beamed at the sound of my name.

"Glad to have you, welcome," Elizabeth told me.

She was about my height with a halo of blond hair and bright eyes. She had the smallest nose and I felt a pang of jealousy. At brunch, Natalie had said she was some kind of psychologist. How had she ended up facilitating a group of transgender people? How did regular people get interested in us? Did she know someone or were we research to her? Or could you actually make money with a psychology practice aimed at the transgender community? Maybe in the Cities it was possible.

We had a few more minutes before the session started, so Natalie introduced me to more people with a dizzying array of descriptors, including trans, MTF, FTM, but also nonbinary, genderqueer, genderfluid. Was I allowed to be confused about this? I just wanted to be a girl.

I met Renee, a woman in her mid-fifties who had recently started transition and looked like someone's plain grandmother with the hands of a lumberjack. Renee had been talking about her kids with beautiful, brown-skinned Vivianna who had the body of a ballet dancer and her black hair up in a cool, asymmetrical messy bun.

"She's half-Spanish, half-Korean," Natalie whispered to me, though I hadn't asked.

"But why is she here?" I whispered back.

"Because she's like us. She transitioned seven years ago. Except she didn't get the surgery. She says she doesn't need that to be a woman. I can't imagine."

"Oh wow," I said and quickly added, "I mean, I wouldn't have guessed she's trans. I can sort of understand about the surgery.

I'm definitely getting facial surgery first. So many more people see my face than my…parts."

Natalie sighed at me. "Don't you think that would be different if you didn't already have a girlfriend?"

I shrugged because this wasn't something I wanted to talk about. Nodding toward an average-sized white guy with short brown hair and a goatee, I asked, "Shouldn't he shave?" I couldn't stand my own facial hair.

"Steve's FTM."

My brain took a second to translate: female-to-male. I looked again. It was impossible to tell. He could've been any of the guys on the swim team with me.

Next to Steve, three people had settled into a close circle of chairs. I thought they looked like men in dresses, with at least one trying very hard not to look like a man in a dress, then mentally kicked myself. I'd hate it if anyone thought that about me. And I probably looked like that sometimes because I was still learning how to sit and move. It wasn't like I could practice sitting like a girl at home.

"Those two are just cross-dressers," Natalie said. She indicated the third. "And she's a little off-balance but super sweet and knows everything about the 1800s, so if you don't know what to say, ask about that."

Steve had moved closer to us when he heard Natalie say his name and cleared his throat, "'Just cross-dressers?' Nat, why do you have to be like that?"

He introduced himself to me and I told him, "You look great. Is that okay to say?"

"I never tire of hearing it." He turned and called across the room, "Badri, come meet Emily."

The short person who crossed the room to us wore a bright blue flannel and a gray fleece vest that reminded me of my dad's collection of pocketed vests. Dark brown skin framed the kind of smile that made me feel we were already sharing an inside joke.

We introduced ourselves and I learned that Badri's pronouns were "they" and "them." I was going to have to practice that.

Then Steve said to Badri, "Nat's being a transphobic trans girl again."

"I am not," Natalie insisted. "I'm only saying cross-dressing isn't the same as medical transition."

"You think I have it easier than you because I don't take hormones?" Badri asked.

"That's so not fair." Natalie waved at the women in the chairs. "Those ladies can afford anything they want. They just don't want to leave their wives and their comfortable lives."

I had a flash of fear remembering how it felt when I thought Claire was breaking up with me—and we'd only been together months, not years.

"That would be so hard," I said. "Loving someone and being together that long. I'd be so scared."

"Transition doesn't mean you have to leave anyone," Natalie told me, softening as she said it.

"But sometimes they leave you or throw you out," Steve said. "Even if they do, you find your people." He put his arm around Badri's shoulders.

Elizabeth called the meeting to order. We all went around and gave a few details about ourselves and what was going on in our lives. Renee had been at the same job for twenty years and still dressed as a man to go to work. She was trying to figure out how to talk to her HR department about coming to work as a woman. But she worked as a children's librarian and was terrified, with good reason, that she'd be fired as soon as she came out.

I wished I'd had someone like her around when I was a kid going to the library.

Vivianna gave an update about her and her husband's quest to adopt a child. She'd changed all of her records, updated them to "female" but was still afraid that if people found out she was transgender, they wouldn't let her adopt.

When it came around to me, I tried to think of something intelligent to say. "I'm Emily," I said, feeling ridiculous using that name with my deep voice and lanky body. "I'm in high school, and I'm trying to figure out how to talk to my parents. I have a good therapist and a really great girlfriend."

There was scattered applause and welcomes.

"That therapist will really help," Vivianna said. "I worked with one for almost a year and when I came out to my parents it was such a non-issue. I was in my early twenties and living on my own by then, but my parents said they'd always suspected and my mother said she always wanted a daughter. I have three brothers. I hope it's like that for you."

Steve spoke next. "Mine said they understood, but they keep screwing up my name and my pronouns. My mom asked me to shave and wear a dress to my cousin's wedding. I didn't go."

"Oh that sucks so bad," Natalie told him. "It's so invalidating. And it's ridiculous, you look like such a guy, no one would read you."

To "read" someone was to assume they were trans, and it could happen even to people who weren't. Being read as a trans person could mean real danger. Even if you weren't trans but someone thought you were, you could get thrown out of places and beaten up.

Natalie was right that no one would see Steve as anything other than a guy. How embarrassing to look like a guy to everyone and have your parents call you "she." And how cruel to get reminded in every sentence that these people who were supposed to love you didn't want you to be yourself.

"I'm still working on forgiving my parents," Badri said. "They didn't formally throw me out of the house but they made it clear I wasn't welcome if I wouldn't do gender the way they wanted. I ended up homeless for a year. I'm so grateful for the Host Home Program here." Badri looked at me and added, "It's a foster program for queer and trans kids. My foster parents got me through college and now, I feel that I should forgive my birth parents, but I don't know if I ever want to see them again."

"You don't owe them," Vivianna insisted. "They should know how hard it is. Shame on *them*."

"Yeah," Badri said with a sad laugh. "Brown trans kids on the streets don't have that many options. If white folks think I'm a guy, they're scared of me, but if they think I'm a girl, it's worse."

Steve caught Badri's hand and held it, muscles clenching in the side of his jaw. I felt so grateful for Claire and Dr. Mendel, for my home—and afraid of what I could lose if I came out to Mom and Dad. Was it worth it?

As the group broke into smaller conversations, Elizabeth sat next to me. "Was it helpful to come today?" she asked.

"It was good," I said. "I have a lot of work to do."

She looked me in the eyes. "You won't regret it. If it's what you want, you'll never look back."

"I know," I said. "It just seems so hard."

"Everyone has to go through a journey to become themselves. It's just more of a challenge for some than others, but a greater challenge also means a greater opportunity."

"Right," I said, unconvinced.

She opened her purse and pulled out her wallet, sliding a small picture out from behind the credit cards. "I don't show this to a lot of people," she said. "But I think you need to see it."

In the photo, a young man glared angrily at the camera, his hair hastily brushed to one side and his brows lowered menacingly. He'd set his lips in a tight line, but that didn't disguise the full bow shape of his mouth and how it looked exactly like Elizabeth's. I stared at her. The only similarities were the shape of her face, her lips and her nose. Anyone else would have assumed they'd been siblings.

"No," I said. There was no way that had been her. I felt like an idiot for assuming she wasn't one of us, and at the same time, I was thrilled.

"Twenty-seven years ago," she told me.

"Wow, you think I could look like you?"

"No, I think you could look like yourself. You'll be beautiful." She took the picture back and put it away. "You're welcome here anytime."

"Thanks," I told her, beaming.

On the way back to the car, Natalie asked, "Isn't she cool? She went to Europe in the eighties to get the surgery."

When I dropped Natalie off at her house, she paused and fished in her purse. "Hey, this isn't really kosher, and I wouldn't do this for anyone else, but with you stuck out there in the boonies and everything…" She handed me a small prescription bottle.

The label had her name on it. I turned it over in my hand. "How? You can't give me yours."

She smirked. "I told my doctor that I accidentally threw out my hormones when I was cleaning up and got a refill. That should last you a month or more. You might start with a half dose and see how you feel. Then maybe we can figure out how to get you your own supply. I don't think my doctor will go for the 'lost it' thing more than once."

She clicked the clasp on her purse open and shut, staring out the window at the front of her house. "My mom would kill me if she knew about this. But I remember how bad it felt when everything about my body seemed against me, you know?"

"Uh, yeah."

"Every day I was hairier and rougher and further from who I wanted to be. Maybe when I'd been a little kid, if I'd dressed in girl clothes and had a girl's name, being seen as a girl would've stopped all that hate from building up. But I don't see you getting to show up as a girl in your life right now, so this is what we've got. It might be different for you, but when I started on hormones, I started to like my body. I treated myself a lot better. I don't think you should have to wait for that. You have to live in your body every day. It should feel like home."

"Not like I'm stuck on Mars?" I asked and, hearing what I'd said, laughed.

"Mars, exactly."

"Thank you so much."

"Take 'em with a meal," she said and flashed me a grin. "And for goodness sake, hide them well. It's easier to explain hard drugs to your parents than hormones."

I hugged her. "It's wonderful, thanks."

The whole drive back to Liberty, I imagined what it would be like to be able to go through my days without always having to remember to be a guy. Elizabeth transitioned twenty-seven years ago and she was only in her middle age now. She'd already lived more than half her life as a woman. What if I could be myself all the time?

When I got home, Mikey was watching TV with Dad. Mom was in the bedroom we kept as an office for paying bills and stuff. I went up to her and leaned on the filing cabinet. She sat at the desk sorting through a pile of mail with her hair messy like usual on weekends. She wouldn't wear sweatpants around the house, but she had on a pair of loose terrycloth pants and a sweater jacket.

"How was your trip to the city?" she asked distractedly.

"It was cool," I said. "I saw something unusual."

"Hmm, what?" She dropped an envelope onto a short pile on the desk and opened the next piece of mail.

I'd thought about the right way to say this on the drive back. I couldn't say "trans woman" or "a woman who'd been assigned male at birth." That was way over Mom's head and she'd want to know where I'd gotten that language. She'd know this wasn't a casual, passing thing. Right now I had to keep pretending.

So I said, "A woman who used to be a man."

"What?" she pivoted her chair to face me. "How?"

"I guess surgery," I said, trying to sound super-super casual.

"How did you *know*?" she asked. Her eyes narrowed and her lips pressed together tightly at the end of the question.

"She told me. She said sometimes women get born into men's bodies—"

"You were talking to strange...people?"

"In the middle of the mall, it was harmless," I said. "I can take care of myself. I thought it was interesting that that's possible."

"Chris," Mom said in her stern voice. "I don't want you going into the city alone, and you certainly don't need to spend time talking to freaks like that. If that happens again, you get up and leave."

I managed not to flinch. Barely. I knew I should get out of this conversation now, but I had to defend something. "It was just a conversation, Mom, she wasn't hitting on me."

"You don't know what people like that are thinking. You're a good-looking young man and you need to be more careful. Promise me you'll watch out for yourself."

"Sure, Mom." The metal shutters had come down the front of my body and I was back to being a robot.

She stood up and gave me a kiss on the cheek. "Don't tell that to your dad, he would flip."

"Okay," I said. "I guess I'll go work on my homework."

I went upstairs and lay down on my bed feeling torn in half. One half was happy and excited about life. She'd gone to a support group meeting and got hormones and she had a girlfriend who loved her.

The other half was a papier-mâché shell that looked like a guy on the outside and was hollow within. His emptiness rang with echoes of my mom's voice saying "freaks like that," "you're a good-looking young man," and "your dad would flip."

I fell asleep staring at nothing and dreamed that the papier-mâché man was choking me to death.

CHAPTER FOURTEEN

I took a fraction of Natalie's hormone pill with breakfast the next morning. I didn't expect to feel different right away, but I did feel lighter when I went to school. That was probably the placebo effect, or pure hopefulness. Yes, my mom thought transgender people were freaks—that wasn't unusual for a woman who'd spent all her life in rural Minnesota. Not to mention that most of her life had been without Internet. She'd come around when she saw how happy I was. Right?

During science class, I imagined the hormones soaking into all the cells of my body, reassuring each little bit of me that everything was going to be all right. I sailed through the day. In psych class I gave Mr. Cooper the decoy paper that Claire had emailed me the day before. I'd changed a few details, but her story was very good at imagining what it was like to be a boy waking up as a girl. A lot better than my version.

The week waltzed by and on Thursday I met Claire after school to go to Dr. Mendel with me. I'd told Mom she didn't need to come along to make sure that I was going. When that failed to convince, I added that I planned to bring Claire so we could talk about "boy-girl" stuff. That did the trick.

Claire and I sat on the couch in Dr. Mendel's office. Claire's fingers tapped out a pattern on the arm. She kept crossing her legs one way and then the other as Dr. Mendel closed the door and settled into the chair across from us. Claire might have worn extra black for the visit: she had on black cobweb earrings and black bracelets in addition to the usual black shirt, jeans and boots. I'd made it all the way down to sweater number six this week, a light tan, and Dr. Mendel was in a cream colored jacket over a plum shell and gray pants.

"Thank you for coming," Dr. Mendel said to Claire. "I've heard a lot of wonderful things about you. And you also game together?"

"I play a paladin mostly," Claire said. She thought Dr. Mendel asking me what kinds of characters I played was supercool, so I was glad Dr. Mendel started there again.

Dr. Mendel said, "It's no wonder you're Emily's protector in the real world then."

"You think so?" Claire asked. "That I'm a protector?"

"Yeah," I said without waiting for Dr. Mendel to answer. "I'd be in a lot worse shape without you around."

"But I kind of freaked out there at the start," Claire admitted.

"That's natural. Emily had years to figure this out. You had to adapt to a lot of new knowledge in a few weeks," Dr. Mendel told her.

"When you put it that way, I guess I am pretty awesome," Claire responded with a grin. "So, what do we do here?"

"I was hoping I could help answer any questions you have so that Emily doesn't have to field all of them, and then if we have time I'd like to hear more about Emily's early experiences of herself, and I bet you would too."

Claire looked at me and then back at the doctor. "Totally," she said. She uncrossed her legs and put her hands on her knees. "Questions, hmm. I read a ton of stuff and it's all jumbled up in my head, so I'm sorry if I don't say things the right way."

"It's okay," I told her and squeezed her shoulder. I wanted to know what questions she had. And Dr. Mendel was right that I felt grateful not to be the only one to answer all of them.

"What's the difference between transgender and transsexual and gender nonconforming?" Claire asked. "Like, lots of cultures seem to have had men who dressed like women, or who lived as women: ancient Sumer, Greece and Rome, Native American cultures. And it sounds like some people are okay dressing as women or living as women but not having all those surgeries. How do you know what's what?"

"I don't want to just cross-dress," I said.

Dr. Mendel held up her hand before I could go on. "Emily, let Claire have her questions. It's a good question. First it's important to remember historically that surgeries and hormones might not have been an option. We don't know that people were okay only dressing as women or if that's how their culture allowed them to be women. Many cultures *have* included other genders in different ways, using the medical knowledge they had at the time. Some cultures have not only third genders, but fourth genders and more."

She paused, grinned and said, "Did you know Jewish law recognizes six genders? We have to be careful not to put our current beliefs about sex and gender onto other cultures."

"Oh cool. I get that," Claire said. She'd pressed her hands together, the way she did when she listened intently.

"Gender nonconforming is a much larger category than trans or people with gender dysphoria," Dr. Mendel said. "It's also how we prefer to label young children, rather than saying they're transgender, because there are boys who love dresses and the color pink who don't later identify as transgender. And there are plenty of girls who are tomboys."

"Or who like cars," I said and Claire grinned at me.

Dr. Mendel went on, "I think everyone has had some experience of gender nonconformity. When I went to college in the sixties there were quite a few people who felt that women wearing pants was gender nonconforming. I'm glad we got rid of that idea. When my husband took a few years off teaching to raise our children and research a book, he really had to struggle with cultural opinions about a man staying at home with the children."

"My mom thinks my goth look is gender nonconforming because I don't wear bright colors and show off my boobs and paint my face," Claire offered.

"Precisely," Dr. Mendel said. "Now, gender dysphoria specifically refers to the distress a person feels when their gender identity doesn't match the gender they were assigned at birth. And even gender dysphoria isn't an unchanging condition. There are children who experience gender dysphoria but it doesn't persist. Not every feminine boy or masculine girl is transgender."

"Aw, I was just about to go around diagnosing my other friends," Claire said with a grin.

Dr. Mendel smiled back at her with genuine humor. "I did a lot of diagnosis from the sidelines when I was in school. I do want both of you to know that if gender dysphoria is present in childhood and persists into adolescence, there's a very high chance that it will remain into adulthood unless treated."

"Mom shouldn't wait for me to grow out of it then," I said.

"Neither should you." Dr. Mendel pointed out.

I thought about that. "You're right, there's still a part of me that keeps thinking if I do the boy thing enough it will stick."

"There are plenty of trans women who've joined the military or taken up extremely masculine professions to see if they could get maleness to stick to them and not have to come out as women," Dr. Mendel said.

"I don't want to do that," I told her. A chill shuddered down my back. In junior high, for over a year I'd been convinced I wanted to go into auto mechanics when I grew up. What a disaster that would have been. Not the profession, but the fact that I'd have tried to keep acting like a guy.

"So it works?" Claire asked. "This transition thing?"

"That's what the studies are showing. Overwhelmingly when teens and adults get to live in accordance with their gender identity—and have access to hormones and surgeries if they want those—they're as happy with their lives as any person. No one's life is perfect, but rates of depression and anxiety drop significantly."

"Well yeah," I said. "I'm scared all the time that I'm going to do something that'll show people I'm a girl and they'll beat me up. Of course we get anxious. And, this might not be a perfect analogy about depression, but what if you knew beyond a doubt that you could never write again for the rest of your life?" I asked Claire.

"I'd...I wouldn't want that life. Writing is part of me. That's why you get so sad? I never thought of being a girl as something like a calling or an art, but they do overlap, don't they? It's all ways of expressing in the world, and if I couldn't write it would be like I couldn't be myself ever again."

"I don't know about anybody else, but I'd say that's why I get depressed," I told her. "Everyone's telling me I can never be the person I want to be."

"Why don't we talk about what you do want," Dr. Mendel prompted.

The rest of the hour was great. I told Claire more of the stories from when I was little, like dressing up in Mom's clothes and playing with the girl who lived down the street as if we were two girls.

* * *

Maybe it was all the talking and support that made me feel bold that weekend. I didn't plan ahead. I got in my car on Saturday and drove in the opposite direction from the Cities until I reached Annandale. I pulled over in a residential area in front of a dark house, and got the duffel out of the back. It now had Claire's makeup kit in it as well. It took me over half an hour to change in the car and do my makeup in the rearview mirror. I didn't know what else to do. I couldn't very well go into either gender of bathroom as a man and come out as a woman.

The other problem was that I didn't have any good shoes. I had some black boots that were more punk than anything, so I'd thrown those in the car with me and they'd have to do with the long skirt. They looked vaguely stylish. At least as men's boots, they didn't have much heel so I wouldn't be toweringly tall.

I only had a hat for my head, no wig. The good news was that my hair had grown long enough in the back to hang down past my collar in a few thick curls. The bad news was that it still looked too short for my taste, but I couldn't do anything about that now.

I tried to get a good look at myself in the mirror, but it's hard to see yourself in a two-by-six-inch reflection. If I turned to the right, I looked pretty girlish, but from other angles, not so good. If I kept my eyes down, I should do pretty well. I'd shaved my face to within an inch of my life that morning and the foundation was thick enough to cover any lingering trouble there. Plus I felt like the estrogen was softening my skin already, though it was probably way too soon.

I figured I'd try a really quick trip into a store and see how I did. With my winter coat on, most people would see puffy down and a long skirt, a cute hat and little curls. If I moved delicately, it might be enough. I went to Walmart. There were enough people there that I could blend in, plus I needed to buy a purse before I went anywhere else.

I walked in and across the store without actually taking a full breath. My shoes slapped too-heavy steps on the floor. Out of my peripheral vision, I thought I saw a woman turn and stare at me, but I didn't stop to find out. My heart was beating against my breastbone like a person pounding on a door.

In an empty aisle of purses I had to stop and fill my lungs a few times so I wouldn't pass out. The store smelled like lemon cleaner and the dark musk of leather. I smelled like iron-edged fear.

I tried to browse individual purses, but my hand shook when I took one off the long metal rack. I put that one back, it reminded me of my mother's, and grabbed a small, plain black purse on my way to the cash registers. Then I paused. I was supposed to buy control top pantyhose. Someone online said that was the key to "tucking" successfully. I had no idea what size or where to look, but the store had only a couple dozen people in it and so far no alarms had gone off and no one was staring at me as far as I could tell.

I followed the signs to lingerie and stared down the long aisle of pantyhose. Tiered row after row of white, gray and tan packages with colorful labels stretched into the distance. This would be a good time to ask for help, except that I hadn't worked on my voice enough. I couldn't say anything without giving myself away.

Good Lord, I was an idiot. I took a deep breath and then another.

I walked down the row until I saw "control top" and tried to read the sizing chart on the back. I had a few options, so I took one of each and made for the registers.

I picked the checkout line with a dark-skinned girl with a headscarf. For all I knew, she could've been second-generation Somali-American, but she had great posture and I was hoping this meant she hadn't grown up watching a million hours of TV. I wanted to seem like just another American oddity to her.

When she said, "Good morning," in heavily accented English, I started to relax. After ringing up my items, she said, "That'll be twenty-eight fifty-three, miss."

My heart soared. I unfolded two crumpled twenties from my palm and handed them to her. The change went into my new purse, the stockings into a bag, and I stepped out into the fresh, cold air.

"Miss" reverberated in my head all the way back to the car. I'd done it! For the first time I was out in public as a woman, and at least for a few minutes, I passed. That elation mixed with the caffeine from the depth charge coffee I'd sipped all the way out here and it seemed like my heavy boots floated inches above the ground. I felt goofy about being so excited, but after years of having "boy" and "son" land like shrapnel in me, being called "miss" felt amazing.

I downed the rest of the coffee and drove the next two miles to the little mall in Annandale. Now that I was out in public, I didn't want to have to change back into my boy clothes and go home.

Okay, I told myself in the mall parking lot, *this has got to be a quick exercise; I'm going to walk through and out because I can't actually talk to anyone.* I had to practice with my voice a lot more in the near future. Maybe I should take voice lessons. I wondered if Mom would go for that.

It wasn't noon yet and the mall's main corridors were almost empty. Two women with babies in strollers walked along one side of the main corridor. I picked the other side, to avoid them. An old woman holding onto the arm of an old man passed me but didn't look at my face. I went from one end to the other and started to stroll back. I really needed new shoes. This mall had a DSW, which was a discount shoe warehouse that skimped on staff to keep their prices low so you had to pick out your own shoes and try them on without assistance. Through the windows, I contemplated a few pairs. I should be able to try on something in there without having to fend off a salesperson in pantomime.

Quickly I found the section of women's boots, but I didn't know much about women's shoes and had no idea what size I was. I should've brought Claire with me. I put two different shoes next to my foot and guessed that I was a size eleven or twelve in women's, but I wasn't nearly comfortable enough to take off my boots and try one on. What if someone came up to me? Would I end up running out of the mall with my boots in my hands?

With a sigh, I gave up and headed back in the direction of the car. Claire wasn't terribly fond of shopping, but if I threw in a movie, she'd come with me. Three junior high school kids walking in front of their parents stared at me as I passed and my heart started thrumming hard against my breastbone. Did they know? I turned away from them and walked faster. I should've waited until I could do a better job at this. Thank goodness no one here knew me.

Unfortunately, my racing heart along with the huge bottled coffee meant that I had to pee so badly it hurt. All the people in the mall were down at the other end where the better shops were. This end held the administrative office and the restrooms.

I paused in the hall to the restrooms and waited for a few long minutes to see if there was anyone in the women's. No one came out. I really wanted to see what I looked like in something larger than a rearview mirror, and I was literally hopping from one foot to the other. If I went out to the car, I'd have to wait until after I changed and then go find a restroom at a crappy gas station.

I ducked into the women's restroom and stared at myself in the mirror. The hat looked cute and so did my makeup, but my eyebrows were terrible and the whole size and ratio of my body still looked wrong. A passerby might think I was a girl, and then again might not. It all depended on what their sense of reality included; I either came across as very boyish girl, or a boy very much in drag.

My outfit was great for avoiding the loud and dramatic, but I desperately needed to work on my ability to walk and to speak. For the first time out, though, it was a huge victory.

I turned toward the stalls. There were so many of them and no urinals. This was for sure the first time in my life that a restroom made me happy.

You don't have time, I told myself sternly. *What are you going to do if someone comes in? Go.*

I quickly stepped into a stall and sat down to pee. It was so clean in here. Not only the floor but the walls of the stall were almost bare. I'd never been to this mall before, but in Liberty's two tiny malls both of the men's bathrooms were covered with disgusting graffiti. I didn't have anything against graffiti. It was the subject matter that disgusted me. The scrawls tended universally toward antigay sentiments, woman bashing and bragging about sexual prowess. In this stall there was a sticker about breast cancer awareness posted on one side and on the other in looping handwriting the message, "You are really beautiful."

The restroom door opened and closed and then a heavy fist pounded on the stall door. I leaped off the toilet and pulled up my underpants so fast I nearly tore them and the skirt right off.

"All right, sir, come out of there," a man demanded.

When I got the door open, a potato-shaped security guard was glaring at me.

"Come with me," he said.

I did. We ended up in the mall security office, which was a large closet off that same short hallway, furnished with a desk, one chair behind it and two in front of it. I got one of the chairs in front of it.

"All right, son," the man said. "What do you think you're doing?"

"I'm sorry," I replied, while frantically running through stories in my mind. My voice sounded awful because it was not only too low but also rough with fear.

"You're damn right you are. Jesus Christ, look at you. What's your name?"

"Jim," I said. "Jim Harding."

"You better not be lying to me. Let's see some ID."

"I didn't bring any," I said, honestly. I opened the purse and showed him it was empty except for the money.

"Where you from?"

"The Cities," I said.

"They tolerate this kind of shit there?" he asked and then sat back in the chair. "What do you think you're doing in a ladies' restroom? You're some kind of pervert, aren't you? You think you're going to see something in there? You looking at girls or just like to pretend you are one?"

I felt so far outside myself I might have been in the next county. This had gone beyond nightmarish into the bizarre and unbelievable. I knew my heart was beating unbearably fast, but I couldn't feel it anymore. My body had turned cold and numb.

"No," I said with some emphasis.

"I suppose you're some kind of fag," he suggested.

"No," I said, equally vehemently.

"Well then what, exactly, are you doing trolling around in women's clothing, boy?"

For a moment, I considered telling him some version of the truth, which might feel like less of a betrayal of myself than lying outright. I could tell him that I was transgender and that my doctor suggested I spend a certain amount of time living as a woman. I was certain he had no idea there were internationally accepted guidelines that health professionals used to support the wellbeing of people with gender dysphoria.

As good as it would feel to be honest, I worried that he could try to hold me here and make me call my parents. I did *not* want him saying anything about me being transgender to them.

My neck shook with the effort of not putting my head in my hands. If my parents had to come here and see me in a skirt...I was doomed. They'd never let me out of the house again, or they'd never let me into the house again, and Dad would certainly stop talking to me. I had to find another way out of this situation, even if I had to lie through my teeth to do it.

"I lost a bet," I said. "I'm on the swim team, see." I flexed my shoulders for verisimilitude, a gesture that I'm sure looked monstrous in that outfit. "And we had a race and the loser, who clearly was me, had to dress up like a girl, with makeup and everything, and go to a mall and buy something. So I tried to pick a mall where none of the guys would see me."

"But the restroom?" he asked.

I shrugged. "I drank a lot of coffee. I couldn't go into the guys' like this, and it's freezing outside."

He shook his head in disgust. "If I ever see you in this mall again, I am hauling you to the police station, understand? And, if you want my advice, don't lose any more bets. Get out."

I ran for my car and drove out of that messed-up town. At a rest stop I pulled over and, when I'd stopped shaking enough to use my fingers, awkwardly changed clothes in the car. I wiped off all the makeup and got out of the car to throw the used wipes away at an outdoor trash can, not bothering with my jacket. The cold made me feel real.

I stood out there for a long time thinking about how incredibly stupid I was. What the hell made me think I would ever make it in the world as a woman? The whole scene with the guard had been miserable, but the worst part was lying, making up that whole ridiculous story about losing a bet, having to pretend I was a guy all over again. How could I make my way in the world if I couldn't stand up for myself?

I glared at the big green trash can in front of me, wondering if I should throw away my girl clothes and give up. Except that everyone did that at least once. Then they showed up years later in places like GenderPeace and Natalie's support group saying they wished they'd never done that. I wanted to learn from someone's mistakes, even if I wasn't so good at learning from my own.

And for that second when I'd considered coming out to that guy, telling him I was transgender, under all the fear and dread, it felt good. Deep down under the pounding heart and the sweat breaking out on my skin, under my burning eyes and clenched throat, I knew who I was. Did I have the courage to be that person?

The World Professional Association for Transgender Health's standards of care suggested that transgender people spend some time living as the gender they were transitioning to before surgery—if they wanted surgery. The standards also recommended working closely with a therapist. I could have recited all that to him, chapter and verse. I could've given him Dr. Mendel's name and number and told him to call her. I could've stood up for myself. But I couldn't risk telling him the truth. Not when my parents didn't know, and I didn't know how they'd react.

I turned back to the car and slammed myself into it. What was the use of knowing all this information that I couldn't use?

When I got back to the house I was still shivering, which turned out to be the start of a fever.

CHAPTER FIFTEEN

I missed school on Monday and Tuesday, miserably situated in front of droning daytime television with a head full of snot. It almost kept me distracted from reflecting on Saturday's horror, but every few hours that would unfold in front of me again and play itself out. I'd be left second-guessing myself over and over. I shouldn't have used the bathroom. I should have told him the truth. I should be on real hormones, not some I got from a friend. I should tell my parents. I should leave town. I should drink more hot tea and stop acting like a morose idiot.

Claire called and checked on me every day. She knew something was wrong. I didn't tell her what had happened. It was too stupid to bear repeating.

On Thursday, she came with me to Dr. Mendel, but I asked if she'd hang out in the waiting area this time. She agreed and opened the book she'd brought for just such an occasion.

I told Dr. Mendel what had happened, and she had tears in her eyes by the end of the story.

"I'm sorry," she said. "You should never have been treated that way."

"I was stupid," I grumbled.

"Just impatient," she replied. "What actions are you taking for yourself?"

"I'm working on my voice," I said. "Sometimes after school when I have some time alone in my car. And…a friend gave me some of her hormones. I know it's illegal, but it's only a little bit."

Her eyebrows went up. "I understand that you want to be on hormones very badly, but there *are* medical risks."

"Give me a break. Millions of women take hormones."

"With their doctor's supervision," she pointed out.

"I'm so sick of waiting. You don't know what it's like. Some mornings I look in the mirror and I don't know who that is!" I was yelling and made myself take a breath and lower the volume a notch. I didn't want to be heard in the waiting room and I didn't want to yell at Dr. Mendel.

I explained, "There's this stranger with hair on his face and sharp angles and it's one more day of faking it. I have to force myself into that face. I look at family photos and it's Mom and Dad and Mikey and some guy who moved into my house and took my life away. Do you know what that's like?"

"No," she said. "The hormones help with that?"

"Everything helps. Getting to wear the clothes that make sense to me—I don't know why that should matter. Girl pants and guy pants are really similar, but they're not. And suddenly the shape of my body matches what's in my head and I can relax. It helped when Claire called me 'Chrissy' before she knew my name's Emily. Every second of that is a vote on the side of me being a real person in the world. And the hormones and feeling like my skin's softer and I'm not so angry, maybe it's all in my mind, but yeah, it helps so much."

She sighed and turned the ring on her index finger. "Here's my dilemma, Emily. I want you to be yourself. And I have concerns. Taking hormones can put stress on your heart and liver. You could be at risk for diabetes, even a stroke. Plus you'll decrease your fertility, which is a real problem if you want to have biological kids someday. I know doctors who work with women through their transitions. Please consider pausing the hormones until we can get you to one of them."

I considered it. For a whole second. Right now, no way. Maybe in a few days I'd think about it again.

"I'd need my parents' permission to see a doctor, wouldn't I? Since I'm underage and insurance and all that."

"Yes."

"They're going to freak out," I said. "I've been hinting to Mom and it's not going well."

I told her what had happened the two times I'd tried to bring up anything trans. She started laughing out loud at the impotence story and I laughed along with her, feeling each burst of air loosen my chest a little.

"Sometimes it takes a while for parents to adjust," she said. "You and I can come up with a plan together. You have to be prepared for them to be upset at first and not assume that's the end of the world."

"Okay," I told her, though I was fairly certain it would be the end of the world.

"Before we get to that, I want to spend the rest of this visit and our next few sessions talking about the ways in which people approach the transition process and what you want for yourself. There are people with gender dysphoria who choose only hormones and not surgery and some who opt for neither."

"I know, I know," I said. "I've been looking at all of this for years. I know there are risks to the surgery and some people decide they don't want it. And there are trans women who never wanted surgery in the first place. I know I don't *need* surgery to be a woman. But that's years down the road. I can't even afford it yet and anyway, I want facial surgery first."

I paused and took a deep breath because she was watching me with that open, clear sky look that made me feel like no matter what I said it was okay.

"I'm sorry, I feel like everyone wants to challenge me on this," I said.

"That's not what we're here for. We're going to create the life you want for yourself. I'm asking that we start at the beginning and go through all the steps."

"I can do that," I told her. "Where do we start?"

"I have some basic psychological tests I'd like to give you. I see that Dr. Webber tested you for depression but I'd like to get my own results. It's common for trans people to struggle with depression and anxiety, and I want to get a good feel for how much of that you're dealing with."

I cracked a big grin. "You mean I shouldn't lie on the tests this time?"

She chuckled. "That is precisely what I mean. And I want you to understand that if you come out of this office with a diagnosis of gender dysphoria, that does not mean that you as a person are disordered or diseased or that there's anything wrong with who you are."

"Thank you," I told her.

We decided to start the tests on the next visit so that I'd have plenty of time for them and ended the hour chatting. As Dr. Mendel walked me to the door, she said, "Take care of yourself. And the next time you go shopping dressed as a girl, get support, don't do it alone."

In the waiting room, Claire stood up as I came out of the office. "Is everything okay?" she asked Dr. Mendel through the open door.

"Yes," Dr. Mendel said. "Absolutely fine, but you've got someone here in need of cheering up, and maybe a shopping trip in the near future." She went back into her office and Claire raised her eyebrows at me.

"Shopping?" she asked.

"I want to go shopping as a girl," I said quietly, after making sure there was no one near.

Claire sat back down in the chair she'd been waiting in. I worried that I'd frayed her patience past the breaking point and, when she pulled out her phone, thought she might be calling her mother to come get her.

"What's Natalie's number?" she asked.

It took a moment for the question to register, and then I told her, following it with, "Wait, why are you calling her?"

Too late. She had the phone to her ear. "Natalie? Hey, it's Claire, you know, from the boonies. Yeah. Yeah. Right here.

Yeah, but we need a favor. She wants to go shopping. Sure. Yeah, it's my cell. Cool."

She put her phone in her purse and stood up. "All right, she's calling me back."

"That's it?" I asked.

She shrugged. "No, I reserve the right to freak out about this later when you're not looking."

I looped my arm over her shoulders. "You are so cool. Do you know that's the first time you've called me 'she'?"

"Don't rub it in. Come on She-Ra Princess of Power, take me home."

We'd been stuck watching a He-Man movie while babysitting Mikey a few months ago. Those characters seemed a lot funnier now. I asked, "Does that make you He-Man?"

She laughed. "I guess so. Gender nonconformity, here I come!"

* * *

The next morning on my way to study hall, Claire handed me a note. It said: "Overnight in the city. Set it up with your folks. Have them call Nat's mom tonight. She'll handle the 'boy thing.'"

What boy thing? I thought, but that was answered as soon as I got home and broached the subject with my mom.

"You can't have a sleepover with two girls in the city—one of whom we don't even know!" she said.

"Oh, yeah, you're supposed to call her mother." I handed Mom a sheet of paper with Natalie's home number on it.

"How do you even know this girl?" Mom asked.

"We met online. She plays the same games that Claire and I do. We've hung out with her a few times. Her mom's a successful lawyer." The part about games wasn't true, but that last bit was the important part. It was meant to convey a sense of safety to my mother and a sense that I was spending time with the right kind of people.

Mom sighed and went to the phone. The conversation went: "Hello? Yes. Yes, Chris's mom. Good to meet you too,

Susan. Online games, he said. Well, I wonder that too." Pause and a laugh. "Really? Oh separate rooms, of course. A daughter in college, that's nice. Princeton? My goodness. And you'll be there all night with them?" Pause and laugh again. "Oh no, no that's not necessary. Yes, that would be nice. Yes, thank you. Goodbye."

She hung up and turned to me. "Well, I suppose it's all right. They sound like very nice people. She said you'll have your own room for the night. She even offered to drive out here so we could meet her. Isn't that nice?"

"Yeah," I said, thinking that Natalie's mom had to be fantastic to make that offer.

"Go have a good time," she said. "And tell me all about it. I bet they have a wonderful house."

I smiled. "Okay, Mom."

* * *

I picked up Claire at four on Saturday and we drove into the city. Her mom had also talked with Natalie's mom and experienced a similarly reassuring conversation. What was it they thought we'd do without parental supervision? Maybe an all-night drunken, pot-smoking orgy. Of course if Mom knew what we were really up to, she might have preferred the orgy.

Natalie's family lived in the northern part of the western suburbs in a sprawling two-story house. When we pulled up, Natalie came out in a coat with a line of white fur around the hood and tan boots that had white, furry cuffs on them, to help lug in our overnight bags along with the secret duffel.

"My brother's at a friend's until tomorrow afternoon," she said when we all crammed into the entryway. "And Dad's locked himself in the master bedroom. He tries to be cool, but this girl stuff weirds him out sometimes. So we have the house to ourselves." She turned and yelled into the house, "Mom, they're here!"

I expected Natalie's mom to be kind of glamorous, but she wasn't. She had dark hair shot through with gray that she'd looped into a bun at the base of her neck. She had the same big, dark eyes as Natalie, but a smaller chin and nose.

"Welcome," she said. "You can call me Susan, I much prefer that to 'Natalie's mom' or, heaven forbid, 'ma'am.' Come on in. We have enough beds for you if you want, but I thought you girls might like the lower level for a full slumber party atmosphere."

She went toward the downstairs and Claire followed, but I didn't know what to do. She'd said "girls"—did that include me? At the top of the stairs she paused and looked back at me, beckoning. I guess I *was* one of the girls. Grinning, I followed.

The lower level had been set up as an entertainment center, with a big TV and a huge L-shaped couch. Three rolled-up sleeping bags rested at the end of the couch and a small stack of blankets lay next to them.

"Make yourselves comfortable. I'll go put the pizza in the oven," she said and headed back up the stairs.

I followed her.

"You told my mom I was going to be in a separate room," I said.

"Yes," Natalie's mom—Susan—said. "If you're more comfortable, you can have Natalie's sister's room, but if you want to sleep in the lower level, you could roll a sleeping bag out on the left side of the TV, which is, technically, a separate room, or at least would be if we hadn't torn down that wall. It's still listed as separate on the property report."

I smirked at her. "You planned that."

"Natalie did," she said with a wink. "She said it would be good for you to have a girls' night and promised me no funny business."

"No ma'am," I said, unable to stop grinning. "Why are you so cool about all this? I think my mom would epically freak out."

She pulled two pizzas out of the freezer. "I did some freaking out," she admitted. "But, I don't know if you'll understand this until you're a mother, there are much worse things in life than gender dysphoria. There were nights I'd lie awake and wonder if Nat was going to kill herself and why it was happening and if I'd be able to stop her. I'd try to think of how she might do it, and to take away anything I thought she could use to hurt herself, but it was never enough for me to know she'd be safe. I had some rough nights after she told me what the problem was, why she was so depressed, but I knew…after that I knew she'd live, that she'd grow up and have a good life. That's a gift. That's what a parent really wants for their kids. I think your mother will come to understand that too. She does love you and she wants you to be happy."

"She's not as…educated as you," I ventured.

She laughed, a big, open-mouthed laugh. "Law school doesn't prepare you for this, believe me. Your mom can learn the same things I did. Now come on, Claire said you need shopping therapy tomorrow, and we have another little surprise."

The surprise turned out to be a couple of the wigs Natalie wore before her hair grew out and that her parents hadn't gotten around to giving away yet. The fit was tight, but with the right bobby pins, the wig with plain brown, wavy hair worked. I spent an hour in the bathroom staring at myself with the hair falling past my shoulders. Without makeup, I looked too coarse and plain, but I could start to see how it would come together.

I counted my lucky stars that I'd been born at a good time. In earlier decades, earlier centuries, people like me had had to content themselves with only dressing as women, but I could change my body to match my sense of myself. I lifted the hair off my forehead and considered the ridge under my eyebrows. I definitely needed to save up a lot of money this summer, and the next and for a few after that, but I would figure out how to get the facial surgery that would take away the caveman aspects. Natalie hadn't needed it and I envied her.

Claire banged on the door. "You going to stay in there all night?" When I came out she added, "You are *such* a girl."

I'm not sure she meant it as a compliment, but I took it as one anyway. Then we all sat around, including Nat's mom, and painted our toenails. We talked fairly unsuccessfully about makeup and movie stars for a few minutes, but I had a lack of knowledge and Claire protested the whole thing, so we ended up talking about school and politics and what the world had been like when Natalie's mom was a kid. Okay, during that last part we just listened politely.

Natalie's mom showed me where to put a sleeping bag so that I was technically in another room, and Natalie scared up a pair of silk pajama bottoms that fit me rather than the boxer shorts and T-shirt that were all I'd had.

I lay awake for a long time feeling my heart floating in my chest.

CHAPTER SIXTEEN

Claire

Claire lay awake for a long time. *If my boyfriend is a girl*, she wondered, *what does that make me?*

Sure she could say "a lesbian" half-joking, or "bisexual" for real, and leave it at that, but that didn't address the doubts gnawing at her. From what she'd seen and read, even a lot of lesbians weren't too keen about girls who dated girls who'd grown up as boys. If she continued through all this with Chris, would she wake up one morning to find there was nowhere in the world where she belonged?

She half laughed at that thought. When had she ever been worried about belonging? But she'd never felt this kind of isolation before. When she provoked other kids at school with her goth look or by spouting esoteric bits of poetry or religion, or her mom by talking about being bisexual—she was drawing the boundary and saying what groups she was and wasn't in. Suddenly, a whole lot of lines had been drawn *for* her.

She pulled apart the different aspects of it. Number one was that she could end up even more of an outsider. Number two, much as she hated to admit it, was that Chris was getting more attention than she was. He'd been the quiet guy for most of their relationship, and now, at least here, all the attention was on him. Claire didn't begrudge him that; he certainly deserved some care. She just wanted more of the spotlight, but she could learn to share.

Number three was uglier than the first two. She accepted that Chris didn't have a choice about this situation, that he…or she, rather, had been born this way and had to go through all kinds of hell to get to a life that worked. But Claire had a choice about loving Chris. She could walk away, she could explore whether that fairly normal-looking kid in her history class really was interested in her.

She glanced at Chris in his sleeping bag across the room. Who loved someone like that? Was she that desperate to be weird? Was there some way in which all of this was still about her?

No, she didn't want to walk away. This whole business about sex and gender didn't change the person she'd gotten to know. Well, except for making her a girl. But in some way she'd always been a girl, just in an amazing disguise.

Claire stared up at the ceiling's gray waffle-board pattern. She missed the plain white of her bedroom. Why was she here? Had she really needed to come along on this mission? She could've sent Chris to spend the weekend with Natalie and stayed home.

Sometimes when she prayed or talked to God she had the feeling of a huge intelligence looking at her, usually smiling. It was there now, surrounding her. *Trust me*, it seemed to say.

She rolled onto her hands and knees and crawled across the basement floor to where Chris was lying on top of his sleeping bag with a light blanket over his legs. His eyes were still open. Claire snuggled down against Chris's side and he put his arm around her. She took a deep breath and stopped—he smelled different. He'd always smelled like salt and sand and warm metal, but now the metallic part was fading. Claire knew she was smelling the lotion he'd put on earlier, but still there had been a change to his underlying scent. An edginess was gone and she kind of missed it.

This was good too. Would his scent keep changing?

But that wasn't the most important question. *When are you going to stop thinking of Chris as him?* she asked herself. *You know she doesn't like that.*

Oh shut up, she told the highly evolved part of her brain, *I want to hold onto something of him.*

But why? She draped her arm over across the warm, familiar body next to her. This was all she needed to hold onto, she thought. Just the person.

CHAPTER SEVENTEEN

In the morning, Natalie's mom made us eggs and bacon. Her dad came down for a few minutes to eat with us. He had a thick gray-and-brown goatee but had shaved his head to help disguise how bald he was on top. When he saw me, he blinked a few times but didn't say anything other than to ask how we were all doing. After a quick cup of coffee and eggs, he excused himself to go to the gym.

"What's up with your dad?" Claire asked when Natalie's mom was out of the room.

"He's my stepdad," she said. "But he and Mom have been married for, like, twelve years, so I figure he gets to be a dad too. He's pretty sweet about the whole trans thing, even though it scares him. Like he's afraid that someone's going to show up in the middle of the night and take his guy parts away and turn him into a girl."

Claire snorted at that, but I wondered how often nontrans people reacted badly to trans people because somewhere inside them they were afraid it was going to happen to them.

"How about you?" I asked Claire teasingly. "Are you afraid the bad fairy is going to turn you into a boy?"

She cocked her head, thinking hard. "Kind of," she admitted. "I was thinking about that when I did your homework last week." She paused and poked my arm for emphasis. "If I woke up as a guy, it might be kind of cool, but if I had all the memories of being in this body, and all the girl experiences I've had, and the dreams for my life, then yeah, I'd be totally freaked 'cause I'd know that wasn't really me, you know?"

"Boy do we," Natalie said.

Claire's mouth hung open. "Oh yeah," she managed. "I guess that is how it is for you. Everything inside you says one thing, but no one believes you. Wow, I never thought about it that clearly. It *is* how I'd feel if I were hit with the 'boy gun.'"

Natalie's mom came back in and Natalie started clearing the dishes. "Okay," her mom said. "Here's the plan. We have two showers, so Nat and Emily you're first. Then, Nat, you're doing Emily's makeup. Claire and I will sit in the living room and talk about politics." She grinned so we knew she might be joking, though I suspected that was how it would go. "Then we are going to Southdale Mall to get Emily a decent pair of shoes and whatever else strikes our fancy. Natalie says you're not great with your voice, so you can fake laryngitis. Anything you want to say, whisper to one of us. We'll provide the cover story. Sound good?"

I nodded, thinking that heaven was populated with people like this.

Natalie gave me the upstairs shower and took the one in the basement, a generous gesture that I understood when I got into that shower. It had all sorts of fancy shampoos and soaps and scrubs. Except for the lure of shopping, I could have spent an hour in there.

Natalie knocked on the door as I was drying off. When I cracked it open, she pushed in and looked at me. "Nice legs," she said.

I kept the towel around my waist and tried not to blush.

"Here, use these in your bra," she told me, and set down two fist-sized packets of an indeterminate nature.

"What are they?"

"Birdseed in pantyhose. They're pretty close to the feel and shape of real breasts but if your parents find them, you can say they're for a school project—*unlike* silicone inserts. You can keep 'em."

"I've been thinking about the inserts, but I feel like that would be so weird if Mom or Dad found those in 'Claire's' duffel bag."

"Girls who aren't trans use stuff like that all the time," Natalie said. "That's why it's so easy to find. You can get padded bras that'll make you two sizes bigger too. Put that with the silicone and you can get to a C-cup easily. It's what the other late-blooming girls at your school are doing, I'll bet."

"Thanks!"

She slipped out and I dressed quickly in case she was going to barge in again. I wanted to wear the brown pants, so I used the control-top hose that I'd cut off mid-thigh to tuck up between my legs and brace the parts that didn't really fit in girls' pants. Then I put on my bra and fit the falsies into the cups. Natalie had a point, they filled out the bra much better than cotton balls. I pulled on my sweater and examined myself in the mirror.

I looked odd. My body looked like an athletic girl's body, but with no waist. My face read as half boy and half girl. "Jeez, I'm an alien," I said, and pushed out the door in search of Natalie and makeup.

Half an hour later I was back in the bathroom looking much better. Natalie's mom had pinned the wig on in a way that gave me short bangs and long brown hair. I wasn't sure I'd wear my hair like that if I had a choice, but I was not going to argue right now. The wispy bangs covered my typically male sloping brow and the ridge over my eyes. Natalie's makeup job partly hid the other masculine planes of my face. I didn't exactly look pretty, but I could pass if I didn't talk.

When we got close to the mall, I started getting extremely nervous, almost panicky. All I could think about was the stupid attempt I'd made by myself, and that jackass security guard. I took Claire's hand and she squeezed my fingers.

"You look good," she said.

I couldn't tell how much of that was true and how much was her trying to make me feel better. But no one we would run into at the mall would want to go toe-to-toe with Natalie's mom. She wore jeans but she'd put on a silk T-shirt and a navy blazer, along with thick gold hoop earrings. I could see a hint of how tough and capable she must look in court.

She parked a few hundred feet from the doors because the lot was almost full, and we had to carefully avoid the frozen-over slush puddles that were the land mines of a Minnesota spring. With a light dusting of snow on the ground, you'd think you were going to step on solid land until your foot broke through the paper-thin sheet of ice and a couple inches of freezing water soaked your shoe.

Inside the mall, it was hot so we took off our scarves and jackets right away. I carried mine under my right arm with my purse looped over my left shoulder. Natalie said the purse looked amazing for a thirty-second Walmart purchase. I hoped that was a compliment.

"I can't believe you tried this alone," she told me. "I wouldn't have had the guts."

"I figured if I screwed it up, no one would know," I said quietly, and indeed they didn't know the horrible details.

Natalie's mom beelined for a shoe store. "What's your size?" she asked.

I shrugged. "Eleven maybe?"

Three minutes later I was sitting on the shoe bench with four pairs of boots around me, a salesman running to the back room for more, and Natalie and Claire arguing over styles. Boot in hand, I took a deep breath of shoe leather and polish. If I'd kept a photo album of life's central moments, I'd put this in. I wanted to be able to remember everything: the crazy fluorescent lights shining harshly on the red highlights of Natalie's hair, the way Claire bit her lip when she was listening to something she disagreed with, Natalie's mom calling all three of us "the girls," the way the salesman called me "miss" without even thinking about it.

Everything around me seemed so real, as if it had more weight and density than my former everyday life. I must have spent a lot of time not really looking at things until now. That made sense because I spent so much of it looking at myself and making sure I wasn't going to screw up.

I dropped right into the bit about laryngitis and figured out how to laugh soundlessly so I could join in the jokes Claire was making about women's shoe styles.

"Not the pointed toe," she said about one pair, and I leaned in to whisper to her, "Too witchy?" She cracked up and repeated it to Natalie and her mom.

The sales guy caught it and grinned. "Sorry about your voice," he said as he dropped off another load of boxes.

I smiled and shrugged.

"Does it hurt?" he asked.

I held up my thumb and forefinger with a small gap between them to signify "a little."

He laughed. "Girls, nothing keeps you from shopping, does it?"

I shook my head, but I couldn't stop grinning.

I felt like my heart had expanded to fill the whole store. It might sound silly, but I'd been crushed inside myself for so long that now that the binding was off, I wasn't sure I wouldn't keep on expanding until I encompassed everything.

"Earth to Emily," Claire said. "Bring the Moon landing home."

"Sorry," I mouthed.

She patted my shoulder, "Don't worry about it, you look like a kid at Christmas. I think you should get the brown pair. They'll go with the pants you love."

I did, along with a pair of black flats that Natalie recommended: my first girl shoes. I wore the brown pair out of the store, putting my guy boots in the bag.

We strolled down the mall, peering in windows and talking about who needed what. Natalie got interested in a new scarf, but she didn't really need one, and her mother gave her the "you're over your limit" look. Claire suggested we hunt for a sweater sale. The end of winter was always a good time to pick up half-price finds.

A few stores turned up nothing worth buying. Natalie's mom proposed lunch and we all filed into P.F. Chang's for tea and shared appetizers.

"Where are you girls from?" the waiter asked. He was a thick guy, probably a wrestler for his school, I thought.

"We're from down the street," Natalie said. "And these are our country mouse cousins from Liberty in to the see the big city."

"Do you like it?" he asked Claire and me.

I nodded.

"She has laryngitis," Claire said. "The cold, you know. We love it. We want to come to school here."

"Let me bring you some hot tea," he said to me. I nodded. He added, "Put a little honey in it, that'll help."

He went off for the tea and Claire poked me in the ribs. "I think he's flirting."

"Oh right," I whispered.

But he behaved in a radically different way than if he thought I was a boy. He'd probably have left me to think of the tea myself, or expect that the women around me would take care of me. Strange.

After lunch we figured we'd see a movie, a "chick flick." There was a new romantic comedy that Natalie and her mom both wanted to see. They agreed that Natalie's dad would never care about having missed it, so we ended up with popcorn and Junior Mints in the dark theater.

"Hey," Claire said. "Scrunch down, I want to try something."

I scooted low in my seat, propping my feet against the seat in front of me and bending my knees. Claire sat up tall and put her arm over my shoulders. I rested my head back on her arm.

"This is cool," I whispered.

"I'm just checking it out," she said.

"You're great."

She shrugged. "I'm just me."

After the movie, we wandered, blinking, into the afternoon sunlight of the lobby. "Okay girls," Natalie's mom said, "time to go and put our secret agent back into deep cover so I can get you home to your parents before my credibility slips."

CHAPTER EIGHTEEN

Claire

On the drive back to Liberty, Claire kept stealing glances at this person next to her. The transformation to Emily had been surprisingly effective. Emily was big for a girl. But as they walked through the mall and Claire examined the other women, she saw so much variety. A few were over six feet tall, some were muscular, some heavy, one had eyebrows like caterpillars. There were women with huge butts, women with flat chests, women with chests bigger than Claire's butt, women who looked like models, women who looked like adolescent boys on purpose. Claire was glad that she got to date someone who looked good as either a boy or a girl. How many kids at her school could say that about their date?

She rested her forehead against the cold window and let herself doze, exhausted. In hazy dreams her body shifted and changed, getting bigger and more spacious. When she woke with the car pulling into her driveway, she felt larger than usual, as if she extended outside her own skin.

Her hazy eyes focused and she thought first: *Chris*. And then: *Emily*.

The idea of Emily came with so many other ideas about Claire herself, her identity, her place in the world. A little exciting and a lot scary.

She kissed the grinning person in the driver's seat and scooped her bag out of the trunk. There was a lot more mystery in the world than she'd thought.

Her own bedroom looked different to her, as if she'd walked into a stranger's house. She didn't feel as solid as usual but instead of being alarmed, she thought that she could choose which pieces of this life she wanted back and which she wanted to let go. How many people got that opportunity?

She got out the T-shirt and sleeping shorts she wore to bed, but then paused in front of the full mirror by her closed door. She pulled off her shirt, bra, jeans and underpants and stood naked in front of the mirror. This was her. Maybe she wanted slightly larger breasts and worried that she'd put on weight on her butt when she was older, like her mom was starting to do, but there was no question in her mind that this body was right for her. She touched her arms, her belly, her thighs.

What was the opposite of gender dysphoric? Gender euphoric?

Claire grinned at herself in the mirror. Yes, she was gender euphoric. She'd have to remember to tell Emily.

CHAPTER NINETEEN

When I got home, Mom was helping Mikey with homework in the dining room, or rather, standing over him and making sure he was actually doing it. Dad sat on the couch, watching TV with his feet up on the coffee table, wearing his one pair of sweatpants. Must be laundry day. He still had a gray-pocketed vest on over a worn T-shirt. I settled onto the couch next to him.

"How was the city?" he asked.

"Great," I said, with real emotion behind the word for once.

He turned away from the TV and examined my sweater and jeans like he was trying to guess if these were my good clothes or not.

"Who's this other girl?" he asked.

"Someone I met online who turned out to be cool. She's in my same grade." I added that last bit so he wouldn't think she was some kind of Internet pervert.

"You like her?"

"Sure," I said, then thought through the implications of that question. "Oh, you mean do I *like* her?"

He looked at me as if I'd lost a few brain cells.

"Dad, if I was cheating on Claire, I wouldn't take her along, would I? Natalie's just cool. She's from Chicago."

He made some grumbles of agreement and leaned back into the couch. "How's that other problem?"

I had to roll back the movie in my head to recall what he was talking about. Right, my alleged impotence. "It's fine," I answered. "I'm doing good."

"Good," he said.

That was it with the questions. Dad was funny that way. He'd have these spurts of concern and the rest of the time it was like the family was made up of supporting characters in the drama of his job and the cars.

I watched TV with him for a while and then went upstairs to lie in bed and relive the day over and over again. For so long I'd thought I was trapped in this life and now I could see the way out and I knew I could take it. Now it was a matter of moving through the obstacles. My next milestone was set for my appointment with Dr. Mendel on Thursday.

* * *

"You said I should come up with a plan," I told Dr. Mendel. "I want a plan."

"Good," she said. "I think you probably already have one, you simply haven't formalized it."

She was right. I told her how I planned to work as much as I could all summer and for the next few years. I'd go to community college until I could get the money together for the physical transformations that I wanted.

"What about hormones?" she asked. "Are you still taking the ones from your friend?"

"Yes."

"We need to get you to an endocrinologist and do this right. We need a plan for talking to your parents."

I sighed. "It's going to suck."

"Do you want to do it here?" she asked.

"You're brave."

She smiled. "It's my job."

"Yes," I told her, with tremendous relief. "I do want to tell them here." It was so good not to be in this all by myself anymore.

"Okay, let's talk about when you feel you'll be ready."

I liked that she left it up to me to decide. It was late March now with spring break coming up next week and the potential for a few more trips to see Natalie. I didn't want to risk losing that. Then I was in the crunch to the end of the school year.

"Can we do it in June?" I asked.

"Sounds like a good time to me. What are you going to do at home between now and then?"

"Be a good boy," I offered, raising my eyebrows at her.

She laughed.

For the next week, I was a good boy at home and it seemed so much easier now that I could get out of the boy role with Claire and Natalie and Dr. Mendel. Playing the good boy felt like a long dress rehearsal for a play I would never star in.

I did some heavy-lifting chores around the house and even managed to play with Mikey a couple times. He was always making up these games in which superheroes from his favorite cartoons and comic books had to fight each other, and he never minded that I took the women heroes for my characters.

* * *

A whole week of playing the good boy felt long. By the following Friday night, I sat at my desk looking at my calendar. To the surprise of absolutely no one, Dad had gotten me another "Girls & Cars" calendar like last year and the year before. I left it on my desk where I could put things on top of it or fold it over to write on the days without seeing the hypersexualized women pretending to show off the muscle cars.

I'd liked February though, and left the calendar open for that month, propped against the wall behind my desk. Mom had scowled at it a few times. The February model wore loose-legged pants, not short shorts, and she'd tucked them into the top of cute little boots. I loved the way the fabric of the pants billowed out at the top of the boots. If I had pants like that, people wouldn't see how skinny my legs were. Plus the fabric looked so soft, like the new brown pants that I loved.

I tore that photo out of the calendar, folded it and stuffed it into my backpack. I'd show Natalie and Claire so they could help me find pants like that. If Mom or Dad came across the calendar image, I'm sure it would fall somewhere between "possible impotence cure" and "oh good, our kid isn't gay."

March's model wore shorts small enough to be underwear. I'd returned to folding the calendar back so only the dates showed. I paged to April: she had on cowboy boots and a hat. I could use a few more hats, but not cowboy hats. By May and June, the calendar had gotten into bikinis.

School ended the last week in May, so I figured I'd be coming out to my parents in Dr. Mendel's office on either Thursday, June 5, or if I chickened out, a week later on the 12th. That was ten weeks away, and I'd run out of the hormones from Natalie in about six. I should save them to take closer to the end of the school year, for finals and extra confidence around coming out. But then I'd have to go through the rest of March and the first part of April without them.

To do that, I'd need more help. Good thing I knew a paladin.

* * *

Saturday, I went over to Claire's early, picking up donuts and coffee on the way. Her mom worked all day every Saturday, since it was a big sales day. I rang the bell anyway, in case her mom was late leaving. I didn't want to tip her off that I had a key. Claire opened the door, pulled one of the coffees from the holder and went back to the couch where she'd been curled up with a book. She was in loose black pants and a black sweatshirt, her goth loungewear.

I put the donut box and napkins on the coffee table and dropped my duffel by her bedroom door.

"Tell me you're not cheerful," she said. "It's too early."

"Motivated," I told her. "I'm going to come out to Mom and Dad at Dr. Mendel's in June."

Claire sputtered, grabbed a napkin and pressed it to her nose. "Holy…what? Your *parents*? June of *this* year?"

"It's months away."

"What are you going to do if they freak out?" she asked. At least she hadn't said: *when* they freak out.

"Duck behind Dr. Mendel's chair and let her explain it all."

Claire sipped at her coffee and snagged a chocolate-frosted chocolate donut from the box.

"That's not the worst plan," she admitted.

"I need help setting it up," I told Claire. She was chewing and nodding at me, so I went on talking. "I'm kind of sucking in school right now. Not English, but everything else is around the C level and I need to look like the best kid in the world before I come out."

"How are you getting Cs?" Claire asked. "You're smarter than ninety-nine percent of the school."

"I thought I was bored but it's more than that. It's not that I don't care about school, it's like I *can't* care. I'm paying attention all the time to a million things and I don't have any brain left for homework. I have to remember how I'm supposed to act. I have to make myself forget that I feel like a girl. People treat me in ways that don't make sense; I have to think about what they're doing and why and how I'm expected to respond."

"Like what?" she asked.

Tearing my donut in two I put one half on the napkin and took a sip of coffee.

I told her, "After lunch when I've been sitting with the swim guys, I get to class and I don't hear anything the teacher says. My brain's spinning back over everything to make sure I did it right. And that's when I finally get the joke that Ramon made, that I had to fake-laugh about—and realize I didn't get it when he told it because it was based on the idea that we're all guys together— then I'm freaking out that I laughed wrong and they're going to know. By the time I try to do whatever assignment I missed the instructions for, all that comes up again and I don't want to think about it, so I go as fast as I can to get it done. And then half the time I forget to turn it in."

I bit into the top of my donut, where it was mostly sugar, and washed that down with more coffee. I explained, "When I get up in the middle of the night and put on girl clothes, it's a lot easier to do homework. All that other noise isn't there. But I can't keep that up. I need more sleep."

"Okay, so?"

"I want to do homework at your house," I said.

"You want to be a girl here all the time when my mom's not here so you can do your homework?" The end of Claire's sentence rose in disbelief.

"Yes!"

She started laughing hard, bending forward, shaking. I grabbed her coffee cup so it wouldn't spill. She wrapped her other hand around mine and held on tight. Good thing or I'd have thought she was laughing at me.

When she'd recovered, she said, "You know in-game when guys are playing girl characters and they're always like 'if I were a girl, I'd spend the whole weekend playing with my boobs?'"

"Uh, yeah." I'd heard that too.

"Homework," she said, smirk-grinning. "You just want to be a girl so you can do that stupid social studies assignment and maybe some math."

"And psychology, definitely need to pull my grade up in that," I told her, grinning back.

"It's on. Go change. Mom's gone until after dinner."

I took my duffel into her bedroom, still smiling.

She yelled after me, "And you'd better stop sucking at math. The world needs more math girls!"

I put on the brown pants and my favorite sweater and my one cute hat. Claire offered to do my makeup but stopped halfway with a sigh and handed me the tiny brush, admitting that I was better at it. Then she had to change into a sweater because she said I was out-classing her by too much.

Sitting on Claire's couch, I got a ton of homework done. She did some with me, did her chores, heated up soup for lunch but made me stop and figure out what we could have for dinner. We watched TV while eating and then Claire looked over my assignments in Psych and Soc because she was better than me in those two.

Mid-evening, I changed back into boy mode and drove home, warm and happy. I went into the house humming and Mom called from the kitchen, "Good time at Claire's?" with a note of suspicion in her voice. Like I'd be stupid enough to hum cheerfully after sex, if we'd been having sex.

"Claire helped me get this monster paper done for Soc," I told her as I hung up my coat and kicked off my boots.

"You seem happier. Dr. Mendel's really helping?" she asked. She was at the stove making a huge batch of something to carry us through the week. Looked like spaghetti sauce as I went over to give her a quick hug from behind.

"Yep, helping a lot," I said and spun out of the kitchen before she could ask more and I could say too much.

Dad was in the garage as usual, sitting inside the Bronco with the dash open, fiddling with wires. I saw one booted leg and part of his pocketed-vest, the rest of his body leaned across both front seats.

"I've been thinking about the wall of parts," I told him, waving in the direction of the back wall of the garage with its bin after bin of old car parts, even though he wasn't looking. "We could list them on eBay, make some money on the ones you're not going to use?"

"Spend it on more parts?" he asked with a muffled chuckle, still focused on his wires.

"You know it," I said with what I hoped sounded like masculine enthusiasm. "But I want a cut."

"What for?"

"Faster computer. Maybe take Claire out more. You know."

He snorted and we haggled about my percentage for a minute. Then he put down his pliers and turned around in the driver's seat to face me. I don't know what he was planning to ask, but his mouth hung open for a moment and the questions that came out were, "What the hell is on your face? Is that makeup?"

Shit and double shit. I'd checked. There couldn't be much.

A big inhale and I dropped my voice further into my chest. "Claire's on this guyliner thing," I said as grumbly as I could. "Wants me to look like some movie star."

"You take that shit off. Stand up to her. Don't let her try to make you soft."

"Sure," I said.

"No girl's going to respect you if you go around looking like a—"

"Dad, I got it," I cut him off. "I'm going."

I hurried out of the garage before he could say anything more. I didn't want to hear whatever slur was on the tip of his tongue. Good thing I'd gotten a week's worth of assignments done today, because the only words in my head the rest of the weekend were going to be the ones he'd already said and the ones he might have if I hadn't stopped him.

CHAPTER TWENTY

Most of April passed without Dad, or anyone, catching me in "guyliner" again. Every Saturday I went to Claire's and did as much homework and studying as I could. We left extra time at the end for her to examine my face and make sure every last trace of makeup was gone.

My grades trended up. I ticked off days on the calendar. Too many days to the end of the school year, and too few days to my birthday.

My birthday isn't my favorite time of year. It's near the end of April, so the world outside is slushy. At least the smell of hope is in the air, gently warm and green, and every year I let myself believe it's going to be different than the year I got a toolbox, or the model car, or the neckties, the suit jackets, and so on. I used to hope I'd get gifts I wanted, but now I pray I won't get anything too awful. I asked for a couple computer games and some graphic design software, in case I ever want my own website.

Mom asked if I wanted a party, but I said not really, so she suggested we all go out to dinner, the family and Claire and one of Mikey's friends. That didn't sound like a particularly fun evening to me, so I added, "Can I invite Natalie and her mom?"

They were more than happy to come out for my birthday, but by the time the evening rolled around, I was regretting my invitation. We had only one nice restaurant in town and I picked that because I didn't want to have to drive too far with my family. Plus I thought it would be fun for Natalie to see downtown Liberty in all its glory. But when we pulled up in front of DaVinci's, I wanted to turn around and head home. The restaurant seemed super small and kitschy compared to those in the big malls in the cities. I worried that my family would be too strange and at the same time I worried they'd realize Natalie was a trans girl.

When my momentum stalled outside the restaurant, Claire grabbed my elbow and dragged me into the red and gold waiting area. Natalie and her mom sat on a low, red velvet bench, both a little dressier than our day at the mall. Claire made the introductions because my mouth was too dry for me to talk, and then we were all seated at a long, rectangular table. Mom quizzed Natalie's mom about what kind of law she practiced, which left Dad to interrogate Natalie.

"So, you're in the Cities?" was his first attempt.

"We moved from Chicago a couple years ago. I'm a junior at Maple Grove," she said, deftly tearing off a piece of garlic bread with her manicured nails. I envied Natalie's hands. Her fingers tapered toward the tips, so even though she had wide hands, she still looked graceful with the long, thick manicured nails she wore. My hands were square the whole way, from the base of my palms to my blockish fingers.

"And how did you meet?" Dad continued, though I'd already told him.

"We met online," Natalie said. Claire and I had prepped her thoroughly on what we'd told my parents. "Gaming. We've been playing together for, what, four months? And I just thought that Em—uh, Chris was really cool." She kept going, but Dad had heard it. And I'd heard it so now all the blood in my body was rushing to my head, making it feel like it would burst open.

"What were you going to call Chris?" Dad asked.

"Amalia," Claire said. "It's one of Chris's characters. Sometimes we get so caught up in the game, we call each other by those names even when we're hanging out together. My character name is Vaorlea."

"The Mighty," I added reflexively, though my voice came out as a squeak.

"You play a girl?" Dad asked me.

I nodded. Couldn't talk. I was having enough trouble breathing. After the "guyliner" thing a few weeks ago, this looked worse than it would've on its own.

"Most mages are girls," Claire lied. "Natalie plays a guy because she's a barbarian. I mean, warrior."

That jab wasn't lost on Natalie, who flinched when Claire said it, but she went with the flow. "Yeah," she said with a pointed look at Claire. "It's kind of weird sometimes, having to be a guy. But it's also kind of cool to see how differently people respond to you. It's an expanding experience."

"But you're a girl," Dad said to Claire, meaning in the world of the game, though he didn't say that.

"The whole time," she said, trying not to smirk. "But my character is a paladin so she also uses magic. You get bonuses to your magic if you're a girl character. I'm not a barbarian like Natalie." She paused and shot another glare at Natalie.

Natalie coughed quietly into her napkin, and I couldn't tell if she was embarrassed or trying not to laugh. Probably both.

Claire continued, "The gender-based stat bonuses are pretty important. Chris's character is very powerful. He can wipe out a whole tribe of orcs with his flamestrike. Well, it's not only that, he's also got these dots…that's damage over time spells. One of them makes the monster explode…"

She trailed off as Dad's eyes glazed over. Claire often said that the quickest way to get parents off a topic was to start going on about gaming. And Dad seemed to buy the "girl characters are magic, boy characters are warriors" excuse, even though Claire had made it up on the spot. No game I knew was ridiculous enough to bonus characters based on gender. But I guess it meshed with Dad's girl/boy stereotypes well enough to avoid scrutiny.

Mom changed the topic by asking Natalie's mom about their house and pulling Dad in to talk about our house's past renovation. Under the cover of that conversation, Natalie glared at Claire and whispered, "A barbarian, huh?"

"You're just lucky his magic user is named Amalia," she shot back in a deadly whisper. They were sitting next to each other, both facing me, while Dad was on my left, so I barely heard what they said.

Natalie looked at me wide-eyed. "I'm so sorry," she mouthed.

I shook my head because I didn't trust my voice yet. The inside of my skin felt like Jell-O still quivering. I tried to eat some spaghetti, but my throat was so tight it hurt to swallow. I wanted my mom and dad to know and understand so badly, but how could I survive telling them if I got this nervous about one slip?

The rest of dinner passed uneventfully, except for Mikey and his friend trying to throw meatballs at each other. We dropped off Claire, and Mom gushed the rest of the way home about how smart Natalie's mom was. But when we got home, Mom took me aside in the kitchen.

"They're very nice," she said. "But I'm not sure you should go into the Cities to see Natalie alone."

"Why not?"

"I think Claire's jealous of her," Mom said. She called to my dad, who was still taking his boots off in the entryway, "Jerry, don't you think Claire's jealous of Natalie?"

"Yep," he shouted back. A minute later he stood in the kitchen entrance. "There was something going on between those two. That Natalie's an attractive girl."

Mom nodded. "And she has a great way with her makeup. Most girls her age either don't wear any or they put on way too much or, well, all that dark eyeliner isn't doing anything for Claire's complexion. Natalie is tasteful. But if you like Claire better, you need to let her know that. She's probably feeling threatened."

"And maybe you should try being a barbarian for a while," Dad added on his way to the garage.

Mom shot me a quizzical look, because she'd missed that part of the conversation, but I shook my head.

"You and Claire have been dating for awhile," she said. "Is it serious?"

"Yeah, I guess so."

"I remember when I was dating your father in high school," she said with a smile that made her face young and wistful. "Some of the other girls thought I shouldn't stick with one guy. Do you get that?"

"Some. Other guys on the swim team date around more, but I don't really want to."

She put her hand gently on my upper arm. "You don't have to do anything you don't want to, honey. I want you to have someone that you love. Someday I'll get to come visit you in a nice house with your children and your wife, and whoever that is, I hope she makes you very happy."

I wondered if she had too much wine at dinner. I think she was trying to let me know that it was okay to dump Claire for Natalie, or not, whichever I wanted. As long as I got married and had kids. I could almost see the picture in her mind of me growing up like her, or rather like Dad.

"Sure," I said.

"You're going to make some woman very happy some day," she added.

I managed a smile. "I hope so."

I went upstairs to send Natalie an email about my parents' compliments to her. I also wondered about what they'd said about Claire. I wasn't attracted to Natalie, but I don't think I'd ever said that out loud. Maybe I should do something nice for Claire. She took such good care of me, and she'd saved my butt at dinner.

CHAPTER TWENTY-ONE

Claire

The Saturdays they spent together had been having an effect beyond bringing up Emily's grades. Every Saturday morning, Claire saw the person she'd known as Chris show up with breakfast food and coffee, go into her bedroom, and come out as Emily.

Except that didn't describe it. More and more, Claire could see Emily was there all the time, only most of the time it wasn't safe for her to be seen. So she acted a role while wearing the most complete Halloween costume of all time.

Much of the information online talked about transitions and transformation, like people turning into other people, and on the outside that made sense. This person did show up looking one way and then change to look another way. Emily put on a sweater that softened the shape of her shoulders, put on a bra and filled it with whatever Natalie had given her that looked pretty darned real. Makeup blurred the angles of her face, smoothed over the places she'd shaved, emphasized her expressive, dark eyes and downplayed the brow ridge above them.

But also Emily let herself be visible in a different way. She'd laugh more and let her voice be lighter and softer. She'd tuck her feet up on the couch, gesture fluently and beautifully with her hands, and do this peering-up-through-her-eyelashes thing that made Claire feel fluttery inside—and also like she wished she could steal that expression.

She wasn't sure what to do about the fluttery. It was good, of course, kind of exciting, like she was getting to date a new person who was also the person she'd known all along.

Emily flirted with her like a girl. She'd never been girl-flirted with before. She'd done it, but it was so different being on the receiving end of all the little touches and questions and being paid attention to. Claire wasn't sure if she liked it a lot or a whole lot.

But she didn't know how she was supposed to respond. So she went with the feeling of envy first. Much simpler to understand.

"Why are you better at girl flirting than I am?" Claire asked on one of their study breaks. They were on the couch, each sitting against an arm, feet tangled together in the middle and Emily's toes had been playing with hers in a very cute way.

Emily gazed up thoughtfully. "I practice at it more?"

"How?"

"I've always watched women I want to grow up to be like. Don't you?"

"I spend most of my time around a woman I want to grow up to be completely *unlike*," Claire said. "But yeah, there are a lot of women writers, women theologians that I'm always paying attention to. I want to know how they think so that I can be like that. But how'd you get flirting?"

"TV. I have to remind myself to watch the guys too sometimes, so I know how people expect me to move."

"You identify with the women?" Claire asked, voice small under the weight of that realization. Had Emily grown up the same way she had? Did Emily automatically watch the women around her and the women on TV to pick out the ones like her—or the ones she wanted to be like in some blurry, distant, imagined future?

The first time Claire had seen Abby on *NCIS*, all in black with tattoos and platform heels, she'd felt so electric. She'd had a sense of kinship and wonder, of wishing Abby were a real person and that Claire could raid her wardrobe. She felt the same way about religious scholar Karen Armstrong, except she was a real person and Claire wanted to raid her bookshelf.

She remembered being ten years old and going with her dad to visit his sister, who was a reporter in St. Cloud. Claire's aunt had given them a tour of the newspaper, everything smelling of paper and ink. Claire thought her aunt was the most amazing person and wanted a job like that when she grew up. But not only the job: Claire had wanted to wear those kinds of no-nonsense slacks and shoes, carry a slender reporter's notebook and a bunch of pens and a minicassette recorder, and wear intricate silver jewelry that looked pretty and serious at the same time.

As a kid it seemed natural to her that it all went together: being a woman and a writer and a thinker meant looking and moving in the world the same way her aunt did.

All this time, had it been the same for Emily? No, not at all the same. Emily could watch the women around her and pick out the ones who made her feel excited for her own future. But any time she tried to emulate them, she was punished. Emily had told her about the time her dad whipped her with his belt for trying on her mom's dresses. And recently Claire had noticed the cutting looks Emily's mom gave her whenever Emily, back in her role as Chris, gestured too soaringly with "his" hands or fluttered "his" fingers instead of making karate chops or whatever guys did.

"Do I identify with the women?" Emily repeated Claire's question while she thought about it. "It's hard to say when I know intellectually that I don't look that way. But yes. Sometimes it feels like 'oh, that's me' and other times more like 'I wish I could be that.' I hate when I'm watching a show and I'll think 'that would look so good on me' and then I realize even if it would fit on this body, and look okay on this body, I wouldn't be allowed to wear it."

"You can wear it over here," Claire said.

"That reminds me, can you help me find pants like this?"

Emily pulled a folded calendar page from her bag and scooted to the middle of the couch. Claire moved next to her and looked at the woman leaning against a low-riding muscle car. Emily's shoulder touched hers. Emily's fingers rested lightly on her thigh. Not the way I'm-being-a-guy-really Chris would've slung an arm over Claire's shoulders, but she liked this too.

She wrapped her fingers around Emily's and leaned closer.

* * *

Claire got so used to hanging out with Emily alone at home on the weekends that she had to be extra careful at school. She dreaded a moment like the one at Emily's birthday dinner when Natalie had nearly blurted out the name "Emily" in front of her parents.

Perhaps sensing this, Emily didn't hang out at her locker as much and didn't seek her out in the halls. Whole days could go by with the two of them barely passing notes. Emily had started signing her notes with a big curving sideways arc, like the letter C, crossed by a small line. It could pass for an artsy "C," but Claire knew it was "E."

It felt like they were sharing a whole volume of inside jokes, most of them more sad than funny.

The weekend before finals was coming and they had a marathon study session planned for Saturday, but Emily passed her a note on Thursday that said, "Let me take you out to dinner tomorrow night."

Two kinds of fear slithered up inside Claire. One easy: finals coming, big stack of books next to her computer, stacks of notecards to study. One hard: going out in public with her "boyfriend."

After school, she called Emily, remembering to ask for "Chris."

"Are you asking me out on a date?" Claire asked when Emily picked up the line.

She could hear the smile in the reply, "You *are* my girlfriend." But tension ran under the words. Going out in public together as boyfriend and girlfriend again would be harder on Emily than on Claire.

They picked the new seafood place and an early time to avoid having to wait in line for ages. Emily said she'd come get Claire with a few minutes to spare in case Claire's mom wanted to coo over them.

Or…should Claire be thinking "he'd come get her." She'd better remember to switch to male pronouns, which she wasn't used to doing outside of school.

She rolled her neck and stood up from the desk. How Emily kept her identity straight all those years was amazing. Now that she persistently saw the presence of Emily, even when Emily had to be Chris, Claire found names and pronouns colliding in her head all the time. She wanted to only think "Emily" and "she" to keep herself used to that and to honor the person Emily was—but they spent so much time together at school and in places where people could overhear them, that she had to keep saying "Chris" and "he."

But sometimes when they were alone, she'd slip and say "Chris" and feel like dirt. Emily had so few places to be herself, she shouldn't have to deal with Claire not having it all together.

Pretending she hadn't slipped up felt worse than saying, "I'm sorry," so Claire defaulted to that.

"I know," Emily had said the last time. "And it helps that you say that."

"It does? I don't know what to do when I screw up. I don't think of you like that but it's habit."

"Say you're sorry and move on. You knew me as Chris for longer than as Emily, I get it. But knowing it's important to you—"

"You're important to me," Claire had interjected and then it all got too cuddly for talking.

* * *

Emily and Natalie had been hanging out more while Claire was busy with the yearbook committee and all her classes. Of course Emily had plenty of schoolwork too, but she hadn't taken as many AP courses as Claire because she wasn't aiming for a top college. She would eventually end up spending more money on surgeries than most kids took out in student loans. While Claire toiled away at home on Sundays, she covered for Emily's trips into the Cities to hang out with Natalie and go to the support group. She and Emily had their Saturdays and swapped notes in school every day. Claire kept wishing Emily would shell out for some kind of mobile device so that she could text her.

Getting out of the shower before their first real date in months, Claire stood in front of her closet puzzling out what to wear. As Emily came out more, Claire felt herself changing, in ways she liked.

In the last two months, she'd learned more about makeup than she ever imagined she would—including the fact that a bit of indigo eye shadow really brought out the gold tints in her hazel eyes. When she watched women like her mother who put on makeup religiously to be more attractive to men, it scared her. She never wanted to feel like she needed a person so much that she'd add all that mirror time to her day.

But when she watched Emily and Natalie, a whole new view opened up. For them being beautiful wasn't a burden, it was a self-expression they were willing to fight for. Their feminine beauty was the battle standard for claiming their own identities. She'd never realized that femininity could be a radical act because she'd never seen a feminine woman as strong in her identity as Emily or Natalie, or even Natalie's mother.

Now that she knew what powerful beauty looked like, she noticed it in other women all over the place. Many of the women in the Bible exemplified it. Michelle Obama definitely had it. Closer to home, Claire's English teacher wore her makeup so her dark skin and eyes gently grabbed and held the attention of anyone looking at her.

Claire drew thin black lines around her eyes. She brushed shimmering tan eye shadow under her brows and applied the indigo color on her eyelids the way the girls had taught her. Foundation and blush would be too much, but she chose a pink lip gloss from the basket full of the cosmetics her mom kept bringing home and applied that. She picked small silver hoop earrings and then crossed the hall to riffle through her closet until she found a blue-gray shirt with a cute collar to wear with her black skirt.

"Oh my God," her mom exclaimed from the kitchen when she saw Claire. She stopped scrubbing the countertop and straightened up. "What have you done with my daughter?"

"Chris is taking me out to dinner," Claire said. "Are you going out later? Can we watch a movie here afterward?"

"I'll probably be home at ten, if that's not too early for you," her mom said with the patronizing lilt that reminded Claire she didn't have a choice. She added, "I think Chris is a good influence on you."

"I know he is," Claire said with a grin and only a slight hitch before "he."

When Claire heard the car pull into the driveway, she said a quick goodbye to her mom and scooted out the door, into the close warmth of the car. Emily was playing "Chris the boyfriend" to the teeth: dressy gray men's pants, light blue button-down shirt and tie under a dark gray V-neck sweater, hair combed and gelled close to the scalp.

But when those warm, dark eyes turned to look at Claire, Emily was still there, the shared, sad joke between them again.

Emily blinked a few times, closed her eyes tight for a second and opened them. "Are you wearing blue?" she asked. "And eye shadow?"

"Yep. Come on, drive. I don't want to have to wait in line forever."

As they headed for the seafood place, Claire rested her hand on Emily's leg just above the knee.

Claire said, "When I see how hard you have to fight to get to wear makeup, it made me realize that it's not all about being some stupid girly girl."

"Well not stupid..." Emily said and laughed her higher-pitched natural laugh at first, but then corralled it into a masculine range.

"Oh you know what I mean."

At the restaurant, Claire regretted the makeup when the host cooed over them while steering them to a quiet table off to one side of the main dining room.

"I feel like we're the cover photo of a travel brochure that says 'welcome to heterosexuality,'" Claire whispered after they were seated.

Emily cleared her throat in a very Chris-like manner and managed not to laugh.

They proceeded to eat an obscene amount of crab, clams, shrimp and butter. At points it was like any other time they'd eaten out together. But Claire kept having flashes of what would happen if they were exposed as two girls together, dating, being bi and lesbian and trans all at the same time.

Those scenarios started with people yelling and throwing things. The more cheerful ones ended with her and Emily sprinting out of the restaurant and making it to the car.

She'd never questioned how safe she'd felt with Chris. After the bullying in junior high, she'd assumed the safe feeling came from being with a more popular person. But a huge amount of it was being with a guy. Not only the unassailable normalcy of it, but the fact that as "the guy," Chris was supposed to protect her.

When two girls went out together, who was the protector? Did they take turns?

Claire leaned back in her chair, cradling her overstuffed belly in her hands, relaxing as much as she could. They'd been in the restaurant well over an hour and the worst thing to happen had been an older couple pausing at their table to say how cute they looked and using the term "handsome" three times for Emily.

"Did you want to catch a movie next?" Emily asked.

"Let's go watch one at my house. Mom's out for a while, and I like when we don't have a bunch of other people around." Claire didn't add that she wanted to make sure she didn't have to fight about who was paying for the movie. Emily had already dropped plenty of money on her with this dinner, and Claire knew how much she needed to save it all.

Plus she was tired of thinking of routes to the car if they had to run for it.

"Thank you," she added. "This was perfect. Apparently I needed to consume a pound of protein covered in butter."

Emily chuckled. "It's for how sweet you've been. And I wanted us to have a real date again."

"Real dates are nice," Claire said.

She smiled, but Claire saw a flash of tension around her eyes.

"What are you worried about?" she asked.

Emily shook her head and paid the bill. When they were outside, sitting in the car with the sweet spring air rolling in the open windows Emily asked, "Are we going to end up just friends?"

"I'm not planning on it," Claire said.

"You don't kiss me like you used to."

"We've had a lot going on!" she protested.

True, of course. But also she didn't know how to kiss Emily. She'd known how to make out with Chris. That was fun, especially because he'd been easy to tease and fluster.

It wasn't the same. But right now it was pretty close or maybe better.

Claire scrutinized the parking lot. People walked to and from the restaurant without paying attention to the cars. And anyway, right now the two of them looked like the picture-perfect hetero teen date.

She climbed awkwardly as far into Emily's lap as she could get. Since she was small and Emily's car had a big front seat, they'd made out like this before. But not like this. Half from reflex and half bravado, Claire kissed Emily hard. Emily's arms came up around Claire with a tight desperation as their lips met.

When they broke apart, Emily's eyes were still questioning her. And Emily looked too much like Chris. Claire's head hurt from the inside out with the weight of being in the world with Chris but wanting to figure out how to kiss Emily.

She carefully got back into her seat.

"My house," she said.

The sun sat low over the houses, but wouldn't set for a while yet. Her mom's car was out of the garage, and Claire figured they had at least two hours until they could expect her home. She took Emily's hand and pulled her through the living room toward the bathroom. "I'm picking the movie," she said. "You do the makeup."

"What?"

"Put some on, I'm serious. And please take off that tie."

She flicked on the TV and started flipping though the On Demand movies, though she didn't care what they watched. Something shallow for background noise that they didn't have to pay attention to.

Emily came out a few minutes later with a light touch of makeup around her eyes, solid foundation, a hint of blush and a lip shimmer. She'd fluffed her hair as much as she could, but it was still too short. Her pants and sweater were gender neutral enough to work either way and she'd taken off the button-down and tie.

Claire beckoned her to the couch. If she'd thought this through, she realized, she could have cued up "I Kissed a Girl" on the iPod speakers. When Emily sat, Claire leaned forward and gently traced the side of her face. She didn't know what to say, or to expect, so she kissed her.

It wasn't radically different from every other kiss they'd shared. They'd been kissing since Emily had come out to her, just not making out at length like they used to. Emily's lips were warm, soft and familiar. But the presence of lip shimmer made the kiss sticky.

Claire pulled back. "This is silly."

"What?"

She hopped up and got tissues and makeup wipes. "The other girl I kissed wasn't wearing anything on her lips and my lip gloss on your shimmer is yucky."

Emily wiped off her lips. "You might be trying too hard," she said.

"All the time," Claire replied as she wiped off her makeup.

"Movie?" Emily asked.

She'd turned to the screen and picked up the remote, but Claire saw the flash of sadness in the dark of her eyes. If girls together took turns, it was definitely Claire's turn. She pushed off the couch and got in front of Emily, fingers on her jaw, tipping her face up. She put her lips on Emily's, kissing with increasing pressure until Emily's hands went to her waist and pulled her down to the couch.

This time no sticky lip gloss got in the way. For the first few minutes of making out, part of Claire's mind stood apart from the experience, waiting to see if anything felt new in a bad way. Emily smelled sweeter than Claire was used to and her kisses felt more tentative, but that was easy to understand.

Claire's favorite parts of the experience hadn't changed. She still loved strong hands on her back, and it didn't matter if those were a boy's or a girl's. She appreciated being kissed carefully and thoughtfully. And she loved the feeling of melting into another human being that she cared about. She let her whole mind dissolve into that.

So much so that an hour later, she almost didn't hear the garage door going up. At least Emily had. She lunged off the couch and into the bathroom to get her makeup off. Claire scrambled back into her shirt and clicked on a movie, fast-forwarding it to the middle so her mom would think they'd been watching it.

The downside to that, she hadn't realized, was that Mom now expected her and "Chris" to watch the second half of the movie together, with Mom at home. Upside: she'd hastily selected *Transformers*, so at least Mom didn't try to join them. Emily had already seen it with Mikey, but she settled in next to Claire and took her hand, entwining their fingers.

Nodding at the screen, after Mom had gone into her room to change, Emily whispered, "Is this your first attempt at a trans joke?"

Claire blinked at the image of car turning into a robot. "It is now," she said. "Maybe you can use this with Mikey when you tell him."

"He'll expect me to have super powers."

"Don't you?" Claire asked and leaned into Emily.

"If turning from a robot into a person counts, then yes."

CHAPTER TWENTY-TWO

The big day was coming. I'd gone back and forth about when to come out to my parents—but I solidified my resolve when I started seeing the bottom of the pill bottle around the few remaining hormone pills. I'd started taking them again in May and the last few weeks I'd felt a difference in myself. I wasn't so angry all the time and on the darkest days, the fierce edge of the blackness seemed to dull.

More exciting was the fact that my skin softened all over my body. As I let the hair grow back in on my arms, it seemed lighter than it had been. I could begin to understand how much my body would change in this process, how I really could stop trying to be a man altogether and become the woman I knew myself to be.

Homework at Claire's for two months had brought my grades into the B-to-A range. And going out with her—no, not going out, but coming back to her house, her making out with me like she used to—gave me strength.

I told Mom and Dad that I had something I wanted to talk to them about and asked them to come see Dr. Mendel with me that Thursday. They looked alarmed, but agreed to come with me when I refused to say more. Dr. Mendel said she'd set aside a couple of hours in case it took longer than our regular session to talk to them. I had stashed a few books at her office the week before that I thought would help them understand.

I was so nervous on the way over that I couldn't sit still. Dad drove and Mom kept turning around in her seat to squint at me as I wriggled in place.

"I don't know why we have to do this in her office," Mom complained. "Why can't you just tell us?"

"It's okay," I said for the hundredth time. "It's easier this way."

"Did you get Claire pregnant?" she asked, apparently her worst fear.

"No, Mom, we're not having sex, honest."

I willed the car to move faster, though Dad was a speedy driver to begin with. At the same time, I wondered how long it would take Mom to get to the right question. I worked out the math in my head. She was asking a question about every ninety seconds, which was about 960 questions a day, except that we'd need time to eat and sleep, so let's assume 480 questions a day, or 2,880 questions a week. With Sunday off, would that be enough for her to get around to asking if I was a girl in a single week? Probably not.

"Are you sick?" she asked.

"No, Mom."

"But you needed an appointment to tell us about this?"

"Yes."

We finally pulled into the parking lot, and I ushered them through the doors and up the stairs to the second floor lobby. I almost knocked on Dr. Mendel's door I was so eager to get this over with, but she opened it less than a minute after we rounded the corner.

"Come in," she said. "Mr. and Mrs. Hesse, it's good of you to come today. Please have a seat."

Mom and Dad sat on the couch, so I took the comfy chair on the end. Dr. Mendel sat in her usual spot facing the couch. Everyone in the room had dressed up for this appointment.

I'd put on my darker jeans and a light blue button-down shirt. Mom was in one of her work outfits with slacks and a V-neck sweater that made her look younger and pretty. She even had on earrings and makeup, though she'd been home from work long enough to take them off if she wanted to. Cleaned up from his construction outfit, Dad wore khakis and a long-sleeved pullover shirt with a collar. And Dr. Mendel was actually in a long, gray knit dress with pearls looping down over her ample bosom and hanging in delicate silver drips from her ears. I bet she'd dressed more stereotypically female so that she'd have more authority with my parents about gender-related topics. Good call.

I tried to take a deep breath, but my chest didn't expand, so the attempt ended up long and shallow. Okay, what was the worst that could happen? They could throw me out. I'd turned seventeen in April, so I was almost old enough to make all my own decisions legally. I could probably stay at Claire's for a while and finish school, or at least that was a nice fantasy. I'd hold on to that one.

"Chris," Dr. Mendel said as if introducing me or maybe reminding me I didn't want to be called by that name the rest of my life. We'd agreed that I had to tell them, rather than her. She was there for support, but I had to do this.

"Um," I said, rather inelegantly, and braced my hands on my legs. "Thanks for coming. So, ah. Well, I don't know how to say this so if it comes out funny I hope you'll hear me out. It might not make a lot of sense right away, but I think with time it will make a whole lot of sense."

"You're gay," Mom blurted out.

"I'm a girl," I said.

Dead silence.

"No, you're not," Mom said.

"Yes, I am."

"Christopher," she said in her low-pitched warning tone.

"Ever since I can remember, I've known I was a girl," I said, glancing back and forth between them and my hands. Dad's eyebrows were tilting out at angles, and Mom's mouth disappeared into a thin line. "When I was little I tried to hang out with the other girls, but everyone said I was a boy and so eventually I played along, but I've always known I was a girl."

"No you're not," Mom repeated. "You are very clearly not a girl." She turned toward Dr. Mendel and demanded, "What on earth have you been telling him?"

Dr. Mendel remained silent while I took another long, shallow breath. "Mom," I said as firmly as I could manage. "Sometimes kids get born with the brain of the other sex. It's called being transgender. It means that although I have a boy's body, inside I really am a girl."

"So you like to wear dresses?" Dad asked. He looked confused and incredulous. His normally tanned face was as pale as parchment.

"Well sort of," I said. "But that's not the point. The point is that I feel like a woman inside, and I want the hormones and surgery so I can live my life as a woman."

"Oh," he said. "Oh God."

The room fell silent.

Dad's hand, resting on his thigh, twitched open and closed. Dr. Mendel sat like a rock and watched them, her face calm but intense. I shifted in my chair and failed to find a position where I felt like I wasn't about to get hit by lightning.

"If this is a joke…" Mom started.

"Mrs. Hesse, it's not a joke," Dr. Mendel spoke up. "Your child has a rare but treatable condition. I think you've noticed that over the last few months, more self-expression for Chris has led to greater confidence, better grades, less depression."

Dr. Mendel very diplomatically avoided using pronouns in her statements. At this point I think female pronouns would have sent my mom through the roof, and male pronouns would have made me feel like crap. Yeah, I had a good doctor.

"Chris is a boy," Mom insisted. She sat back against the couch and folded her arms tightly against her chest. Her eyes narrowed to hostile slits. "He needs to learn to live that way, not have his head filled with this nonsense."

Silence stretched out again until Mom stood up.

"We're leaving," she declared.

"No," I said. "We're not."

She looked at Dad to back her up. "Let's hear all of it," he said grimly as if he were talking about a list of war casualties.

Mom sat back down and crossed her arms again with her hands in fists. "All right, but I don't believe it."

"It's scientifically proven," I said. "And besides, what really matters is that when I get to be a girl, I feel like myself. All these years I've had to pretend to be someone I'm not." My voice rose. "Don't you want me to be happy?"

"Chris," Dr. Mendel warned before anyone else could answer. I tried to calm down. She was right, this was a bad time to ask leading questions of my parents before we brought them up to speed on the whole thing. She'd warned me last week that I'd had years to research this and they were probably hearing about it for the first time in their lives.

"Sorry," I offered.

Dr. Mendel picked up the conversation. "Sometimes a child is born whose internal sense of their gender does not match their external sex characteristics, and in some cases, that difference is so pronounced that the child knows that he or she is the other sex from the body he or she was born with," she said in her grandmotherly tone. "It's called gender dysphoria. This is what happened for Chris. While everyone around assumed Chris was a boy, which is quite natural, inside Chris has always felt like a girl. There are over a million people like Chris living in America. Many of them choose to transition their outward appearance to align with their gender identity, and live the rest of their lives as productive, well-adjusted members of society.

"You brought Chris to therapy because you noticed, quite rightly, that your child was struggling with mood problems. The good news is that your child is very bright and socially well developed. Considering what Chris has had to live with, she's an outstanding individual. This is not about anything you did or didn't do. It's a biological condition determined before birth. You have a child you can be proud of. Chris has been very strong in the face of considerable adversity and some of that is due to the values you've instilled. Now she needs your support, more than most kids do, to take the last few steps to adulthood."

Dr. Mendel sat back in her chair. I wanted to bottle that speech so I could listen to it every day for the next year or two.

"Are you done?" Mom asked coldly.

"Yes," Dr. Mendel said. "Though we have a few pamphlets and books for you to look at if you'd like."

Mom looked at me. "Anything else?"

I didn't know what to say to the ice sculpture of her face. I wanted to ask Dr. Mendel to rescue me, but I figured that wouldn't help much. What could she do beyond what she already had?

Dad broke the silence. "There are other kids like this?" he asked Dr. Mendel.

"Yes," she said.

"How do they know?"

"There's a persistent sense of being the wrong gender that lasts for years. It's natural for children to be curious about the other sex, to wonder what it's like, but I think you'll agree that having a persistent sense that you're a girl over ten years or more is something very different from curiosity or a child trying on various roles."

He looked at me. "You always did cry a lot. I thought you were a sissy. But you toughened up."

"I've been pretending," I said.

"So you want to be a woman...does that mean you want to date guys?"

"No," I said. "I still like girls."

"Jesus Christ," he said and all but rolled his eyes. "That makes no sense at all." He picked up a pamphlet from the side table, stood up and crammed it into his pocket. "All right, I'm done with this. Chris, you coming with us?"

"Sure," I said and stood up with a wide-eyed look at Dr. Mendel.

"Would you two wait outside for a minute?" she asked.

After a final glare from my mother at Dr. Mendel, they walked through the door and shut it loudly behind them.

"That sucked," I said.

"Give them time," she told me. "They're going to go through stages. They're in shock right now, and then they'll be in denial for a while. Try not to let them blame themselves, and if they get too angry...if you're afraid, call me and get out of the house, okay?"

"Yes."

"Promise me you won't try to tough it out if it's more than you can handle."

"Okay," I said.

"You can do this," she reassured me. "You have me and Claire and Natalie, lots of people supporting you. Let your folks know that you love them and you're being honest with them."

I nodded and thanked her, then headed out the door. Mom and Dad were already in the car with the engine running.

When I got into the back seat, they didn't say anything at all or look at me; the silence held all the way home. It held even when we picked up Mikey from his friend's house down the street. He knew something was wrong and didn't chatter on like he usually did.

In the house, the air felt icy compared to the warmth outdoors, and it wasn't because of the air-conditioning. Dad made a beeline for the garage and Mikey ran into the living room to turn on the TV.

Mom dropped her purse on the table with an angry clatter.

"What the hell are you trying to pull?" she yelled at me.

"It's the truth," I said.

"You want to be a *woman*? That's ridiculous. Look at you!"

Into the pause in the tirade Mikey yelled from the living room, "Fag!"

Mom turned toward him. "GO TO YOUR ROOM!" she screamed louder than I'd ever heard. He leaped to his feet and tore up the stairs.

She dropped her voice, which didn't help much because now it sounded like a butter knife trying to saw through bone. "Being woman isn't going to solve anything," she said to me. "It's just going to make your life hell. Look at you, you'd make the ugliest woman I can imagine. You'd be a freak. You need to drop this bullshit right now, young man. I don't want to know what put this crazy idea in your head, but you are grounded until you come to your senses. No more computer, no more trips to the city, and I'm going to find another doctor for you. Now you go to your room, too."

I ran for my room. I logged on to GenderPeace and quickly posted a message that my mom had lost it and I might not be able to get online in the near future. Then I sent Natalie a short note, and an email to Claire saying I was going to need help.

Moments after I hit send, Mom threw the door open.

"Get off that," she said.

I stepped back. She yanked the cords out of the wall and picked up the whole computer, carrying it out of the room. A minute later she came back and took my phone. Then she slammed the door behind her.

I waited. The house was quiet. No, I could hear her in the garage yelling at Dad. Then him yelling back. I couldn't tell what he was saying. I thought about putting my ear to the floor, but I didn't really want to know. Instead I snuck out into the hall and tapped on Mikey's door.

"Yeah," he said softly.

"It's me."

He opened the door. His eyes were red and he sniffled a few times, trying not to cry. "I didn't mean it," he said almost in a whisper. "Why is Mom so mad?"

I shut the door behind me and sat on the edge of his bed. He had a Batman bedspread, though I'd heard Mom tell him he was getting too old for it. Right now he looked pretty young even for nine. His brown eyes were huge and red with the effort of not crying.

"Mom's not mad at you," I said. "She's mad at me."

He sat on the foot of the bed, one leg tucked up under his other leg, and idly rearranged the action figures beside him. "She said you want to be a girl?" he asked. "That's weird."

"Yeah," I said. "I do."

"Am I going to turn out like that too?" he asked.

I put my hand on his shoulder. "No. I've always wanted to be a woman. You don't. You're a boy."

"I am," he said with gusto. "Girls are gross. I don't know why you want to be one. Does this mean you're going to turn into my sister?"

I tried to read his face to see if he was going to use this against me later, but his pale skin and tight lips looked genuinely scared and concerned. "In a few years."

"Can they really make you into a girl? I never heard of anything like that. What do they do?"

I didn't know how much to tell him, so I stuck to the basics. "It takes surgery and hormones. They don't just zap me with a laser."

He laughed, as I'd intended. "That would be a funny power to have. What would you call that superhero? Girl Man? I'd zap Zach, he deserves it."

He'd started to grin, and I smiled back. "I think maybe we should only turn people into girls who want to be girls," I warned. "Otherwise it's not fair."

"Yeah," he said. "Is Mom going to be mad at you for a long time?"

"Probably," I told him.

"Can I have your car?"

"You can't drive for seven more years," I pointed out. "What would you do with it? Sit in the driveway?"

"It's cool."

"I still like cars," I told him.

"You're going to be a girl who likes cars?"

"Such creatures do exist."

"But you're my brother right now, right?" he asked.

"Yeah."

"Want to play superheroes until Mom's not mad at you?"

I pretended to think about it. "Can I be the girls?" I asked.

"Yeah!" he said with emphasis. "I don't want 'em." He pushed the female action figures to side of the bed where I sat.

"And I get Warlock," I insisted, snaring that figure and pulling him over. Warlock was an alien robot. Since I felt like an alien right now and might have to be a robot for the near future, that seemed like the smart pick.

His favorite game these days was to compose teams of superheroes and explain how they pounded the crap out of each other. I picked my four favorite girl heroes and lined them up with Warlock. He picked an amalgam of men and aliens. We whaled on each other until Mom called us down for a very silent dinner.

CHAPTER TWENTY-THREE

A large vacuum invaded our house, which is to say: life sucked. Mom rescinded all my communication and travel privileges. She cancelled my appointments with Dr. Mendel and set one up with Dr. Webber. I refused to go. I put up with her other bullshit—I didn't want to find out if Claire's mom would honestly take me in if Mom threw me out—but there were a couple boundaries I was holding firm, and that was one.

We were at a standoff. I spent a lot of time working on cars with Dad who never brought up anything from the visit to Dr. Mendel. I also played with Mikey a lot. My girls and robot team even beat his men and aliens team a few times. I knew I should've drafted more aliens.

With permission, I managed one trip over to Claire's in late June, when she said she needed my old geometry book, and I told her what had happened. I stashed the duffel bag at her house. When I got home it was clear why Mom allowed me to visit Claire. She'd been through my room and taken my copies of Kate Bornstein's *Gender Outlaw*, Jenny Boylan's *She's Not*

There, Leslie Feinberg's *Transgender Warriors* and Julia Serano's *Whipping Girl*. Pretty sure she hadn't taken them to read. She also took some of my X-Men comics, which puzzled me, and the swimsuit issue of *Sports Illustrated*, which was actually Dad's but I had lifted it to imagine myself as those models.

My senior year of high school started in two months and then she wouldn't have so much control over my activities. I would wait her out. After I talked to Dad about it, we set my computer up in the garage so I could keep selling his car bits on eBay. I had a roof over my head and food, and I was making decent money with the eBay work, so I could wait a few months to have my girl-time back. Half the time Dad didn't pay any attention to what I was doing on the computer because he was under a car or deep in its engine. I'd open another browser window under the eBay window and post on GenderPeace. It was amazing to see so many people from all over the world offer support for my situation.

"Remember, it's a process," one post said. "It took me a while to realize that my parents had to go through all this mourning for the loss of their son. My mom was crying almost every day and I thought it was because she was so ashamed of me. But really she was trying to let go of her old idea of me. Then for a while I felt like I was the one who killed her son and that was awful. But now we can talk about it, and she asked if I would come home for a visit sometime this year. Hang in there and give them time!"

"I'm sorry she cut off your good therapist," another said. "Keep coming back here, you need all the support you can get right now. You can do this."

The only funny part of the whole dismal time was a surprise visit from Claire. She brought me some of her science fiction novels and an English textbook that I didn't need since it was summer. While we were sitting in the kitchen talking, because Mom said I couldn't have anyone in my room, Mom came in.

"Did he tell you why he's grounded?" she asked Claire.

She shrugged. "School stuff." She was lying. I had told her everything and she thought it was awful, but she'd had two years of drama club and sensed an opportunity.

"He thinks he wants to be a girl," Mom said. "Isn't that disgusting?"

Claire's eyes got huge. "Oh my God!" she said. She turned to me. "How could you! You said that was only a phase. Chris! I'm so embarrassed!" She stood up and ran out of the house.

"Claire!" I yelled, quite dramatically. I grabbed my car keys off the counter and glared at Mom. "Thanks. Thanks a lot!"

Claire stood by the passenger side of the car, face in her hands, shoulders shaking, pretending to cry. As I got closer, I heard her muffled laughter. I bundled her into the passenger seat. Her mom had dropped her off and was going to come get her in an hour, but I got into the driver's seat and peeled off. Mom could reground me later when I got home.

A couple blocks away I had to stop because I was laughing too hard to see straight. "That was priceless," I told her.

"I hope it wasn't too mean," Claire said. "But I couldn't stand her crap. Maybe she'll feel bad for once. How long do you think it's going to take for you to comfort me?"

"Few hours?" I suggested.

"Good, I'll call Mom and tell her not to pick me up. We can catch a movie. I've got liner and eye shadow in my pocket if you promise to wear shades."

"You're making me feel like a junkie," I said.

"You don't want it?" she teased.

I smiled. "You're wicked."

"Just what you need. Come on, let's go see something mind-numbing while I plot my next performance."

I had one thing I wanted to bring up with her, and I didn't know how to say it. "Claire, would you talk to Natalie and see if there's a way you can order hormones for me? Natalie knows the right stuff, and I'll pay you back for all of it."

I could feel her looking at me, though my eyes were on the road ahead. "That's not legal is it?" she asked.

"No," I admitted. "But my parents aren't going to take me to a doctor and…I need them."

She took a deep breath. "Emily, it's not going to hurt you to wait a few more months…" She sounded like she was going to say more, but I'd pulled over a few blocks from the theater.

I put my head forward on the steering wheel and sobbed. All the tension of the past weeks at home and the awful things Mom had said, plus the hopelessness of running out of the one thing that was making a positive difference, it all came out of me in deep, dry sobbing, my fingers wrapped white-knuckled around the wheel.

Claire rubbed my back with her palm. "It's going to be okay, it's just a matter of time."

"I don't have time," I managed. "Seventeen years and every day is torture. I can feel this stupid testosterone masculinizing me. It's making me all rough and hairy. And now it's worse because Mom and Dad know and they're awful. And I'm so close. I want to be normal…a normal woman."

She rested her cheek on my shoulder. "Honey, I'm not sure you should ever want to be normal. I'll talk to Natalie, but I can't promise anything. I'm not into illegal and no matter how crazy things are, you shouldn't be either."

I dug into my pocket for a tissue and blew my nose. "Thanks. I'm sorry."

"I worry about you," she said. "Maybe you should call the good doctor."

I shrugged. "Maybe."

* * *

I tried being a good kid for three weeks, but Mom showed no signs of relenting. She glared at me a lot. In her softer moments, she'd compliment me on what I was wearing and say how broad it made my shoulders look, or how tall I was getting. I started avoiding her. For a few days here and there, I could lose myself in the work on the Bronco with Dad.

I had two lawn-mowing jobs in the neighborhood, but that didn't take up enough time or make enough money. Pretty sure mom wouldn't go for me applying as a cashier at the crafts boutique, and honestly I wasn't that into crafts. Dad talked about getting me some cleanup work at the local auto shop.

I put up a flier at our church for babysitting. Having my own car helped with that and Mom lifted my grounding enough so

I could work. But in week three Mom got pissed at me all over again because one of the families told her how great it was that I'd play dolls with their girls.

I stayed away from the house as much as I could. I also started staying up later and later at night. In the quiet, dark hours, I could feel like myself again. Even if I didn't have my computer, I could dream about going out as a woman. For hours at night I would lie awake in bed and go through every detail of the trip to the mall with Natalie and her mom, and the few shopping trips I'd had with Natalie in May, and then I'd build out from there, imagining myself with an apartment in Minneapolis and a job, and everyone would call me "ma'am" or "miss." I could wear my hair long, and my skin would feel soft, even softer than it had on Natalie's borrowed hormones.

I wrote a few stories in the back of my chemistry notebook about a girl named Emily. Mom didn't know my name, though I was sure she'd be furious if she found them. I didn't care so much anymore.

Staying up late meant that I could sleep in later. Even after I woke up in the mornings, I didn't get out of bed until I was forced to either by having to pee, or someone knocking on my bedroom door. Most days I could stay in bed until nearly noon, and then I only had to navigate the hours between noon and ten, when Mom went to bed.

I thought I was holding myself together pretty well, existing day to day, waiting for the next and the next so that I could get back to school and eventually escape this house completely. Until the dinner.

The dinner was out at a fancy restaurant in the neighboring town. The financial planning firm Mom worked for hosted it as a summer bonus because the business was doing well. Only the older kids from employee families were invited, so Mikey got to luck out of it and spend the night at a friend's house.

Mom insisted that we dress up for it and make a good impression. "That means a jacket and a tie," she told me.

I wore them. I didn't much care one way or the other. The body in the jacket didn't feel like mine anyway. In the restaurant, we sat at a table with one of Mom's bosses and his family, a wife and three girls.

Mom introduced me as, "Chris, our oldest son," which seemed excessive, but I let it go. She didn't.

"We're very proud of Chris," she slipped in later. "He got a letter in swimming this year. He likes distance swimming best; can you imagine that? Swimming a mile?"

"Really?" the oldest girl asked. She was about my age and pretty in that I-would-kill-to-have-her-brow-line style. Too blond for me to be attracted to her, but slender in a way that made me envy her waist.

"Yeah," I said, sounding like a Neanderthal.

"You two are about the same age," Mom said, pointing out the obvious. "Why don't you come over here so you can talk to each other." She actually got up and switched places with the blond girl.

I didn't know what on earth she thought she was doing, and if it hadn't been a dinner for her work, I'd have stood up and left. Also I didn't want to offend this girl who was clearly caught in the crossfire of our feud. I kept my hands in my lap because they'd started to shake with the effort of sitting still.

Betsy was the girl's name, and she had that same nervous habit of talking that Claire had. We made it through the entrée with her telling me all about her school activities and her sisters, without my having to give more than one-word answers.

When she started winding down, I asked, "Where'd you get that sweater?"

"Banana Republic," she said. "Do you like it?"

"It's great. I have a pair of pants from them, very soft," I told her.

"They have great stuff, don't they? I saw this white quilted jacket I wanted, but how would you ever keep something like that clean?"

I laughed a little with her. It felt good to laugh, and to have some girl talk.

"Your eye shadow looks really good," I said. "Is it MAC?"

"No, it's actually Mary Kay. Mom's a director, so I get all these free samples from her. You like it? I thought it was too blue."

"It brings out the light colors in your eyes, it looks good," I said. "Do you like Mary Kay products?"

"Well, I like the soaps and lotions best," she said. "They make my skin so soft. Feel this." She held out the back of her hand and I touched it. It was as soft as feathers, but without feeling fragile.

"That's amazing, I wish my skin felt like that."

She giggled. "I could do your hands sometime."

From across the table, Mom interjected, "Don't you two look cute together."

I glared at her. She made it sound like we were dating, but she knew I had a girlfriend. I realized Mom didn't like Claire even more than she let on. She'd rather have me with this blond Mary Kay girl than with my goth-haired, kohl-eye-linered best friend in the world.

My glare didn't stop Mom. She went on. "Did Chris tell you about how he restores cars with his father? He's very good with his hands, but he also gets good grades. Well rounded."

"No, Mom," I said. "We were talking about makeup."

Mom's mouth shut in a chiseled line. Luckily the youngest sister chimed in about how she wanted to wear makeup and no one noticed the deadly looks passing between Mom and me. She didn't let me forget that remark, though. As soon as we were in the car, she started in about it.

"Chris, I can't believe you said that at dinner. Talking about makeup, honestly. I want to be able to take my family out to a simple dinner with my office and not be mortified by my own child. Can't you give it up for one night? Do you have to be a freak all the time? I don't know why you want to stand out so much. Your dad and I have given you everything we had, and you persist in this...perversion of nature."

"Sharon," Dad said in his warning tone.

"Don't try to calm me down. Chris is a man, and the sooner he accepts that, the better. I don't know where he came up with this crazy idea, but I have raised him as a boy and he will never be anything other than a man." She raised her voice and glared over her shoulder. "Do you hear that? You're a man, no matter what anyone tells you. Just look at yourself. That's all you'll ever be."

I wobbled on the razor edge of sanity. Dad pulled into the driveway and I opened the car door before he'd stopped. I had my keys in my hand and ran to the front door before anyone could follow me. I dashed through the doorway and up the stairs to my bedroom where I bolted the door behind me. Then, for good measure, I pushed my desk all the way across my room and shoved it in front of the door, panting with the effort and my rage.

I tore off my jacket, tie and shirt and searched for a way to destroy them. In my top desk drawer was a pair of scissors and a hunting knife Dad had given me last year. First I thought I should just cut off the parts of me that had Mom so convinced I was a man. I stood over the desk, bracing myself on my left hand while the knife quivered in my right. I couldn't. Even though I hated that part of myself, I couldn't attack my own body that way.

Instead I sat down on the edge of my bed in my slacks and cut the arms off my jacket. As soon as the scissors bit through the cloth, I felt a clear determination rising inside of my outrage. I took each arm and cut it into strips, then I cut off the collar and used the knife to rip the jacket to rags. I took apart the shirt the same way, and then snipped perpendicularly across the tie, so that it lay on the floor in one-inch wide pieces.

I stood up and stepped out of my pants, which came under the blade next. I was naked except for my briefs and those weren't coming off because I refused to confront what was underneath them. I opened my closet door and looked into the comforting darkness.

Dad knocked on my door. "Open up," he said.

"No," I told him.

"Don't make me break in there, you won't like it."

"The desk is in front of the door, I'd like to see you try," I shot back at him.

He raised his voice. "Chris, open the door."

"No," I said, and then more loudly, "No!" I was screaming now as loud as I could, defying all the bullshit they'd put me through, "*No! No! No!*"

Leaning over the desk, I punched the door. I heard Dad step back from the other side, but it barely registered over my own shouting and hitting the door again with my fist.

I screamed, "No!" and hit the door again, harder, over and over again.

I saw blood on the door and heard my voice go hoarse from screaming, but I couldn't stop. The fury drove through me into the wood as I hit it. Only when my knuckle scraped the edge of the deadbolt and tore off a half-inch of skin did the pain slice through my rage.

I grabbed my right hand with my left and staggered into my closet to curl up in the clothes I'd dragged off their hangers. I was crying so hard I thought I was going to puke.

A booming impact hit the door so hard from the other side that the wood around the hinges groaned. Then twice more until wood splintered and the lock tore loose. I heard the scrape of the desk being pushed back and then Dad was kneeling down in the doorway to the closet. He grabbed my bloody hands and turned them palm up. He was afraid I'd slit my wrists.

"Didn't...cut...myself," I managed through my heaving breath. "Knuckles."

"Ah Chris," he said and closed his hand over the back of my neck. He gave me a tiny shake. "Jesus."

He left. I curled deeper into the clothes pile, wishing it would all go away. My head felt crushed. My eyes and sinuses burned with a damp fire.

Dad came back a few minutes later. I was still crying, but not so hard. The tears rolled down my face whether I tried to stop them or not. Dad had a stack of washcloths, bandage pads, tape and a bag of ice that he put on my right knuckles once he had a washcloth in place to stop the blood. He cleaned up my left hand and then very carefully ran a damp cloth over the right.

"Shit," was the one word he said during this process. He opened a couple of sterile bandage pads, pressed them over the knuckles and taped them loosely.

Then he helped me pull one of his baggy sweatshirts down over my head. I didn't realize how cold I was until he put the shirt on me. I started shivering uncontrollably.

He looped an arm under my shoulders and helped me across the room to my bed. Dragging my desk chair across the room, he sat next to the bed and put the ice pack on my bandaged hand. I struggled to come up with words but before any came I fell into an exhausted sleep.

CHAPTER TWENTY-FOUR

When I woke up in the late morning, my right hand had a swollen lump that joined the knuckles together in a puffy, blue-purple mass. As loose as the tape was on the bandage, it still strained from the swelling. I gingerly pulled up one edge and peeked underneath. A line of scabs crossed my knuckles where the skin had split and torn. Most of the skin that should have been on my middle knuckle was gone, leaving a raw, red patch.

It hurt with both throbbing and burning pain. I couldn't close my hand. I went and stood in the shower for a long time, holding the bandage out from the spray and wondering if I could leave home now. I could get in my car and drive to the Cities and find a job doing something stupid, but I'd be a kid from the sticks with no high school diploma.

Back in my room I put on jeans and a T-shirt and then listened to the sounds of the house, trying to figure out where my parents were. I was hungry enough to feel my stomach growl, but not hungry enough to walk into the kitchen if Mom was there. I noticed that Dad had cleared out the remnants of my torn up clothes from the night before and moved the desk back to where it belonged. The bolt on my door had torn its casing out of the molding, leaving two ragged holes where the screws had been. The casing hung off the end of the extended bolt at a ridiculous angle. I pulled it free, dropped it on my bed, and pushed the bolt back along the door.

My parents weren't making any of their usual Sunday noises. After ten minutes I began to worry that they were sitting in the kitchen waiting for me to come down. I wasn't going to give them the satisfaction. I'd starve myself first. I lay back on my bed and folded my left hand behind my head, staring up at the white ceiling.

After a while, Dad's footsteps came up the stairs, heavy and slow. He knocked on my door. "Chris?"

"Yeah," I said.

He pushed the door open. "You coming downstairs so we can talk?"

I shrugged. "Is Mom going to rail on me again?"

"No."

He sounded so tired that I sat up and looked at him. His carpenter pants and shirt were as wrinkled as if he'd slept in them, and his face was deeply lined, eyes sunken and dark.

"Okay." I stood up more because of his face than what he said. I cared about him, and I felt a little afraid of him, but today he looked as beat up as I felt, so I figured I'd stick with him, at least until things got ugly.

I followed him downstairs and into the kitchen. Mom sat at the table, hands wrapped white-knuckle tight around a cup of coffee. If I decided to spend the rest of the day in my room, this would be my one chance today to eat something. I got myself a bowl of cereal before sitting down at the far end of the table, away from Mom. She looked at Dad.

He settled into his usual chair and said, slowly, "We think you should go see someone again. Someone who can help you."

"You're the ones who stopped the visits with Dr. Mendel," I pointed out.

"We want you to go back to Dr. Webber," he said.

If I hadn't cried myself out the night before, I might have started yelling at them about what a jerk he was. But I was so tired and worn out, and I wanted to know my options. I had nothing left to lose here. If it didn't get better fast, I was leaving.

"What's in it for me?" I asked.

"A chance to be well," Dad said.

I rolled my eyes. "I know what's wrong with me. That is not going to make me well."

Mom sighed. "Honey, would you try to have an open mind? Maybe you're wrong about all this, have you thought of that?"

"What if I'm not? How long are you going to make me prove myself?"

They looked at each other. Dad shook his head and Mom frowned. "What is it you want?" she asked.

This was clearly not the time to bring up surgery or going out dressed as a woman. "I want to see an endocrinologist, to go on hormone therapy," I told them.

"What is that?" Mom asked.

"It's part of the process of transition…to a woman," I explained. She opened her mouth, but I said, "Listen. I'd start taking hormones for a year or two and the effects are reversible. If it turns out I'm wrong, I can stop."

I wanted to tell them how much better I felt when I was taking the hormones, more like myself and in charge of my life, less angry and hopeless. But then I'd have to admit I'd been taking someone else's prescription and that would get both me and Natalie in trouble.

"You want to take women's hormones?" Mom asked, her voice rising sharply at the end.

"You will when you hit menopause," I said. "Lots of people take hormones."

"I'm a woman," she said harshly.

"So am I," I shot back.

The three of us lapsed into cold silence. I wondered where they'd stashed Mikey and if he was going to pop out of the other room at any moment and shout "fag" at me or if he was upstairs again trying not to cry. Then it occurred to me that they must have left him over at his friend's house so they could have this talk with their unfortunate "son."

"All right, look," Dad said abruptly as he stood up from the table. He put his palms on the tabletop and leaned in toward both of us. "I'm no good at this shit and I'm sick of it. Chris, you're going to see Dr. Webber for the next month, and Sharon you go with him if you want. At the end of August if you still want to go, I'll take you to a hormone doctor and we'll see what he says. I don't want to hear any more about this."

He stalked away from the kitchen and a moment later the slam of the garage door echoed through the house.

Mom went upstairs. I washed my cereal bowl, dried it and put it back in the cupboard so it looked like I'd never been in the kitchen. Then I put on my coat and boots and left. Let Mom tell me later if I was still grounded.

I drove around for a while and then went to the public library to update my friends online about everything that had happened. I wanted to see Claire, but I was afraid that when I did, I'd start crying again. I sent her an email instead. Then I went home to a very quiet dinner.

Monday morning, Mom and Dad went off to work as usual. I watched Mikey in the early part of the day, but then he went over to a friend's house. I drove to the nearest Home Depot, which wasn't all that near, and bought a new piece of molding for my doorframe. Then I went over to Claire's house. She put her arms around me as soon as she saw me in her doorway and dragged me to the couch. She didn't let go for about three hours.

* * *

Mom got us in with Dr. Webber as soon as possible. It was only two days later that I took a short, silent car ride to his office. She came in with me, so we ended up in that dreary office, with her on the couch and me in a chair. I sat back, crossed my arms and waited to hear what the doctor was going to say. His hair was still closely cropped and neatly combed as if it hadn't grown at all since the last time I saw him six months ago. He looked like an actor playing the part of a psychiatrist in a commercial for an antidepressant.

"Chris, I hear things have gotten worse since I saw you last," he said with a slight, tense smile.

Now that I hadn't been to Dr. Webber in months I saw him differently, even through my anger. On the surface he seemed so perfect from his distinguished graying temples and close trimmed nails to his sharply creased pants. But the overly tense way he sat in his chair made him always off balance. Dr. Mendel could sit up straight and relaxed at the same time. I never saw her *trying* to sit up straight; she just did it. Dr. Webber swayed and caught himself, straightened up and shifted his shoulders into place like he was always trying to find a midpoint and missing each time.

I told him, "Actually, things got better for a long time, and then my parents freaked out, and since then it's pretty much sucked."

Mom sighed loudly. "He wants to be a woman," she said.

Dr. Webber turned his chair more fully toward me and leaned forward. "Is that true?"

"Close," I said. "I am a woman, on the inside. I'd like my body to match my internal sense of myself."

"How do you know you're a woman?" he asked.

"How do you know you're a man?" I asked back. "It's a feeling you have, a sense of yourself. I've always known I was a woman—or a girl, when I was a kid—and I was confused about why everyone always stuck me with the boys."

He swiveled his chair back toward my mom and this started another sway, shift, straighten sequence. "Did you notice effeminate behavior in Chris when he was younger?"

"No," Mom said, "not really. He's always liked cars and girls and adventure games. He likes being outside a lot, and he's been on the swim team since he started high school."

"Chris, when did you start thinking you wanted to be a girl?" the doctor asked.

"I didn't start thinking it one day. What I remember is being surprised that other people didn't treat me like a girl. Mom, remember in first grade when I wanted a girl's name?"

"Aha!" Dr. Webber said. His hands pushed down on the seat of his chair, propping him up even straighter. "How old were you then, five, six? What was going on in the home at that time?"

He directed that second question to Mom who gave him a half shrug and raised her eyebrows. "I'm not sure I can remember."

"Was there any instability in the home?"

"I'm sure there was some. Money was very tight. I'd just taken a job, my husband was out of work for a while."

"Interesting," he said. "Well, Chris, I think we can work on this. I suspect what happened is that you've idealized women and degraded men, probably having to do with that stressful time in your early childhood. You saw your mother as capable and your father as helpless and decided it's better to be a woman. You may also have had some trouble bonding appropriately with your father and decided that you wouldn't make a good man. What we need to do is to rewire these patterns."

I sat very still and tried hard not to roll my eyes. He went on, "I'm going to come up with a treatment plan for you. Now what is important for you to understand is that this problem of yours is not physical, although it may seem that way, it is psychological. To attempt to treat it physically, is to go in the wrong direction. You can take hormones and get plastic surgery, but a 'sex change' is a misnomer. You will never be able to change your biological sex. You need to think about what kind of person you want to grow up to be."

He turned his awful attention toward my mother. "You and your husband need to set a good example for Chris of a well-balanced marriage with strong masculine and feminine poles. I'd like the two of you to come see me, and I'd like Chris to come see me on his own next week."

Mom said something in agreement and thanked him. I wasn't listening. I hated him with a black, hopeless rage.

"See," Mom said when we got in the car. "He believes you can be cured psychologically. You don't need to go through all this craziness to become a woman. You can be fine the way you are."

She and Dr. Webber were the ones living in a fantasy with a super simplistic notion of biology and sex and gender. I could've explained so many problems with his thinking to her, but she'd never listen. She'd heard what she wanted to.

"How many times do we have to go?" I asked.

"As many as it takes until you become the man you were meant to be."

I stared out the window. That would be one hell of a long wait. I'd be out of the house in a year anyway.

When we pulled into the driveway, I said, "I'm going over to Claire's."

I slammed into my car and left before she could protest. At Claire's house, she said what a jerk Webber was a few dozen times, but was surprisingly quiet for Claire. Her eyes had a hard, dark look to them.

"I'll hurt him if I have to," she said at last. "I don't know how, but I'll find a way if he keeps treating you like that."

I felt comforted, and a little scared. Claire was scrappy and had a healthy disrespect for authority, but I didn't want her to get herself into serious trouble over me.

CHAPTER TWENTY-FIVE

By the next week, I was ready to change my mind on that last point. Mom and Dad went to see Dr. Webber and after they came home, we started having family dinners together every night where Mom would try to get Dad to talk about his day and Mikey would interrupt every two minutes with a story from school or a TV show he'd seen.

I confronted Dr. Webber about it when I was back in his office. "Do you think all that family dinner stuff is going to make a difference?" I asked.

"I understand that you have a lot to be angry about," he said. "But you have to understand that people can change. Your parents can change and you can change. Now, Chris, I have a delicate subject to bring up with you, and that's your sexuality."

"What about it?"

"Your mother tells me you have a girlfriend." He leaned forward, slipped a mint into his mouth and held the tin out to me. I wanted to smack it out of his hand, so I ignored it.

"Yeah," I said.

"Are you sexual with her?" he asked.

"We make out and stuff, we haven't had sex. Why?"

"But you enjoy it?"

"Yeah," I said. "I love Claire."

"Then why would you want to be a woman? Don't you understand you'll become a lesbian?"

I must have stared at him for a whole minute before I could get my incredulous lips to move. "Look, Dr. Webber, do you think I'm stupid? Of course I know that. Do you think I haven't thought this whole thing through, over and over again? Do you think it's a whim?"

"What do you think of when you think about being a woman?" he asked.

"I think about going to school," I said. "Same as now, except I'm a girl."

"Do you think about going into the girls' locker room? Looking at the other girls?" he asked.

"Not particularly."

"But you think about yourself, dressed as a girl. Do you ever find that arousing?"

I shrugged. There was no way I was touching that land mine.

"There is a condition that some people develop which causes them to be turned on by the idea of themselves in the clothing of the opposite sex, or even having a body of the opposite sex. Do you get turned on thinking about being made love to as a woman?" He didn't pause long enough for me to answer, for which I was deeply grateful. "Because you're a normal heterosexual male, I think this might be what's happened with you. You're aroused by women and by the thought of yourself as a woman, and we need to rewire that to fit a normal heterosexual male pattern."

"I am a woman," I said, but with less emphasis than I intended.

"Chris, I want you to pay attention to what you think about when you imagine yourself as a woman, and what role arousal plays in that, and come back next week prepared to talk about that."

I did the first part of that assignment. I couldn't help it. Once he suggested it, every time I thought about being a woman, I questioned what I was really thinking about. But there was no way in hell I was going to talk to him about it.

* * *

I was already watching Mom obsessively, wanting to stay out of her path as much as possible. Some days hearing, "You look so handsome today," felt stupid, but the more I saw Dr. Webber, the more Mom's compliments felt like kicks aimed at me. She didn't mean it that way. She was trying to encourage me. But it felt like I'd opened the lid of a box, started to climb out and she was determined to kick me back in.

She took me shopping for more guy clothes. Wanted to know if I needed a gym membership so I could stay in shape for swimming. Kept making eggs and steak for breakfast. Was letting me know in every way what body I was supposed to feel at home in, what body I was supposed to want. Like I didn't know. Like I hadn't already tried all of this.

But I did some of it. She bought me short-sleeve Henleys because apparently the Henley is the most masculine of all the shirts, according to an article she'd read. And of course they were steel gray and army green and one raglan style that managed to combine two boring gray colors that looked worse together and terrible on me.

I wore them. And rolled the sleeves and tried to pretend I was a 1950s butch, which worked not at all.

I started watching Dad too. Could there be anything to the idea that I didn't want to be like him? I didn't like how silent he could get, unreactive, but I respected it and found it calming. I wanted more emotions. Did that make me a girl or was that because I already was one?

By the end of the third Dr. Webber visit, I felt shaky inside. He said more things about "arousal" and got anatomically specific in ways that creeped me out. He seemed to think that my attraction to girls was the reason I wanted to be one. Never mind that billions of straight guys could be attracted to girls without wanting to be women. And never mind all the lesbians and bi women in the world.

When we got home, I went directly to the garage. I didn't want to stay in the house with Mom.

"How was it?" Dad asked, closing the hood of the Bronco.

I shrugged, pretty sure that he'd walk away if I started crying.

"You learning anything?" he asked.

So many new ways to hate myself, I didn't say. What could I tell Dad that wouldn't make him hate me too? I couldn't live in this house with two parents hating me.

I pictured the guys on the swim team. Pretended I was one of them. Thought about what they'd say.

"Masculinity's pretty cool," I said. That sounded stupid, but it worked.

Dad gave me a nod. "I'm going to the shop. You coming?"

"Sure."

I got in the passenger side of the Bronco and cranked my legs out at a ridiculous angle, in that way guys do. I couldn't quite remember what to do with my arms. I'd had my hands in fists for most of the Dr. Webber show, so I let one stay that way, rolled the window down and spread the other hand on top of the door frame.

The shop was a classic car showroom and garage about a mile from our house. Dad hung out there a lot. He didn't need help on the cars, but he liked showing off what he was working on and the guys would all stand around and talk about the car he'd brought and the others on the showroom floor.

He pulled into one of the spots by the garage and right away his favorite mechanic friend came out of a garage bay to walk around the Bronco. I wandered around the showroom, looking at the colors of the cars, the shining chrome, the decades of history enclosed in these bodies.

When I returned to the back lot, two other guys had joined Dad and the mechanic. None of them were wearing Henleys. All had on jeans and T-shirts except for the one sales guy in a short-sleeved button-down and slacks.

I pretended to study the cars in the garage bays while I listened to them talk. Dad said a lot more here than he ever did at home. Of course at home no one would discuss cars for more than five minutes, except me in a good mood, which was rare these days. The guys thoroughly interrogated Dad's work on his car. Then they talked about one of the guys who'd gotten engaged, teasing him about settling down, then debated football before circling back to the car again.

I didn't hate this. The way they teased and challenged and roughly complimented each other. The way the conversation got so intense about the work each of them loved. Dad was having fun. I could see in a few years how Mikey would fit in here. Maybe not the cars, he wasn't that into machines, but the football for sure. His feelings about NFL teams were already about as strong as his feelings about Marvel vs. DC heroes.

I didn't hate it, but I didn't want it.

Dad waved me over so I squared my shoulders and went to talk about how I'd gotten the car's radio to work again and whether the swim team would place in regionals next year. They were impressed about the radio. And then they wanted to me to explain eBay, which I did. Twice.

The mechanic said, "You're going to be one of those computer geniuses, aren't you? Make a billion bucks. Buy all these." He waved in the direction of the showroom.

"Yeah," I said. "Have a car for each day of the week."

He laughed. Dad clapped me on the shoulder and they all fell to talking about which cars were the right ones for Mondays vs. Sundays vs. Thursdays.

If Chris *had* existed, he'd be having a good time right now.

I tried to feel enjoyment. I had some relief that Dad was back to treating me like his kid. That he'd patted me and was grinning at me. I got a shred of happiness about the compliments. It felt far away, on the other side of some murky plexiglass with little slits in it, so what should been happiness was just being okay for a minute.

On the drive home, taking the long way to feel the purr of the Bronco's engine, Dad said, "They like you there. They've got work for you. Nothing fancy but it pays all right."

"Great," I told him, but it came out flat.

We went a few more blocks. The air was perfect, mid-summer hot but dry, so as it blew through the open windows, we got a little cool.

"You doing okay?" he asked.

"Not really."

More silence. Either he didn't know what to ask or he didn't want to know. And I wasn't going to say anyway.

"You spend too much time in your room thinking," he said. "We'll get you started at the shop this week, maybe pick up another car. You got to keep busy."

Compared to Mom taking me shopping and hammering on me with compliments, compared to Dr. Webber creeping me out with his weird theories, it sounded like the best plan in the world.

"Sure." I managed to get some enthusiasm into the word. "Can we get a busted-up computer too? I want to try to fix one."

"Yeah, Son. Sure will," he said.

"Thanks, Dad."

I didn't cry until I got up to my room. Then I sat on the foot of my bed, next to the crisp new wood of my repaired doorframe, and let tears run down my face and drop onto my shirt, making wet black spots on the steel gray fabric.

If I had to survive being Chris and play the good son for one more year in order for Dad to love me, I'd find a way.

CHAPTER TWENTY-SIX

Claire

Late June to late July was one long slide into darkness. Claire kept feeling like they were in *Lord of the Rings*, taking the ring to Mordor. Except there was no ring to rule them all (she'd probably have used it if there was) and she worried that Emily was the one about to go over that dark edge into a pit of lava.

At least Emily wasn't grounded and could come over and try to describe the creepiness of Dr. Webber and cry when she needed to. But after the second visit, she didn't want to talk about Dr. Webber anymore.

Emily curled in on herself and stopped talking in full sentences when one-word answers would do. Claire dragged her out to movies, but Emily would slump down in the seat like a bag of sand. Claire couldn't tell if she was watching the movie or brooding on what the doctor had said that week.

She also stopped changing clothes, even if Claire's mom was away for the day. When Claire asked about that, Emily said, "It's too hard right now. It feels like something I can't have. And like I'm going to screw up being Chris and I can't. Not right now."

"You're miserable," Claire pointed out.

"But there's an end point. Dad said he'd take me to an endocrinologist if I do this."

"You don't have to do it all the time."

"It's worse if I don't. Like I get to breathe one day a week. For now I want to forget what it feels like to be happy, okay?"

It wasn't the least bit okay, but Claire didn't have a better answer.

Mid August, two weeks before the start of school, Emily invited her to come with the family to a church dinner. Emily's mom had been dragging them to the local Evangelical church most Sundays. Claire worried about what this Evangelical congregation would do to Emily's relationship with God and wished she could bring Emily to her church.

But she relished this chance to get inside the enemy's camp. Not that she wanted to think of other Christians as the enemy, though sometimes with what she'd seen online, she was sure they could be called Christian.

"Mom wants to know if you're coming with us to that church dinner tomorrow," Emily said late that Saturday afternoon, sitting on the couch in the crisp, dim, air-conditioned cool of the living room, wearing the gray-and-gray shirt that made her look undead. Or maybe that was just her misery.

"Does your mom know I'm…" Claire trailed off because she didn't want to say something oblique and cutesy like: *I'm in the know.*

Emily watched her carefully.

Claire asked, "Does she know I'm dating Emily?"

A smile flashed across Emily's face, like a burst of sun in the eye of a storm. But then clouds again, darkness. "No," she said. "As far as she knows you're still mad because you thought it was a phase."

"Maybe that's good."

"You're not going to change her mind. Don't even bother. Come with me and be like we used to, okay? This church is weird. I'd rather do this with you."

"I wish you'd come to my church. It's so much better. Or, I'll bet there are some in the Cities—we should ask Natalie—ones that are accepting and friendly."

"I don't want to go to church," Emily said.

"I'll come to the dinner, don't worry. Can I go full-on goth?"

"I don't see why not," Emily told her, smirking.

Claire didn't want to go without feeling like she had armor on. She chose a black dress but also sandals because of the heat. She did her eyes heavier than usual and wore her ornate cross.

Between the church building itself and the busy street beside it was a wide strip of lawn with trees. *A perfect place to hold a picnic that advertised the fellowship and community of this church, like a bunch of show-offs,* Claire thought angrily. Over a hundred people had gathered, sitting on the lawn with picnic blankets and around a few folding tables that had been brought out of the church building.

It felt like half of Liberty was there. That couldn't be true, but Claire saw a few families from her neighborhood, a bunch of kids from high school, even two of their teachers. Could be the late summer heat or the rumors that one of the younger pastors cooked the best bratwurst in town.

They got out of the car and Mikey ran to find the kids his age. Emily's mom carried the dish she'd brought to the long tables of food, other women gravitating toward her as she walked. They were all in dresses, pastels and some bright colors, and Claire wished she'd worn pants.

"Guess it's up to us to stake out a spot," Emily's dad said. He popped the trunk of the car and tossed a rolled-up blanket to Emily, then lifted a box that rattled with plastic cutlery and closed the trunk with his elbow.

"I can carry something," Claire said, but Emily gave her the don't-bother-because-guys-carry-things look.

Emily set her shoulders in her most Chris-like stance and went off after her dad, Claire trailing both of them. They set up in one of the last shady spots under a tree, nearer the church building than the road.

"We should socialize," Emily told her when they had the blanket down. Her dad had already gone to check out the grille. "Mom will be less on me if I put on a good performance."

"Is the performance a comedy?" Claire asked. "Can I be your straight man?"

That got a tiny snort from Emily. "Pretty sure I'm the straight man."

"Pretty sure you're not," Claire said in a whisper. She caught Emily's hand and didn't let go as they wandered into the mass of people.

Emily was doing a great job as Chris. Everyone around them saw a tallish guy with short, curly hair and toned swimmer's shoulders. Claire caught a few looks of envy from other girls. Months ago, she would've enjoyed a bit of envy. But now every time she got a glimpse into Emily's eyes, she saw a person drowning.

Through their joined hands, she felt the tension in Emily's body, the subtle way she froze when people said things like, "Chris, look how tall you're getting." How she flinched, not more than a twitch of her fingers, when people dropped their voices to talk to her, switched to monotone. Like there were two languages and you could only be emotive to women.

They made it through three groups of adults and then spotted a picnic table surrounded by teens.

"Is that Ramon?" Emily asked, nodding toward a group of students from their school.

"Can you see who he's with? Rumor is, he met a girl at camp."

"Not from here, come on."

At the edge of the high schoolers they were intercepted by a young pastor on a mission. He was a stocky, barrel-shaped guy, not much taller than Claire, with black hair, light brown skin and a ready smile.

"I'm Pastor Song but you can call me Alan. I lead our youth worship groups here."

"Chris and Claire," Emily said.

She took his offered hand and got a, "Nice grip."

Claire made a point to close her hand strongly around Pastor Alan's when she got the chance, but he didn't offer her the same compliment.

"We have a vibrant youth group here," the pastor said. "Come meet some of them. Kids, have you met Chris and Claire?"

A blockish body rose from the bench, his back to them. Claire gripped Emily's hand, knowing before he turned around that this was Jason from her history class, the one she'd hit with her textbook last spring. When he saw her, the grin dropped from his face and his eyes squinted.

"You called me a blasphemous heathen," he said.

"I'm glad to see you're doing something about that, going to church and all," Claire replied.

Pastor Alan raised his eyebrows at her. "I'm sure that was a misunderstanding."

"She thinks homosexuals and trans-whatever, sex change people are okay," Jason said. "Don't you?"

"Of course I do and so does the Bible. Did you know that the first person baptized—and I mean the first ever—was gay or trans or both, depending on how you read the translation."

"How do you know *that*?" Jason asked. "You have some 'Gays in the Bible' guide? Because maybe you *need* one?"

"I'm not—" Claire stopped. To say she wasn't bisexual meant erasing Emily and herself, but to say she was meant endangering Chris's reputation, which Emily needed to hide behind.

"Let's all take a deep breath and moment to reflect," Pastor Alan said, to no effect.

"Your girlfriend's a queer, man," Jason told Emily.

"Don't try to get him to fight my fights," Claire growled. She dropped Emily's hand and took a step toward Jason but Emily put a hand on her shoulder.

Stupid gender roles. If Claire got into a fight, as Chris, Emily was supposed to be the one protecting her. She remembered Emily telling her, after she'd blackened Jason's eye with her textbook, that she'd told Jason he could beat up Chris if he had to take his anger out on someone.

"I'm not worried about my girlfriend," Emily said in her deepest, slowest, most threatening guy voice.

"Stop it! You," Claire turned to Emily, "I can speak for myself and you know it." She whirled back to Jason. "And you, blasphemous heathen, God's not a bigot, only you are."

"Now everyone, let's remember to let the peace of Christ rule in our hearts," Pastor Alan said. "Claire, you have a great passion. I'd love to talk with you more. Can we go into the sanctuary?"

"Yes. Chris, I'll meet you back at the blanket."

"You don't want me to come with you?"

"It's going to be a bunch of religion stuff. You'll get bored."

Not to mention that this was the best way to protect Chris, and therefore Emily, from Jason.

Claire followed Pastor Alan into the building. The front entryway opened into a large sanctuary, plain except for Bible quotes in artsy stencil on the walls. At the front of the sanctuary was the pulpit and a semicircle of chairs facing the empty chairs of the audience. On the left stood a large wooden cross. Claire watched it as they went up to the front of the seats, trying to draw strength from it.

Pastor Alan sat in a front chair and patted the seat next to him. Claire wanted to believe he could be an ally.

But then he said, "You seem to have some confusion about how God made people. He made a man and a woman."

"Uh actually the Bible says 'male and female He created them.' It doesn't specify in that verse that it was only one man and one woman. And you should know I don't hold to a literalist interpretation. I think that's woefully reductionistic."

He stared at her for what felt like a whole minute and then grinned. "You have a very keen mind. But you must know that God's plan for humanity is for men and women to have families together. Remember, Genesis 2:24 tells us 'Therefore a man shall leave his father and his mother and hold fast to his wife, and they shall become one flesh.'"

"And Galatians 3:28 says, 'There is no longer male and female. For you are all one in Christ Jesus,'" Claire replied.

"Don't you believe Christ came to update the laws? At least for Christians?"

"He could have been speaking about equality, not doing away with men's and women's distinct roles. We know that this is a broken world and there are many ways for people to fall away from God's love," Pastor Alan said. "Homosexuality is one of those ways."

Claire wanted to yell at him that he was describing control, not love. But not here, in front of the cross and the sense of peace it brought. She asked her next question more to the cross itself than to Pastor Alan. "What do you do when the world's so full of hate and ignorance?"

"That's why we need God more than ever. And we need to show others how to be his faithful followers in the world and enact the plan He created for us..." he went on, but she wasn't listening.

A kid entered through the door to the left of the sanctuary from the back of the building, maybe fourteen, tallish and scrawny, face dotted with acne, hair short and lank. Hard to tell if the kid was a boy or a girl. Probably girl, Claire thought, because she was carrying a basket with a cloth over it and wearing an apron, some flour across her sweatshirt. Then she smirked at her own assumptions.

The flour-spattered person came over to Claire and the Pastor.

"Hey, sorry, these are fresh, thought you'd want one." Slender fingers pulled back the cloth to show perfect rows of golden rolls.

Claire took one and cupped it in her palms. "Thank you."

Even though it was a hot day and warm inside the building, the heat and the weight of the fresh baked roll seeped into her hands, making them feel more alive.

The Pastor's words flowed around her. He'd made it from the brokenness of homosexuality to saying something about "transgenderism." Probably because Claire had said the first person baptized was gay or trans or both, so he figured he'd better cover all the bases.

"Transgenderism isn't a word," she told him. He paused long enough for her to say, "People are transgender. It's not an ideology."

As if she'd said the exact opposite, he continued right into how the transgenderists were rewriting history. Pretty ironic, since that's what he was doing.

Claire tuned him out. Pastor Alan's words were meant for someone who wanted the conventional, the picture-perfect, the safe. They didn't pertain to her life. The bread in her hands smelled yeasty and hearty. The warm scent created a boundary between her and Pastor Alan.

The cross drew her attention again with its plain, solid strength. She'd always liked the teaching that the arms of the cross represented the sacred world reaching down through the material world. She worshipped a God who reached down into the world, like the top of the cross, and held it up, like the bottom. God took care of people and didn't make life harder than it already was.

She could listen to Pastor Alan's arguments and refute them, but he'd keep arguing. It came down to a choice between two worlds. Did she believe that God made some people bi, lesbian, gay, transgender, queer just so they would have to overcome that? Or did she believe in a God who so loved variety and diversity that He created all manner of things and loved them all?

Not only was it in the Bible that queer and trans people were beloved of God—but it was obvious in the physical world. Hundreds of animal species had homosexual pairings. Some animals had a lot more than two sexes. There were animals that changed sex, some more than once a day. People were the ones stuck on a frozen, limited idea, thinking that was perfection. God created wonders.

Claire held the roll in her palm toward Pastor Alan and his words paused. She told him, "I'm sorry but I disagree with everything you're saying and I think we should eat these while they're warm."

"What?"

"This is a picnic. I'm supposed to be eating with Chris and his family. Can we talk about this other stuff later?"

"Oh yes." He stood up.

Claire followed him toward the exit. "Who was that with the rolls?"

"Sorry, I'm still new here. I have no idea. Hope to see you at church."

She went into the bright afternoon sunshine. The basket of rolls sat on the end of the nearest food table and she grabbed one for Emily. And then three more, for Mikey and Emily's parents.

She found them on their blanket under the tree.

"I got rolls. They're really fresh," she said, like that excused her absence. And it kind of did.

"We got you a brat with mustard, Chris says that's what you like? And some salad." Emily's mom held out a plate to trade for her roll.

Claire watched the families with their kids, people walking from blanket to blanket, talking and laughing. Some day, in the not too far future, she wouldn't be welcome here. Not just here, but maybe at her own church as well. And she'd miss the simple ease of fitting in.

She'd enjoyed it last year at school, being Chris's girlfriend, being almost popular or at least acceptable. She liked feeling safe. But what good was it to feel safe if the people she loved the most didn't get to feel that way too?

And she had people to feed, starting with Emily.

CHAPTER TWENTY-SEVEN

I thought we were going to a movie, but Claire told me to drive to Dr. Mendel's office. At first I stared at her because I couldn't figure out what movie theater or restaurant was anywhere near that office park. Plus, Claire was wearing a red T-shirt with her jeans, which made me wonder what was going on with her.

"Why are we going there?" I asked.

"Because you have an appointment," she told me.

"No I don't."

"Come on, drive, we're going to be late. I made you an appointment with Dr. Mendel. Hit the gas."

As I turned the car in the direction of her office, my heart lifted and the headache around my eyes relaxed. I hadn't dared hope that I would get time with the doctor.

"How did you make me an appointment?" I asked Claire.

"It's called a telephone," she said. "You punch in numbers and someone answers, remember?"

At the office building she grabbed my hand and dragged me into the waiting room. Dr. Mendel smiled when she saw us sitting there, but a sad smile where her eyes didn't crinkle. I'd curled slump-shouldered in my chair and Claire gripped my hand as if I was going to bolt. If it had been Dr. Webber instead of Dr. Mendel, I would have. Instead I let Claire pull me into Dr. Mendel's room and push me toward the couch. Claire remained standing.

"Emily's all messed up," she told Dr. Mendel. "She won't tell me all of it, but I'm hoping she'll tell you. Dr. Webber's been saying some crap to her, and I think she's starting to buy it. Can you straighten her out? Err, so to speak."

"I'll do my best," Dr. Mendel said.

Her reading glasses hung over her chest, taking the place of the pearls that she wore when my parents came to the appointment. She had on a bluish lavender knit sweater with short sleeves and I loved the color. It made her bright blue eyes stand out, but when she turned them to me, the lines around them were tight with concern.

"Great, I'll be waiting," Claire announced and skipped out of the room.

I stared at the closed door. "She just told me about this," I said.

"You don't look well," Dr. Mendel offered. She pulled her chair two feet closer to the couch and sat near enough that I could have reached forward and touched her knee. "Have you been taking care of yourself?"

"No," I admitted. "Life has sucked since we left here. Mom grounded me for life, Dad doesn't talk much and I ran out of hormones so I'm a rage-monster again. And then I freaked out after this dinner thing. Well, Mom freaked out first, but I really lost it and started cutting up my boy clothes and beating the crap out of my door."

"Did you hurt yourself?" she asked.

I shook my head. "Not seriously. I couldn't."

"That's good."

"And then they asked me to go back to Dr. Webber and said if I saw him for a month I could go get hormones."

"That's an interesting strategy," Dr. Mendel said neutrally. I got the impression that "interesting" was a euphemism for "screwed up."

"He's crazy," I told her. "He thinks he can cure me of being transgender. He thinks I get off on thinking about myself as a woman."

"What do you think?" Dr. Mendel asked. Something in her voice got me—the way she asked and then got quiet to listen to me. Whatever she believed, one way or the other, she wasn't going to push it on me. She honestly wanted to know about me.

I started crying, the tears hot on my cheeks. Not like the helpless tears I'd cried in the past few weeks, these were pure grief mixed with all the hurt and rage and fear that I needed to get out of me. She handed me tissues and let me cry for what seemed like the whole hour.

"I don't think I'm crazy," I managed at last. "I don't think this is all in my head. I know I'm a girl, that's all. Why is that so hard for everyone to understand?"

"Probably for many of the same reasons it was hard for you," she said. I had to smile at how gently she reminded me that I'd had years to understand what it meant to be transgender and my family only had a few weeks.

After a pause to let her words sink in, she continued. "I know there's a simple answer to this question, but I want you to look beyond it: why are you so hurt by what Dr. Webber says?"

"I feel insulted," I told her, "but that's the simple answer. And I feel invalidated, like he doesn't see me at all. And I'm afraid—sometimes, I'm afraid he might be right."

She nodded, so I went on.

"You know, I have some girl clothes that I've worn out in the world a few times. And before Mom went nuts, sometimes I'd get up in the middle of the night and put them on. I liked to surf the web, do homework and stuff when I was dressed like myself. But sometimes when I'd get dressed up in the girl clothes, I would get aroused, like Dr. Webber says. I get afraid that maybe I'm just deluding myself and maybe I am a guy who gets his kicks dressing up like a girl."

She nodded again. "You're worried that if you get an erection while wearing women's clothing that you're a fetishist and not transgender?"

"Yeah," I said, knowing I was blushing a deep beet color.

"You know there's no test by which we could determine externally whether it's right for someone to transition or not. Only you can say if this is who you are and what you need," she said. "But I can tell you a few things that might help you answer it for yourself. There isn't a one-to-one connection between getting an erection sometimes and being aroused by the idea of wearing women's clothing. As I understand it, you're basically thrilled any time you get to participate in life as a girl."

"Of course," I said.

"And your body doesn't always know the difference between that excitement and arousal. As a teenager, you have so many hormones flooding your body. Have you noticed other times when you get an erection for seemingly no reason at all? Or when you're excited about something but not necessarily turned on sexually?"

"Yeah, I have."

"Do you find women's clothing sexually exciting?" she asked. "It's all right if you do."

I thought about it. "Not really. I mean, not the clothes themselves. But sometimes when I'm in them I think about having a woman's body and what that would feel like to be able to touch someone and be touched without feeling like the Frankenstein monster."

"Frankenstein?"

"Like I have extra parts clumsily bolted on," I said, so embarrassed by this whole conversation that I thought I'd probably melt through the floor before the session ended.

"That makes sense," she said. "You're the only one who can say what's going on in your mind, but it's not unusual for a person who knows herself to be a woman to be aroused by the idea of being made love to as a woman. If you're aroused by the idea of being a man who presents as a woman, we can talk about that. For example, if some of the arousal comes from the idea of being discovered as a man, or perhaps being a man who is somehow forced into womanhood. Those are both also valid ways to be."

"No, I don't want to be a man at all, I never have."

"Then consider that the only difference between you and Claire, for example, is that when you think about sexual activity, you imagine a body different from the one you have now. She takes it for granted how her body is, but I suspect that she also pictures herself, imagines her body, when she thinks about sexual activity. She just doesn't realize it. Imagining your body doesn't mean you're attracted to yourself as a woman. It means that you understand for intimacy and attraction to be present there need to be two bodies involved. Your imagination is simply doing the work of seeing yourself—as you see yourself."

"Oh…yes. I want to be in a body that feels right to me. Otherwise it's hard to feel close to Claire. So when I think about us, I think about me the way I am, not the way I look on the outside. Wow, thanks."

She smiled. "No one else has the right to tell you who you are, no matter what degrees they have. Are you committed to going to the rest of your appointments with Dr. Webber?"

"I want the hormones, and that's the only way my parents are going to let me have them."

"Then let me give you one bit of advice, though I'm not in the habit of doing that: Don't get angry at the rain."

"What?"

"When it rains and you get wet, you dry off again. You know it's not raining on you personally, so you don't get upset at it. You know the rain falls on everyone the same way. You take whatever steps you need to dry off and take care of yourself. Dr. Webber is like that. He's raining and it's falling on you, but it's not personal. He would treat any teen who came to him and said 'I'm transgender' that way; he's not addressing who you are, Emily, as an individual. He's not talking about you."

I'd have hugged her, but she was a therapist and I didn't know if that was cool, so when we stood up I shook her hand for a long time. Before I opened the door, I paused. "My mom and dad don't know I'm here, do they?"

"I doubt it. Claire set up the appointment and paid for it."

"She paid for it? Wow. Can I do that too?"

"Of course you can. Call a few days in advance and we'll set it up."

I slipped into the waiting room and half-lifted Claire out of her chair into a huge hug.

"Hey it worked," she exclaimed. "I got you back."

I kissed her. "You're a great protector," I said.

"Claire the Mighty." She grinned.

* * *

I couldn't say I was looking forward to the next trip to Dr. Webber, but at least I wasn't dreading it as much. I even played with him a little. At one point I volunteered, "I'll tell you some of the fantasies I have about being a woman."

"Go on," he said.

I was trying hard not to smile. "In one, I go out to dinner with my girlfriend, Claire, and the waiter says 'What would you ladies like to order?' Oh, and then there's the one where I'm shopping, and I go to use the women's restroom and there's another woman in there and she looks at me and says 'Nice shoes.'"

Mostly I put up with him trying to guy-bond with me, and talked about my childhood memories of my dad. Dr. Mendel's advice made a huge difference in the visits too. No matter how stupid they got, I'd come home and take a shower and imagine washing off any crap he said. Then I'd towel off and imagine I was drying off the rain.

"It's not personal," I'd tell my reflection in the mirror, repeating it until it sank in. And then I'd go down to dinner.

August continued to be one of the strangest times of my life. Now that I was out to my parents, I didn't try so hard to act like a guy. I started being myself as best I could and a weight lifted off my shoulders and skull. Around the house, though, my self-expression met with mixed results.

"There is no way Sabretooth could beat Starfire in one-on-one," I told Mikey one evening as we sat at dinner, punctuating my points with finger jabs. "If Cyclops can blast him away, so can Starfire." I illustrated the rising and falling arc of Sabretooth's defeated body.

"Well what about Nightcrawler versus Starfire?" Mikey shot back. "He can teleport."

I grinned at him, about to propose Starfire vs. Warlock, when I felt the hair on the back of my neck stand up. Turning in my chair, I saw Mom glaring at me.

"Stop waving your hands around," she snapped.

I crossed my arms and turned back to Mikey. "I think that would be a cool fight to watch," I told him.

A moment later when Mom went to the garage to get Dad for dinner, Mikey whispered, "I bet no one yells at Starfire like that."

I grinned and ruffled his hair. "I bet you're right."

Dad never said anything, but twice while he was watching TV with Mikey and me, he simply got up and left the room. When he didn't come back, I reviewed the last few minutes in my mind. He'd left right after I crossed my legs above the knee and folded my hands together in my lap.

* * *

One afternoon in the middle of the month, when I went into the garage to see what Dad was doing, he put down his wrench and sat back on his heels. "I made you an appointment," he said brusquely. "You need to send a letter."

It took me a minute to figure out what he was talking about. "The endocrinologist?" I asked, incredulous.

"Yes, he's in the Cities. I'm going with you. If he says this isn't safe, I want you to promise me you're not going to make a fuss. You're going to do what the doctor says."

"Of course." I skipped across the room and put my arms around his shoulders, giving him a kiss on the cheek. "Thanks, Dad."

"And you need to talk to that doctor, the one you like, she has to send him some kind of letter about you."

"No problem, I'll do it," I told him.

He grumbled and got back under the car. Knowing I had that appointment to look forward to made the last couple weeks with Dr. Webber bearable. Mom came in with me one time to complain that I was acting effeminate around the house.

"I'm not acting," I said, but it fell on deaf ears. Dr. Webber suggested that my Dad take me to more sporting events.

We compromised and went to a car show. Not only did I honestly enjoy it, but I used descriptions of it to fill up most of the next Dr. Webber visit.

CHAPTER TWENTY-EIGHT

For the trip to the endocrinologist, Dad put on a suit coat. He only had two of them; I was relieved that I got the gray one for church and not his black formal dinner-and-funerals jacket. I wore my usual jeans, but dug out a nice T-shirt. I wondered if I should wear something more feminine, but I was already on eggshells with Mom. I'd given Dad the names of two doctors that had been recommended to me by Dr. Mendel, and he went with one of those, so I was sure this doctor had a good sense about how to work with transgender people.

On the drive in, I couldn't keep my legs still. When I tried to stop them, my right hand danced up and down my thigh, picking at the seam of my jeans. Finally I managed to settle on wiggling my toes in my shoes on one foot and then the other, back and forth. I could tell Dad was tense too, because he didn't bother to make small talk. We listened to the radio most of the way, or at least tried to.

Funny thing: the appointment was just like the physical exams I'd gotten every year since I could remember. The nurse checked my blood pressure, weight, temperature, all that stuff, and then put me in a little room to wait for the doctor. Dad came in with me because he had questions.

The doctor walked in reading my file. His white coat and the bright blue-and-white-striped dress shirt underneath it gave his dark brown skin a gray hue. His short, black hair was stylishly brushed up rather than back, but his walrus mustache looked like something from my dad's generation. He pushed his rectangular glasses up on his nose with one hand and closed the file, then introduced himself to Dad and me as Dr. Dinesh Gopal.

"Looks like you're in good health," he said matter-of-factly. "I received the letter from Dr. Mendel about your gender dysphoria. You want to go on HRT?"

"Yes, totally."

He smiled then, which made him seem a lot younger than my dad all of a sudden. I wondered if the mustache was an attempt to look older. He had a handsome, wide mouth and perfect teeth.

For the physical exam, Dad stepped out of the room. Dr. Gopal called me "Emily" effortlessly and I loved it. But as we were finishing up, when he asked if I wanted Dad to come back in for questions and the instructions about the prescriptions, I said, "You should probably still call me Chris around my dad and use he/him pronouns. He's not used to it yet and I really need him on my side for this."

"I understand," he said and called Dad back into the room.

He detailed the prescriptions he was giving me, how to take them, what to expect. After a pause, he added, "Now some people think more is better when it comes to estrogen, but that is not the case. Taking more won't make the process any faster. You need to stick to this regimen. Okay?"

"Yes," I said. "No problem."

"Also you need to think about, and should talk with your parents about, fertility preservation."

"What?" Dad blurted. "He can't have kids?"

"Of course he can, if he takes steps now," Dr. Gopal said. "I can recommend a good fertility clinic or there are mail-order kits that allow Chris to freeze some sperm for later use."

I winced, but if Dr. Gopal had used another word, Dad wouldn't have gotten it.

"How long do we have?" Dad asked.

"Sooner is better. More time on hormones means a lower sperm count," Dr. Gopal said. "That is generally reversible if Chris stops taking hormones, to a point."

"You're doing this fertility thing," Dad told me. "Or no hormones. You aren't giving up your ability to have kids."

"Okay, yes," I told him. I kind of wanted to thank him for making that call for me, but feared that would set a bad precedent.

"Lower fertility does not mean none," Dr. Gopal said. "If you're having sex, or plan to have sex, with your girlfriend, or anyone else who can get pregnant, you need to use a contraceptive."

I'd mentioned Claire during the exam, when we were chatting. I wished he'd said this then, not in front of Dad. I couldn't tell if my face had gone red, white or both, because my cheeks felt burning cold.

"We're not," I mumbled, but he handed me a brochure with a condom package stapled to it anyway.

I didn't want to look at the brochure less than I didn't want to look at Dad, so I opened it. Bright orange lettering told me that the great news about STDs was how preventable they were. Each page balanced between telling me not to have sex and telling me to use condoms or other barrier protection if I did. I liked that one of the couples looked androgynous but girly and could've been me and Claire. They were grinning at each other under the headline, "Have Fewer Partners," and I totally agreed.

Dad shifted, making his chair creak. "How dangerous are these hormones? What else do they do?"

The doctor leaned back against the white table that ran along one wall and folded his arms loosely into what seemed to be his lecture pose. "There are risks, as with any medication. Chris is in excellent health, and we'll want him back here every few months to make sure his liver and kidneys are processing the hormones well."

"It's all reversible, right?" Dad asked.

"More or less," the doctor said. "Chris will start to notice his skin softening, his body hair will become less heavy. Over a period of a few months to a year the fat on his body will start to redistribute itself. His face will look softer, and he will start to develop breasts."

"Good Lord," Dad said. A muscle clenched in the side of his jaw and he shook his head, but didn't say more.

"Up to that point, he can stop taking the hormones and the changes will reverse themselves. Once he's developed breasts, you would need surgery to reverse that."

Dad's normally tan face turned blotchy, parts becoming pink and other parts a faint yellowish green.

"Dad, please…"

He sat back against the wall and didn't say anything. And that was it. The doctor gave me the prescriptions and told us to come back in a few months. I made Dad stop at the first Walgreens we saw and fill the prescriptions. Then I took one of each of the pills with a candy bar and bottle of water to wash them down.

"Do you want to go to a movie?" Dad asked when I got back in the car.

"That'd be cool."

I thought he'd say more about the doctor's visit, but he didn't. He took us down the street to a theater and bought two tickets to the latest James Bond flick. I wondered if this was another last-ditch attempt to indoctrinate me back into manhood, but I didn't much care.

Sitting in the theater reminded me of being out with Claire and Natalie, and I wondered how Natalie was doing. She'd gone in for her surgery a few weeks back. I'd seen short posts from her on GenderPeace, but she'd been pretty out of it.

As we left the movie, I figured it wouldn't hurt to ask. "Dad, while we're down here, can we go see Natalie? She had to have some surgery this summer, and I'd like to see how she's doing."

"She live around here?" he asked. "We can't stay long. I promised your mom we'd be home for dinner."

"She's only a few miles away."

As I rang her doorbell, I wondered if it was a bad idea to stop by unannounced, but that was one of the downfalls of not having a cell phone. Natalie's mom answered the door with a big smile and my pounding heart slowed down. I'd been afraid that if her dad answered, he wouldn't be cool about the visit at all, though I didn't know that for sure.

Natalie's mom had her hair tied back again and wore the same kind of outfit she had on for the slumber party: loose black pants and a law school sweatshirt. She stepped to the side of the doorway and waved us in.

"What a surprise!" she said and held her hand out to my father. "It's good to see you again, come in."

"Thank you," Dad replied and gave her hand a quick shake. His gaze traveled around the foyer. Their house was a lot nicer than ours—not much bigger, but I knew he was seeing the building materials and how nice they were. The foyer floor was a fine gray stone and the windows on either side of the door had stained glass patterns in them.

"Jerry, would you like to join me in the kitchen for coffee while the kids talk?" she asked. "I just made a pot."

"Thank you," he said again.

To me she said, "Natalie's upstairs in her room, first one on the left, go on up. I know she'd love to see you."

I bounded up the stairs. I paused outside Natalie's door and knocked.

"Who is it?" Natalie asked weakly.

"Emily," I announced through the door.

"Hey!" Her voice picked up volume. "Get in here!"

I pushed open the door. Her room was a rich palette of cream colors and light browns with a bed dominating the far wall where Natalie sat propped amid teddy bears. Two flower arrangements flanked the bed, and I felt stupid that Claire and I hadn't thought to come out together and bring one. Plus now Claire was going to be mad that she didn't get to come on this trip. Natalie's hair frizzed out from her head in a dark halo, and she looked very monochrome with no makeup on, but she was smiling.

"Sit down," she said, gesturing to the chair next to the bed.

"Are you just dropping by?"

"Dad brought me in to get hormones, can you believe it?"

She laughed. "That's great."

"So how is it? What's it like? How do you feel?"

"It hurts," she said, still grinning. "It hurts a hell of a lot. But I wouldn't trade it for the world."

"Tell me everything."

"Well, first I had to go off hormones for two weeks, which sucked as you can imagine. Then Mom and Robin and I flew to Arizona—"

"Robin?"

"My sister. She said she'd make it more like a holiday for Mom so she didn't freak out while I was in surgery. I got prepped and shaved and they ran all these tests, and then they put me under. And when I woke up I felt…I don't know how to describe it. I mean, I was high on all the drugs, so I was feeling pretty happy anyway, but separate from that I felt whole.

"That first day out wasn't so bad, but then the heavy drugs wore off and it hurt like a bitch. Plus the strong painkillers made me sick, and let me tell you that puking after that surgery is unbelievably awful. But after a couple days I could get up and walk a few steps, and after that I started feeling better pretty quickly. I'm still sore, and I'm supposed to take it easy for a few more days, but I walk around some every day now. And, wow, it's so different. I mean, for the last two years I've been living as a girl, but with this freakish part that I always had to hide and pay attention to, you know. It's weird. And now, I'm just me. And in some way I always was, except it all fits together now."

"Cool," I said, feeling envious, but also afraid. I wasn't a big fan of surgery in general.

"How are you?" she asked, and I updated her about all the craziness in my life since I'd told my parents.

I finished by saying, "I guess I should go check on Dad and see if he wants to go. I'll come back out with Claire soon."

I gave Natalie a gentle hug.

"I'm excited for you," she said.

"Same here," I said and laughed.

With school starting in a week, it would be a lot easier to get around without Mom watching my every move. I felt sure that a visit to my trans girl bestie wasn't on the list of Dr. Webber-approved activities for me.

I went down the stairs wondering if I should join a club at school and use that as the excuse to come see Natalie. At the bottom I stopped, hearing my dad's voice.

"... and that's when you stopped trying to fix him?"

"Her," Natalie's mom said, the word gentle but heavy.

Dad grumbled, "Her... I can't get used to it. Always had two boys."

"Did you?"

"It's a thing you're born with then?" Dad asked. "A brain thing? Chris has a girl's brain?"

Natalie's mom hummed a soft sound that combined agreement and question.

"That's one good way to think about it," she answered. "Science hasn't pinned down one single thing that determines gender identity, and that's true for all of us. We don't know why you feel like a man and I feel like a woman. We're starting to understand that genetics and hormones, the brain, and our culture all come together to give us that sense of who we are."

A chair leg scraped as she got up. She asked, "More coffee?"

"Thank you, no," Dad said.

"I'll tell you a few things that really helped me understand," she said. "First, identical twins are more likely than fraternal twins to both be transgender, so there is definitely a genetic role in this. And let me tell you, as a mom, as the person who carried Natalie in my body, that's really comforting. But also I learned that Natalie's body was heading down the 'boy' pathway at six to eight weeks but her brain didn't start to develop the parts that give us our identities until months later. So maybe the hormones she was exposed to changed, or the way her genes interacted with the hormones was different, or all of that."

Dad repeated, "I can't get used to it." I heard the heavy clunk of a coffee mug against the table like a judge's gavel coming down.

Natalie's mom didn't answer. I snuck up a few stairs and came down again, heavily, so they'd hear me.

In the car on the way back to Liberty, Dad didn't say much, but what he said gave me an idea about what else Natalie's mom had said in the kitchen.

"You didn't tell me Natalie used to be a boy," he said.

"No," I said. "She's just a regular girl now. That's how she wants people to see her. She doesn't go around with a big 'T' on her chest."

"T?" he asked.

"For transgender."

"Your birthday dinner, all that time, I wouldn't have known," he said.

I didn't know what to say to that, so I didn't say anything. I wasn't sure if he was going down Mom's well-worn track about how I'd make an ugly woman, or if he was trying to say something else.

When we got home I made sure I thanked him a couple times for taking me to the doctor. He shrugged and left for the car shop. Maybe after all that trans stuff, he had to be around "real guys" for a while.

CHAPTER TWENTY-NINE

Claire

The first week of school, Claire felt the return of a familiar terror from when she'd been in sixth grade and junior high, waiting for the pretty girls to spot her, descend and pick her apart like vultures on a dead body. This fear echoed the night at the restaurant when she'd realized how much she'd stand out if Emily had been out as herself.

Even if Emily wasn't out at all at school, even if she was manning up and doing Chris to the gills—for reasons Claire didn't understand and kind of hated—the other students would eventually figure out that Claire didn't fit in. More than ever, she wasn't like most of the other students here.

And Jason knew it.

She caught him watching her. Was it malice in his eyes or revenge? Was it still about the fact that a girl had given him a black eye? Or had she become the lightning rod for his hatred of all things different from himself?

The other girls in the yearbook club told her about the rumors that spread out from Jason's cheerleader girlfriend/

arm-candy-of-the-month. Guys weren't supposed to gossip like that, right? But Claire knew where the rumors about her being "a queer" originated from. When she wasn't terrified, she kind of liked that Jason had picked the word "queer" instead of "lesbian." Like he was trying to be bi-inclusive in his hate-gossip but didn't know how.

As much as people talked about her, they also talked about Chris and his decision to quit the swim team. He hadn't been such a great athlete, nor was the swim team that popular, that it was a big deal to the school's reputation. But September was a slow gossip month.

Claire jumped any time someone said the name "Chris," even if they weren't talking about her person, her Emily, which was how she overheard the swim guys talking during week two. She'd finished up lunch and gone to bus her tray when she heard them. From the end of the tray conveyor, she moved a few steps left so that a wide, square column blocked her from being seen by the table where the swim team sat.

"Heard Chris's dad is making him work," one guy was saying.

"He told coach it was grades," another said.

"Oh right, his weren't that bad last year. Not by the end." The guy speaking lowered his voice, but not so much that Claire couldn't hear as he said, "I heard he's gay. Got kicked off the team so he won't be in our locker room."

"No, he's still got that girlfriend." That came from Ramon, the captain and the guy Emily liked best on the team.

"You sure that's not for show?" gay-gossip guy asked. "I heard she's for sure queer. Maybe they're covering for each other."

She should go confront them, but she was shaking. The smell of aging, greasy tater tots from the cafeteria swamped her, reminding her of too many lunches alone with books in junior high, waiting for classmates to jeer at her.

"That's farcical," Ramon said. Claire suppressed a laugh at the cleverness of his word choice.

Jason's booming voice cut in. He must've been one table over. He said, "No, it's true. Jessica saw them at Southdale with some red-headed girl. That's probably who that little goth punk is really dating. Maybe your coach caught Chris checking you all out."

Claire forced herself around the side of the pillar, one hand on it for support. She was about to tell Jason how disgusting he was, and what an asshole, and all the things she'd usually say. But that would make life harder for Emily. And she thought about being in the church, the warm bread in her hands, the idea of feeding the good in situations and in people.

"Chris and I are together," she said. "He quit the team for grades and money and because I asked him to spend more time with me."

That last was true. She wasn't obligated to add that she'd asked "him" to spend more time with her as Emily.

Jason made a whipping sound and gesture.

"He's gay *and* I've got him whipped?" Claire asked. "I must have superpowers."

"Or you threatened to stop covering for him."

"Right. What's it going to take for you to get over this old-fashioned homophobia?" Claire asked. "Queer and trans people have existed in most, maybe all, cultures and times. Hundreds, thousands of cultures. You're just being ignorant."

Jason stood up and came toward her, but Ramon put himself half between them. He was as tall as Jason, if not as wide.

"Hey man, Chris is one of us, on the team or not. Let it go," he said.

"Oh maybe he quit the team because you two had a lovers' fight," Jason singsonged.

Ramon crossed his arms over his chest. "Nah, the whole swim team is doing each other and Chris is the only straight guy. That's why he quit. But don't tell my girlfriend, okay?"

All the swim guys cracked up and rose up from their seats, pounding Ramon on the back and saying variants on, "Good one." Jason used the movement of the swimmers to walk away, muttering things Claire was certain she didn't want to hear.

Ramon stayed behind, scrutinizing her. He'd been asking last fall if Chris liked dating Claire. And he'd gone to Chris a few more times for relationship advice, which Emily and Claire had conferred about since neither of them turned out to be an expert on straight guy relationships.

"For real, who was the red-head in the Cities?" he asked. "Chris break up with you?"

"She's a friend," Claire said. "We're still together. Why does no one believe that?"

"You two don't act like you used to. You don't touch him as much. I figured something happened."

Now that made complete sense. No wonder the rumors had so much traction. Claire made a mental note to tell Emily they had to go back to being cutesy at school.

"We went through some stuff," she told Ramon. "But we came out more together. All that stuff before, in the halls, half of it was for show, to make other girls envious and show off my cute boyfriend and now...I know I've got this person in my life that I'm always going to love, no matter what, even if we go to different colleges. That other business about how things look doesn't matter."

"That's some deep knowledge, little goth," he said with a nod to the colored scarf she was wearing. "I like it. What else do you know?"

"This school would be a better place if queer and trans students didn't have to be terrified all the time."

Ramon smirked and said, "Be nice if it was a little less white, too."

"That is so true." She wanted to offer him something and, now that Jason was calling her queer all the time anyway, she didn't have much to lose, so she added, "I am queer, though. The bisexual kind."

"Oh," he said. "Hot."

"Jerk. Like you'd say that if I were a guy."

His face froze for a second and then his grin flashed across it and he shrugged. "You should get over that boyfriend-time thing. We need Chris on the team."

"Do you really?" Claire asked.

"Nah. Going to miss him, though. Middle of those meets gets pretty boring."

"Don't you guys ever just hang out? Like not at meets? You know Chris restores old cars, right? He works on them with his dad. Do you like cars?"

"I could," Ramon said.

"Good, because I find them deeply tedious. I'll ask Chris to invite you over sometime. Bring whoever you want." She added that last without gender in case the frozen look on his face and the quick grin had been him starting to come out to her.

He picked up his lunch tray. "Girlfriend jokes aside, I don't have a whoever right now. But when I do, maybe I will."

CHAPTER THIRTY

School starting brought a welcome relief to the whole family. Despite the high temperatures of the summer, the house had been emotionally cold as a tomb since June. I dove into my classes with fervor, and started going over to Claire's most nights after school, except for the dreaded Wednesdays when I still had to see messed-up Dr. Webber. He'd been taking lots of notes during my visits of late. What were they for? I started to feel paranoid. I had to figure out a way to stop seeing him, but for most of September I was content to have my regular life back.

I fantasized about telling my swim coach the real reason I quit the team. I imagined walking into his office and saying, "Actually, here's the truth. I'm a trans woman and I'm going to start growing breasts this year, so I can't swim with the guys anymore."

Unfortunately, the second part of that imagined scenario involved him outing me to the whole school, so I never went with that plan. Instead I'd pointed out that I wasn't in the top half of the team and that I needed to focus on schoolwork and earning money for college. He argued against it, but I was tenacious.

Dad had more trouble with me quitting than the coach did. Maybe because coach had a crop of new hopeful swimmers to deal with and Dad was stuck with me.

He brought it up a few times in the first weeks of school. Swimming practice didn't start until October and he pointed out that I had time to change my mind.

"You're still a guy at school," he said. "I thought you liked swimming."

"I do."

"You said no one else is as good at distance."

"No one else wants to do distance. They've got a bunch of new swimmers this year. The team will be fine," I told him.

"Don't you want the varsity letter?"

"Dad." I didn't know how to say the obvious truth that he'd forgotten or didn't want to face. I moved the neckline of my shirt to the side and held up the strap of the training bra I was wearing under three layers of shirts.

His eyes got very wide. And then he walked away.

The door to the garage slammed shut.

* * *

Dad avoided me for about a week. I couldn't stand it. I put on my very gray Henley and went to work on the car with him. We didn't talk. But at least he'd let me hang out with him in his sanctuary.

It was early October and the sun set around 6:30. Every evening I went up to my room, sat at my desk and got nothing done, staring out at the dark sky. I caught myself rubbing my arms, the softening skin there, thinking about the future. A year or two from now, I'd be in the Cities, being a girl. Except in that future there was no Claire, she'd been accepted to a college in Iowa, and there sure wasn't Mom, also no Dad. And because Dad's side of the family was the side known for being randomly, weirdly liberal, no Dad probably meant no family at all.

Mom would keep me away from Mikey, so no brother.

At least I had Natalie. But one person wasn't nearly enough.

Now that I'd come out to some people, had chances to be myself around them, it was so much harder to go back to being an automaton. The Chris programs were harder to run and every time I ran them I felt the chasm widen between myself and everyone else.

Knowing what happy felt like, deliberately avoiding it hurt. Not that being happy was all about girl stuff. But the girl identity issue was the bouncer at the door. When I couldn't get past that, when I couldn't have that, it was impossibly hard to get into all the rest of it.

A few times in the first weeks at school I tried wearing a girl T-shirt as a base layer under my other shirt and sweater, trying to feel like a real person. Instead I panicked that someone would figure it out, that they'd X-ray vision through my clothes and see. Claire had told me about the conversation she'd interrupted, about Jason saying she was queer and so was I. When Ramon came over to tinker on the car with me and Dad, he never mentioned it, but I couldn't be too careful.

I liked having Ramon over. Claire told me she thought he might be on "Team Bi." While we tinkered with car parts, he'd tell me about his family and his dreams and the epic fantasy books he loved. But then I'd wonder if I should try to be a guy more like him. At least playing the guy role all the time I didn't worry so much about being outed.

Natalie kept telling me I wasn't being healthy and Claire said about the same thing but not in words.

They were right. I needed a break from the pressure. Feeling ridiculous about it, I got a girls' pajama set: a turquoise top with hearts on it and cute half-sleeves and sleep shorts, striped pink and purple. I ordered it online and had it sent to Claire's house.

The first time I put it on was the middle of the night, when I got up to pee. I'd been sleeping in a T-shirt and boxers, but I changed into the pajamas and stared at myself in the mirror for a long time. I'd been on hormones for two months and I thought I could see the hint of breasts, though it was probably too soon. But the idea made me grin and grin.

Nobody understood, except Natalie and the people in the support group, how for me gender was such a deep human thing that not being a girl meant not being a person, not being real. That telling me to be a boy meant telling me not only that other people were more important than I was, but that I had no importance at all. That I couldn't be trusted to know who I was.

Now I could start to grow up, to become the person I wanted to be. I just wished I didn't have to do it alone.

* * *

A few weeks later, Dad knocked on my door, saying, "Chris, you up?"

I'd been sitting in bed doing my History class reading in my girl pajamas. A gray robe Mom had gotten me hung over the back of my desk chair and I pulled it on to cover all that scandalous color. It hung well past the sleep shorts and covered them up easily.

I opened the door saying, "Yeah, it's only nine."

"You've been going to bed early," he said. "You sleeping a lot?"

I wondered if Mom had sent him to administer the depression checklist, make sure I was okay. They could've just slipped it under my door on a clipboard.

"Reading mostly." I stepped out of the doorway.

He came into the room and closed the door most of the way behind him. I braced myself.

He contemplated my desk with its sleeping computer, mess of papers and the folded over *Girls & Cars* calendar. Looked back at me, brows coming together.

"What are you wearing?" he asked in a tone of disbelief at best, maybe disdain.

A glance down confirmed that the top of the bright turquoise shirt was visible and the upper curve of the big pink heart. I hadn't pulled the gray completely over the bright colors. Subconscious much?

It might send him running again, but I wanted him to see me, even for a minute.

I braced my feet and said, "Girls' pajamas." Untying the robe, I let it fall open. I made myself not cross my arms over my chest, just stood there and let him see me in turquoise and hearts and ruffles. I waited for him to slam out of the room.

He didn't move.

He looked at me so long I had to start talking again.

"I'm trying, Dad. Trying to be your son. But I can't do it all the time. It's like I'm a robot, I'm not a person. I'm frozen in time as this non-thing and…"

"Stop it," he said. He unsnapped a vest pocket and pulled out a bolt that he turned in his fingers.

"I can't stop," I told him.

He shook his head and sank down onto my desk chair. "Sit down."

I crawled across my bed and sat against the pile of pillows where I'd been doing homework. He was across from me, not far, hands between his knees, rotating the bolt over and over.

"You going to look like that girl Natalie someday?" he asked, watching the bolt move in his fingers.

"Yes."

"Is this because you want to be pretty?"

"I'd like to be pretty. I mean, I hope so. But it's because I'm a girl. I know I'm a girl. And even if I didn't know it now, every time I think about who I could be when I grow up, in the future, I'm always a woman."

Another long pause. He weighed the bolt in his palm, stared around the room.

"Did I do this to you?" he asked. "You don't want to be a man."

"No!"

I hadn't ever thought what it would be like to be my dad with all the shit Dr. Webber had been saying about how I only thought I wanted to be a girl because I hated my dad. That must've been awful to keep being told he'd screwed me up. I wanted to hug him and tell him no a dozen different ways.

"Dad," I said. "I love you. This is just something that happens. I knew when I was really little. It's not anything you did. You don't have to blame yourself."

He made a grunt of agreement and turned his face to me.

"Don't you coddle me," he growled. "You aren't the parent here. I'm the damned parent."

He pulled a grayed and folded piece of paper out of an upper vest pocket. From the creases, the dirt and the grease-defined fingerprints, he'd been carrying it around for days, maybe weeks, taking it out to unfold and fold up again.

He unfolded it now and spread it on the edge of my desk: a single notebook page, torn out, written on with blunt pencil. It said:

1.   Brunch
2.   Go for a walk/hike
3.   Golf
4.   Photography
5.   Fishing
6.   Women's sports
7.   Theater

"I've been asking the guys at the shop what they do with their daughters," he said. "I didn't tell 'em why. Didn't think that was their business. Now they probably think your mother's expecting." He snorted and asked, "You like any of this?"

I blinked back tears so I could read the list again. He'd asked his buddies what they did with their daughters? I remembered hearing him talk to Natalie's mom. Him walking away from me after the swimming/bra strap conversation. I'd thought he was mad. But maybe mad was how it looked when he got confused.

I put my finger on number three and said, "You think golf is stupid."

"It's better than theater."

"Where's your pencil?"

He pulled it from another pocket, a half-stub with the lead worn down. I started crossing off and re-writing the list until it read:

1.   Any food
2.   Go for a drive
3.   Cars

4. Computers
5. Hiking
6. Family board game night
7. Action movies

He put his finger on number three, where mine had been. "You still like cars?"

"I'm still me," I said. "More me. And girls can like cars."

"Long as you don't ever pose for one of those calendars." His lips wrinkled, trying to hide a smirk.

I smirked back at him and said, "Yeah, about that."

"I got something better for you this year," he told me.

"You don't have to. This is what I want."

"What? Working on cars with your old man?" he asked.

He pulled the bolt out of his pocket again and held it up, then put it between his fingers and turned it slowly. I watched his thick fingers with the crescents of grease under his nails.

I told him, "I want to be a girl and still have a dad."

His brows drew closer as he asked, "Where'd you think I was going to go?"

I didn't have to answer because he turned his head to stare through my cracked-open bedroom door in the direction of the master bedroom. His jaw hardened. He had to be thinking about Mom, about how she and I avoided each other now, didn't talk unless we had to. He got that I didn't mean he'd go somewhere physically, but that he'd stop loving me. He blinked and rubbed a hand briskly across his face.

Thumping his finger on the list on my desk, he said, "'Course you've got a dad. Anytime. Got it?"

"Thanks, Dad."

He went to the door, then turned back to me. "Talking to Susan, Natalie's mother, she told me I should call you Emily. That from your grandma?"

"Yeah."

"Huh." A half smile, faint and thoughtful. He nodded and said, "Emily."

He went out and shut the door behind him, which was good since I'd started crying a lot.

CHAPTER THIRTY-ONE

I didn't know if I could refuse to go to Dr. Webber without Mom trying to cut off my supply of hormones, but I had to try. Claire and I brainstormed early in the weekend, and then I cornered Mom in her tiny office after dinner on Sunday.

I tried to sound as plaintive as possible, and not demanding. "Mom, I don't want to go to Dr. Webber anymore, he gives me the creeps."

"That was the deal," she said. "You got to see your hormone doctor; you have to see Dr. Webber too."

I sat on the edge of her desk. "When we have appointments and you're not there, he spends the whole time asking about my sexual fantasies," I told her. "It's gross."

Now she turned in her chair to look at me. "Are you lying to me, Christopher?"

"I'm not," I said. "I mean, you know I can't stand him, but if that was it, I could keep going I suppose. He makes me feel disgusting. He wants to talk about masturbation and stuff. It's nasty. And then he takes lots and lots of notes. I'm afraid of what he's going to do with them. Can we find another doctor? You can pick one who wants to change me, just not a...you know, a gross one."

She sighed. "I don't know why you persist in this delusion about womanhood. What do you think it's going to solve? Do you think your life would be easier as a woman?"

I sagged back against the desk, holding myself up with my arms. After months of this, even the first few lines of my mother's argument made me feel like I'd gone three days without sleeping.

"It's not going to make my life easier," I said. "Are you kidding?"

"Then why?" she asked.

"Because I *am* a woman," I said simply. "That's all. What would you do if you'd grown up as a boy?"

"I'd be a boy," she said. "I wouldn't be myself. That's the point, Chris, people don't go from one to the other. You're not a woman. You don't act like a woman, you don't think like a woman. I'm afraid you're going to turn out to be a freak, and you'll never get what you're looking for."

Normally, I'd have fought her and insisted that I am a woman and therefore I think like one and so on. But I didn't. Maybe it was the conversation with Dad, or the mellow weekend I'd had, or the hormones, or being able to be honest to more people than ever before. I didn't feel as angry at her as usual. I could start to understand that she honestly wanted me to be happy but she didn't see how all this could work.

"I'm afraid of that, too," I admitted. "I'm afraid I'll get through all this and I won't look or sound like a woman."

"Then why do it?" she asked.

"Because being treated like a guy all the time, having to pretend I am a guy, I'm lying to everyone. It destroys me. I would rather fail at being myself than succeed at being someone I'm not."

She shook her head. "I don't understand it, and I'm still going to look for another way out for you."

"But not Dr. Webber?"

"No," she said. "Not him. But you're going to church at least twice a month."

I enjoyed church with Claire explaining it all to me, but I knew I had to pretend it was a chore. "Ugh, Mom," I said and sighed heavily. "Fine. If I have to."

I was elated to have the weight of Dr. Webber off me, but Mom's comment about me not thinking like a woman haunted me. Was it possible that even though I felt female inside, my growing up as a boy had changed me forever? Would I never fit in anywhere except for the transgender community? Although I found support there and liked the people I'd met, I couldn't imagine living my whole life inside those boundaries.

* * *

The following Saturday, sitting on Claire's couch with her, I asked her if I didn't think like a girl. It had been bothering me all week, but we hadn't had time alone to talk. Now we were in our usual feet-to-feet position, leaning against the couch arms, reading and eating the egg sandwiches I'd brought.

She deftly pried out of me the details of the entire conversation with my mother. Then she about fell over laughing.

"Why are you laughing?" I demanded.

"Let me get this straight, figuratively speaking," Claire said. "In the middle of a conversation in which you got out of seeing Dr. Webber by insinuating that he has a sexual interest in you, your mother suggests you don't think like a woman. I don't know what girl manual your mom got, but that's in the first five pages of mine. No straight teen guy I know would say some man was leering at him, even if he was." She paused and added, "Guys should be reporting sexual harassment a lot more than they are. My point is: manipulation isn't big in the guy playbook."

I said in my best Valley Girl impression, "So, I'm, like, totally a girl."

"You're more of a girl than I am," she agreed. "You actually enjoy makeup. You're like an eleven-year-old worried that you're never going to get your period. Chill out."

I made myself sigh, look down at my half-eaten sandwich and frown.

"What?" she asked with a hint of real concern.

I said, "You're right, I am afraid I'm never going to get my period."

Claire leaned forward and caught my hand. "You will," she said. "I read about that online, a lot of trans girls get PMS and everything except the bleeding part. Maybe we'll sync cycles."

I felt teary, which happened a lot lately on the hormones. I took a sip of my coffee and swallowed hard.

"Why were you were researching trans girl periods?" I wondered out loud.

"Um, curious." She hopped up and carried her sandwich wrapper into the kitchen.

I followed. "Claire?"

She tossed the wrapper into the trash under the sink and then turned a slow circle, searching the kitchen, as if her mom would pop out of a cupboard. When that didn't happen, she grabbed my hand and pulled me into her bedroom, shutting the door behind us with her foot.

In her room, she dropped my hand and stood by her desk, flicking the pages in her notebook with her fingernail. She'd cut her hair to just beyond her ears this fall and it made her face even more pixie-cute. I'd grown mine out another two inches. At what point would my hair be longer than hers?

I remembered trying to come out to her in this room and all the wrong guesses she'd come up with, so I waited for her to talk.

Claire finally said, "I was looking for ways to, you know, be in bed with you."

"You don't like how we are?"

She caught the stack of pages with her fingernail again and let them ruffle down. "Last winter, before you told me, I thought I had this boyfriend and all he wanted to do was make out and make me feel good. Other girls at school kept talking about how their guys pressured them for sex. And if they did have sex, it was over when he was done and he didn't seem to care if they had a good time too. I figured I'd super lucked out."

She peeked sideways at me and added, "Which I have. Except now I'm starting to feel like I'm the guy in a bad way, like it's all about me. But also like I'm the girl in a bad way, like you get to have me in a way that I don't get to have you. I want it to be different."

I turned away and moved into the open part of her room between her bed and closet. I didn't want things to be about me. Not while I didn't like what I had to work with.

I grumbled, "Boy parts."

"You don't have 'boy parts'," Claire said, sounding angry, but maybe not at me. "I'm sorry I ever said that phrase. You have girl parts that look different than mine."

That seemed implausible. I wanted it to be true, but I couldn't see how. In the nine months since I'd come out to her, we'd slowed way down while she got used to me being a girl, and then slowed down again when I got depressed from the Dr. Webber trips. Only a few weeks ago, we'd gotten back to where we'd been early last spring. That explained why she was researching this now.

But what could she find? I kept my back to Claire and shrugged. "What if I really wish I had different parts?" I asked. "What if being touched like that just reminds me of feeling wrong."

She didn't say anything for so long that I turned around. She'd moved from her desk to the window, rested her fingers on the sill but wasn't looking out. Her eyes had a broken-glass sadness to them.

"Is it that bad?" she asked.

"Sometimes," I admitted. "Most of the time."

She half-turned toward the window, face tilting down, the sound of tears in her voice. "I wish I could make everything feel right for you. When we're kissing and you touch me, I feel so close to you. But then there's this wall and I know it's not your wall—you didn't put it there—but I really want to climb over it."

"You want me to throw you a rope?" I joked, trying to lighten the air between us.

"Yes."

"Oh."

I wanted to give her something, to get us closer again, but I didn't know how. I went into the kitchen and poured myself a glass of water and one for Claire. When I got back to her bedroom, she was still standing between her desk and the window, her eyes red-rimmed. I put her glass down on the desk and drank half of mine, then set it next to hers.

I sat on the end of the bed and said, "The wall—Dr. Mendel said this cool thing—for two people to have intimacy, there have to be two bodies there. Like my body and your body. But you can take your body for granted because it's the way you expect it to be, while I have to imagine my body. There's how my body's supposed to be, but there's also how it looks and feels now, and I have to make up the difference. That's a lot of work. I think that's part of the wall."

Claire ran her thumb along the rim of her water glass. She took a sip and put it down again, returned her thumb to its edge.

"Can I help you imagine your body?" she asked.

"How?"

She took a step toward the bed. I thought she'd sit next to me, but instead she nudged my legs apart so she could stand between them, right in front of me. She wrapped her arms around my shoulders and pulled my cheek to her chest. Her chin rested on the top of my head.

"See, you're tall," she said. "But that doesn't mean you have to feel tall all the time or most of the time if you don't want to. Same goes for everything. It's how we think about it. We don't have to do boy things with your parts. We'll do girl things. We'll call your parts by the same names as mine and go from there."

"Really?"

"Yeah, why not?"

"Because mine look so different."

She moved back enough to look at my face, resting her hands on my shoulders. "If we close our eyes, isn't it all just squishy bits?" she asked with a half grin.

I stared at my big feet and Claire's little ones. "Mine don't squish the same."

Her fingers walked in from my shoulder and brushed my cheek. She asked, "Can we at least try? We'll go slow, but someday I'd like to take your pants off."

That sounded kind of great but really scary.

"Just your pants," she said. "Not your panties. I'm not trying to pressure you." With a half laugh, she added, "I'm not that kind of guy."

I caught her hips and tugged. She came close and put her arms around me again.

"You could probably get into my pants now," I whispered into the fabric of her sweater. Her hold on me tightened and she made a light, happy murmur.

I asked, "What if it doesn't work?"

"If you don't feel good, tell me. We'll go watch *Law & Order* and snuggle under a blanket. It's not like we were great at kissing the first time either," she pointed out.

"How long's your mom gone for?"

"Hours," Claire assured me.

She tipped my face up and kissed me. I liked being the short half of the couple.

Also Claire was wrong; she wasn't the luckiest girl in our high school, I was.

CHAPTER THIRTY-TWO

The strangest thing happened a few days after Christmas. Mom was going through another phase of not talking to me; probably having trouble finding a new shrink who thought they could fix me.

Claire had gotten her acceptance letter to that university in Iowa with the great writing program. I couldn't imagine what I was going to do without her. I didn't have the money to go to a really good school and if I did have the money, I'd spend it on surgery anyway. I planned to a community college for a two-year degree and then transfer to the University of Minnesota for the last two years.

But that remained a long way off and so my Christmas was bleak. Claire went to visit her dad, and I was stuck in the house with Mom glaring at me every time I did something girlish and with Dad wrapped up in his cars. He'd sold the Bronco and picked up a 1977 Ford Thunderbird two months ago. He must've been in love with it, because he worked on it every night.

Two days after Christmas while I was slumped on the couch trying to be interested in the television, Dad opened the door to the garage and said, "Come here."

I followed him into his workshop that was, as usual, littered with tools and car parts. He picked a small, badly gift-wrapped box off his worktable and tossed it at me.

"What's this?" I asked.

"Late Christmas present," he said. "Open it."

I did. It was a small box with a set of car keys. "Dad, I already have a car."

Standing next to me, he turned me toward the Thunderbird. It was still a bit of a monstrosity, but, as he often boasted, for something he'd picked up for twenty-five hundred bucks, who could complain. It had good lines and with all the work he'd put in and the right paint job it would run and look slick.

"Now you have two," he pointed out.

"What am I going to do with two cars?"

"Sell one of 'em," he said, like that was obvious. "What do you think you can get for the Chrysler?"

I felt my jaw loosening, wanting to drop open. "Sixteen," I said with effort. "Maybe seventeen grand."

"Good. There you go."

"For school?" I asked, not quite believing my ears.

"For whatever you want. I don't need to know what you use it for."

Was he suggesting I use it to pay for surgery?

"Dad—?" I started.

He turned to face me fully. "Look, I don't understand this gender stuff. It makes no sense to me. And it doesn't have to. All I know is that you've been angry and sad damn near your whole life, and now sometimes you're happy. I want you to stay that way. You do whatever you need. And if I hurt you when you were little…well, I'm sorry."

I started crying. I couldn't talk.

He threw an arm over my shoulders and tightened it once. "Jesus Christ," he said roughly.

After a minute he dropped his arm and walked across the workshop to his latest project. "What do you think I can get for this shit?" he yelled back to me. "It's shot to hell."

I wiped my face and walked over to where he was standing. "It's worth something," I said. "I'll look it up."

He didn't bring the topic up again, but I spent more time over that holiday working on the Thunderbird with him. And I could've sworn he'd stopped calling me "son" and started calling me "hon."

* * *

Our school had a Valentine's Day dance on Friday, but we didn't go. Who goes to a school dance on Friday the thirteenth? And we didn't feel like trotting out as Chris and Claire again. We had to do that at school all the time anyway.

The rumors about Claire being queer were dying down. Mainly because Ramon was a champion. From the many girls with crushes on him, he'd found one he liked—Claire and I liked her too—and brought her out on a few double dates with us, then talked about it loudly at school. Plus Claire and I kissed each other in the halls often enough that any theory about us not being together sounded ridiculous.

Pretty funny, since we were by far the queerest couple at the school.

For Valentine's Day itself, Natalie had invited us to a party at her house. I was supposed to pick up Claire a bit before dinner and we'd drive to the Cities together, getting something to eat on the way. Her mom was seriously dating the guy she'd started seeing the previous summer and kept bringing him back to the house. At least her mom still worked one weekend day, so we had that to ourselves. And those days together now sometimes involved more undressing than dressing up. But not today. Her mom had the day off and I got a panicked mid-afternoon call from Claire about there being "Valentine's Day grossness."

I drove over and brought her back to my house. Her arrival was the excuse Mikey needed to get every action figure he owned and bring them into the living room. He insisted Claire do battle and she rose to the challenge. They pushed the coffee table back to the couch and set up the field of battle. Mikey crouched on one side in his Hulk T-shirt and Claire sat on the other in a navy sweater with cute white stripes that could almost pass for a superhero uniform if I squinted a lot.

I went to make nachos. We had leftover ground beef from taco Thursday, so I sprinkled that over the chips, cut up tomatoes, and added shredded cheese, feeling smugly domestic.

I headed toward the living room to ask Claire and Mikey what they wanted to drink with the nachos, but stopped when I heard Mikey tell Claire, "My brother's going to be my sister."

"I know," Claire said, her grin audible.

"But you're still his girlfriend?"

"Yeah, I like her a lot. Girls can date other girls. And she's the same person, just more fun."

"I guess," he said. "She's still not as good at games as you are. You should teach her to be better."

Claire laughed. "I'm working on it. She might be too nice."

Then there was a bunch of laser and punching sounds and Mikey yelling, "I'm killing you!"

I was grinning so huge my cheeks hurt, until I turned back toward the kitchen and saw Mom. She stood at the bottom of the stairs, between living room and kitchen, her face a plastic mask.

"What if he says that at school?" she asked.

Now that she'd found me a new shrink, we were on speaking terms. Her new thing was all variations on "what will people think?" and about how hard this would be on Mikey.

"I'm gone in a few months anyway," I said. I didn't want to get into it with her again. Not today.

She pursed her lips in a tight frown. "You don't have to."

Did she mean I didn't have to move out or was she back to saying I didn't have to transition? If she meant not moving out, how would that work?

I saw Dr. Mendel at least once a month, even though I had to see the other shrink too. Dr. Mendel kept telling me that my folks had their own process and to give it time. She didn't get how hard it was to live with this person who was supposed to take care of me and kept wanting the real me to vanish.

I softened my voice and told Mom, "It's better if I'm in the Cities. I'll come visit."

"As…a woman?" her voice held layers of disbelief and worry and maybe curiosity.

"You could always tell the neighbors I'm a cousin."

The microwave beeped and I hurried back into the kitchen. When I'd pulled out the nachos to cool, I turned around to see Mom standing in the doorway watching me.

"A cousin from which side of the family?" she asked and the side of her mouth twitched up a little.

"Dad's?"

She nodded and almost smiled. Before I could ask if she was trying to make a joke, she went back upstairs.

I carried the nachos into the living room and took a pillow to the face.

* * *

When it was time to leave for the party, Mom and Dad were both in the kitchen. Mom sat at the table with the paper in front of her and Dad was unloading the dishwasher. They were talking about going out to brunch tomorrow, just the two of them.

Somehow despite Dr. Webber's advice being awful, they'd managed to ignore the whole "model male and female poles" thing and remember they liked hanging out together. I think Dr. Webber had pissed off Dad enough that he started doing more of the "female" things around the house. He'd been cleaning more and I caught him folding the laundry. He was really good at it too.

"I'll watch Mikey," I said, though they'd probably assumed that anyway.

Dad lifted a stack of plates into the cupboard and gave me a nod. He pulled his wallet out of his back pocket, got out a twenty and said, "You're taking Claire someplace nice, right?"

"Yeah." I hadn't told them we were going into the Cities. I figured it would just freak Mom out. "It's okay, Dad. I've got money."

"Someplace nice," he repeated and held out the twenty until I took it.

I hugged him. And then, because it would be really weird not to, I went over and hugged Mom too. She held on long enough that I started to worry she thought she could squeeze me back into being her son.

Claire came in and said her good-byes. On the way to the car she asked if she could drive. "I need more practice," she said. "For driving back from Iowa. But you have to tell me which way to go, I'm totally lost."

"We're standing in my driveway."

"Yep, not a clue which way to the Cities."

"You wanting to drive—is this a metaphor?" I asked as I got in on the passenger side.

"It is now." She backed out, got us going in the right direction and then said, "Oh hey, speaking of metaphors, check my right jacket pocket."

I unzipped it and felt inside until I hit hard plastic. I pulled out Mikey's Starfire action figure with her insanely skimpy costume and hair down to her knees.

Claire told me, "He wanted me to take her so we could strategize beating his team when we get back. But also he said he thinks she's transgender, so he wants her to hang out with you."

I brushed my thumb over Starfire's big, green eyes. Mom was so wrong about Mikey having trouble with this.

I said, "Starfire is an alien. We don't really know what gender she started as. She could be trans. I love how it's just not a big deal to him."

"How's your mom?" Claire asked. She must've seen us talking through the doorway.

"Still weird. She might have been trying to make a joke. I don't know."

I held onto Mikey's action figure and watched the passing darkness, wondering how much I'd have to leave behind and how much I'd want to. I'd never miss Liberty or that high school. But I'd miss Ramon and a few other swim guys. I'd miss hearing them rag on how bad coach's pep talks were; now that I wasn't on the team, they re-enacted the pep talks over lunch for me. Ramon had gotten into a good school on the west coast and most of the other swim guys who would graduate this spring planned to flee our small town for bigger cities.

I'd miss Claire when she went to Iowa in the fall, so much that I couldn't stand to think about that.

I liked the idea of having my own space, but what would it be like not to see Mikey's messed up hair every morning? Not to hear him running through the house making flying sounds for his heroes? What would it be like to go an entire week without seeing Dad in his fifteen-pocket vests? And, for as crappy as the last eight months had been around Mom, I'd miss talking to her about the news or hearing her office gossip.

I hadn't put all the pieces together until now, talking to Mom and her asking if I was coming home as a woman. Of course that's what I wanted. I'd been planning to go to college as a girl. I'd turn eighteen in April and then I'd change my name and paperwork. By the time I started in the fall, I'd have been on hormones for a year. I didn't want to keep pretending.

When I'd imagined moving to the Cities and going to college, and coming home on weekends—hanging out with Dad in the garage, playing with Mikey and complaining about it but liking it at the same time—I'd assumed I'd be me. I'd be Emily.

Would I have to dress up as a guy again to visit home? Was Mom serious about the cousin thing? She hadn't even touched the topic of me coming out to my grandparents. What would happen when she saw me as a woman? Or when Dad did?

I'd thought coming out to them at Dr. Mendel's would be it, but they had a lot of road to travel, too.

When we arrived at Natalie's, her mom opened the door and hugged us both. Music drifted up from the lower level. I had my duffel bag over my shoulder and Natalie's mom pointed us to the upstairs bathroom. Claire came with me and sat on the edge of the tub while I did my makeup.

"I feel like that scene in every show with a trans girl ever," I said, brushing on eye shadow.

"What scene?"

"The big reveal where she gets all fancy and the viewer sees her…" I put down my brush so I could do air quotes, "…'as a woman' for the first time. It's like every time they have to show this whole business, like it's artificial. Like we're not just who we are all the time."

Claire put her hands between her knees, watching me. She said, "You look like Emily all the time to me now. I mean, you look like yourself. It's your eyes, I guess, or, if you don't think this is too sappy, your soul."

From her it wasn't too sappy. And it reminded me. "I got you a Valentine's gift."

I went into the side pocket of the duffel bag and pulled out a wrapped rectangle: red and pink paper but not garish. Claire ripped off the paper and opened the two sides of the hinged frame. One side was a photo of us that Natalie had taken just after New Year's. I'd been sitting on the couch in Natalie's basement and Claire had come up from behind and put her arms around my shoulders. I was grinning like I'd won the lottery and Claire had this joyful smirk like "Can you believe this girl?" mixed with "Can you believe this is my girl?" It was the first photo I had of me that I liked.

The other side of the frame said: "Do everything in love."

Claire murmured, "I have mixed feelings about the apostle Paul, but this is so perfect. I got you something too."

She opened her shoulder bag and pulled out a compact, wrapped package, all shimmery red foil. I slit the tape with my thumbnail and unfolded the foil to reveal a cell phone box.

Claire said, "I had the girl at the store set it up. My number's in there. I paid the first few months already. And I set the wallpaper for you."

I thumbed it on. The background was her paladin character in full armor. In the contacts, she was listed as, "Claire the Mighty."

"I was going to get one, honest," I told her, grinning. "But I still see you every day."

"And you're going to keep seeing me every day for months, but now you can also text me."

She looked at the frame in her hands, mouth turning down, and I knew she was thinking about fall, like I was.

"Come on," I told her. "Let's go party."

We headed down the stairs. On the first floor landing, Claire grabbed my hand. "This is our first semipublic date as a girl-couple," she said.

"You should've worn a dress," I told her, because I was in my long skirt.

She stuck her tongue out at me and we walked down to the basement. There were about ten people there: Natalie and her new beau, who was a trans guy she'd met at the support group, plus Steve and Badri, and a few people from Natalie's school.

After the introductions, Steve and Badri went back to dancing together, as did two of the girls from Natalie's school. Claire wandered off to get a plate of snacks as I caught up with Natalie.

Once I had all the Cities gossip, I spotted Claire sitting alone in an armchair near the back of the room. I pulled out my new phone, found her number and texted her: *want to dance?*

She felt her phone buzz, read the screen and grinned. By then I was standing next to the chair. I knelt down next to her. "You okay?"

"Are you going to get bored with me now that you have a bunch of trans friends?" she asked.

"Um, no. Are you going to get to Iowa and decide you want to date someone else?"

She shook her head, looked down at her phone, whispered, "I'm going to miss you so much. I don't want to go, but I have to."

"I know," I said. "We have months. Iowa isn't that far and I have a car."

"You're going to drive to Iowa in the Thunderbird?"

"It's sturdy."

I'd sold my other car a few weeks ago and now had an impressive amount of money in the bank—enough for my first two years of college and a good start on the surgery I wanted.

Plus Steve and Badri had cleaned out their four-season porch and offered to rent it to me cheaply until I found an apartment near school.

A year ago, when I'd tried to imagine my future, I could only see what I wanted to look like, who I wanted to be, but nothing else real about my life. Now that I could be that person, the life around me also took shape. I'd live in a cool city with amazing friends. I'd figure out how to visit Dad and Mikey and Mom; we'd get used to being a family with one son and one daughter. I'd be in college learning how to write code so I could make more online spaces for people like me.

"I get to go to college as a girl," I whispered.

Claire lifted my hands and pressed my fingers to her lips.

It hadn't hit me until now that this life—surrounded by friends, music, food and warmth, my hands in Claire's—could be mine all the time. I tugged on Claire's fingers.

"Want to dance with your girlfriend?" I asked.

She stood up and pulled me up with her. "Do you want to dance with yours?"

"More than anything," I told her.

We moved over to where the others were dancing and put our arms around each other. She rested her cheek on my shoulder. Through the window I saw the gentle winking of the soft white holiday lights that the neighbors hadn't taken down yet. Above that, bright stars surrounded a glowing, nearly full moon.

Soon I would live a few miles from here and everyone would know me as Emily.

EPILOGUE

Ten Years Later

A lot changes in ten years. From the time I came out to Claire, spring 2008, to now, transgender became a household word and same-sex marriage was legalized. We watched our country take so many steps forward and too many steps back. Still I'm hopeful as much, maybe more than I'm heartbroken.

Claire wanted our wedding to be ten years to the day that I came out to her. She calls that our anniversary because that's when she got the chance to start dating Emily, instead of the well-constructed fiction of Chris. And she still loves coincidences, only she won't call them that: miracles, divine intervention.

Too cutesy for me—the ten years thing, not miracles. But she's a better planner than I am, so our wedding date turned out to be ten years, a week and a half from when I came out. That is it would be, if we managed to pull off the wedding itself.

* * *

Claire and I had gone to our separate colleges and split up halfway into that first year because the distance felt too hard. I'd moved to the Cities and started community college officially as Emily Christine Hesse. I earned a two-year degree in Computer Science, worked full time for a year, got the surgeries I wanted. Then I enrolled in the University of Minnesota for two more years.

Claire got most of the way through her four years in Iowa and started telling me "I miss you" a lot. It took me longer than I want to admit to get the hint. In her last year of college we started getting together again, carefully, in case too much had changed. She moved to the Cities the summer after her graduation, but we didn't get a place together until that winter—slogging through the January snow to look at duplexes because we were back in love with each other and didn't want to wait any longer.

Claire and I had been living together for about two years—girlfriends for three years, or five, depending on how you counted—when I started wondering if we should talk about getting married. Because I'd grown up looking like a guy, I'd been trained to be the one to ask and I didn't want to. But then Claire had been trained to be the one to wait to be asked, and I didn't know if she'd untrained that.

I found a ring that would be perfect. Super adorable. But then I couldn't ask because I couldn't figure out how to do it without the whole guy-gets-on-one-knee thing. And besides, I really wanted to be asked.

The engagement ring sat in my dresser drawer for months and months. Life went on.

We have a pretty great life. Claire works in (that is, unofficially runs) the communications department for our church. I work for a healthcare company, in their tech department, supporting a phone app that helps people take better care of themselves. It's a big company and the tech department, which includes way more than the app support, is about twenty people at the location where I work.

The day it happened, around lunchtime, one of my coworkers who sits by the window got up, paused, and still peering out the window said, "I think there's a bunch of elves on the lawn. I'm definitely seeing pointed ears."

A few of the others clustered around the windows and then one called across to me, "Hey, Emily, isn't that your girlfriend?"

We all ran down the stairs to where dancing elves twirled ribbons in the air. Claire wore a cute dress and some of her armor pieces from Minnesota's huge Renaissance Festival, just the artsy ones, like the vambraces with their etched metal and leather.

Claire got tongue-tied. She said something about paladins not being much without people to protect and other stuff about magic. I thought she was trying to set something up for Fest next year.

But slowly I was getting the idea that this wasn't a practice run for some future performance piece. Plus Beatrice from HR started crying.

Claire realized if she got on one knee while I was standing, we'd be way too different in height, so she steered me over to a bench and knelt and said, "I want to be your person for the rest of our lives."

I remember that part exactly.

Then I was crying and she was crying and my coworkers all applauded. Thankfully, Beatrice pulled it together enough to say, "She's asking you a question about the rest of your lives. You're supposed to give her an answer."

I stared at Claire in wonder and said, "Oh, of course." That made everyone laugh and the elves started ribbon-dancing again.

Claire had gotten me a gold ring with a diamond, the most perfect ever. And I told her, "I have a ring at home for you. In the dresser."

"You do?"

"Waves of black and gold. I had to buy it."

So I took the rest of the day off and we went home to get it and, since it was conveniently in the bedroom, not leave for a while.

* * *

That was last summer. We didn't talk about the wedding for months. I was afraid Claire wanted a big church wedding, which, if we had it at our very queer and very trans church, wouldn't be too bad. My mom, who ended up being better about me being transgender than me being a lesbian—once she got over that I really was never going to marry a man—seconded the big church wedding idea..

Dad just said, "That Claire's a good one."

And Mikey, who's in his second year of college now, went on about how weddings are great places to meet girls and would I please invite some single girls who like guys. He added, "And I mean all the girls, not only the cisgender ones."

Because my brother grew into the kind of guy who knows that "cisgender" means people who aren't trans and can work it easily into any conversation about him getting a date. He'd also grown into a giant, getting the muscle mass of Dad's side of the family and the height of the men on Mom's side. His hockey buddies called him "Colossus," from the X-Men; he'd grown into a real life superhero.

When I finally asked Claire, "How far out are we supposed to book the church for a wedding?" she gave me a quizzical look and shook her head.

She fished in her bag and then held out a clump of printed web pages stapled together. It was the info for a romance-themed science fiction and fantasy convention in February that would have a wedding chapel set up in a lovely atrium with a different theme each day.

"I love our church, but wouldn't you rather get married on the Enterprise?" she asked.

"You are my very favorite person in the whole world," I told her. "Can we have a fantasy theme? Nobody looks good in a *Star Trek* uniform. Except maybe Nico. But Nico looks good in everything."

"We can't have a *Game of Thrones* wedding," Claire insisted. "I'd be scared the whole time. *Star Wars* cantina, hm, no. Oh wait, look, on Sunday in the afternoon they're switching it over from *GoT* to *World of Warcraft*."

Which is how I came to be standing in an atrium of the convention center with rain beading the dozens of windows, worrying how much longer I might have to wait. Claire wasn't there yet. A third of our guests weren't there. A few of those, like Claire's mom, might show.

Should we postpone the wedding?

Who do you ask?

The atrium was a huge room, windows on three sides with a broad hallway making up the fourth side. Chairs had been set out in rows with a wide central aisle. The ceremonial dais was covered in fake stone with pillars flying banners from *World of Warcraft's* Horde and Alliance factions.

Our friend Ella, from Ohio, stood by the open end of the room as a greeter, looking like a slight, blond elf, even without a costume. She asked people "Horde or Alliance?" instead of "Are you with the bride or the bride?" Claire had taken the Horde faction, saying she didn't want to be stuck as a human.

I couldn't ask Ella about when to postpone a wedding. Her boyfriend had gone back to China, saying he'd get as good as job there as he could in the States and likely be treated better. She wanted to join him but couldn't leave her grad school program.

Our friends Nico and Tucker had driven up from Ohio with Ella, but they'd gone off with Claire and Mikey to watch the end of the costume competition. It must've run long because it was starting to overlap our wedding time. We only had forty-five minutes left for the ceremony before the next wedding group got to come in and set up. We didn't need that much time, but we definitely needed some. And I only planned on getting married once, so I didn't want to rush it.

Elizabeth, Vivianna and most of the support group were here. Steve and Badri might have some wisdom about weddings, but I wasn't sure Steve wouldn't dis me for buying into the patriarchy or something like that.

The front of Claire's side of the room, reserved for family, remained empty. Her dad had sent gifts but didn't come. Her mom hadn't responded to any of the invitations, though we'd only sent paper and email. I kept telling Claire we should go in person, but she'd scowl and tell me I didn't know what her mom's new husband was like. He was the reason for her mom's absence, so I didn't argue.

The back of Claire's side was jammed with people from Claire's writing group and our church. They knew more about weddings than anyone, but I didn't know them as well as Claire did. She should be the one to ask them and she wasn't replying to my texts.

This left me standing at the front of an audience with a minister from our church dressed gamely in a *World of Warcraft* Priest's robe. Claire had even found a robe that looked a bit like one of my old character's favorites: all flowing white and purple. My dress was white with embroidered flowers and a simple, elegant shape. Claire ended up being the one in lace on top of lace, which looked great next to mine. If she'd been here to stand next to me.

I went down the two steps to the front row of the Alliance side, where Mom and Dad sat. "How long do I wait?"

"Wedding nerves happen to everyone," Mom said. "I'm sure Claire's on her way."

Dad grumbled, "You wait all day if you have to. You're getting married today." He waved at my phone, "Text your brother. Tell him pick her up and carry her down here."

I'd already texted Mikey ten times with no reply, which made me think the room with the costume contest wasn't getting cell phone service.

As I went to ask the minister her opinion, I saw a group of drenched people move through the hallway off the atrium, followed by another. They weren't coming in from the rainy outside, they were jogging from the inside to the exit. In the distance, an alarm clanged. A group of half-drowned people in Harry Potter costumes dragged by in their heavy robes.

And there was Claire, running, holding her lacy skirt, Mikey next to her. Our friends Nico and Tucker jogged behind her. As always, Nico looked like a pretty person of indeterminate

gender with curly dark hair, light brown skin and joyful eyes.
Tucker rocked a classic butch button-down style and had her
Mohawk in a topknot. Nico put on a burst of speed and sprinted
to the front of the atrium.

"Someone set off the fire alarm. This whole wing of the
building is getting soaked," Nico told me and my parents.
"Atrium's safe though. But the costume contest is a sodden
wreck. They did it on purpose, to screw up the judging."

Claire, Mikey and Tucker had caught up by then. Claire
turned her golden-hazel eyes to me. I saw pain, sadness.

"It's Angel and Laura," she said. I had no idea what that
meant.

I told her, "We're supposed to get married. Like, now. Who
are you talking about? Is this about your mom?"

"No. Yes. Kind of," she said. She pushed her hair back
behind her ears. The short layers only got cuter from being
damp. "This contest is for the most romantic couples costume.
There's a pair who's doing a great Laura Kinney, she's the new
Wolverine, and her boyfriend Angel—but some of the others
tried to get them disqualified."

She looked like she was about to cry. Over costumes? This
had to be about her mom. I got off the dais and took her hands.
"Love, I don't understand. Do you want to wait?"

"It's not fair," she said, tears collecting on her eyelids.

Nico put a hand on my arm. "In the comic books Angel is
this tall, super-white blond guy and our Angel here is black and
nonbinary and short, plus our Laura is trans. Some jerks are
saying they're not close enough to the originals. Like they don't
have a right to these characters too."

At Nico's shoulder, her hands in fists, Tucker said, "You
should see Angel's wings—so amazing. And they made the
wings all by themself, by hand, every bit of wiring. Oh I hope
they didn't get wet."

I'd seen pics of costume pieces Tucker had crafted for Nico.
Of all of us, she knew best how much work went into that.

"You know they must have," Nico said, putting an arm
around her.

"Or they will as they're evacuated." Claire nodded to the windows where a light rain had been falling steadily all day. "The costume contest has cash prizes for the top three places. Angel and Laura are just kids. I'm sure they could use the money. And these people, trying to disqualify them, pretending it's not racism and transphobia. In *our* fan community…"

She trailed off. This was very much about her mom and the new husband and our country. Claire couldn't fight the way her mom had given in to her husband's ignorance and insistence that she not attend her daughter's queer and trans wedding. But here, today, Claire saw a chance to make one thing right; she was smarter than I was about picking fights she could win.

"How many more costumes did they need to judge?" I asked.

"Two or three more," Nico said, adding with a grin, "I was going to make it to your wedding on time, I swear."

"We do have a lot of room, chairs, a stage…" I looked to the minister.

"I can wait," she said. "But I'd like to change out of this robe if we're switching venues."

"Do you want to?" I asked Claire.

She surveyed her side of the room: all the people from her writing group and our church and no one from her birth family. Her aunt Debbie, the reporter, had said she'd try her best to be here, but she'd been on international assignment for weeks and wasn't sure she could make it back to the States in time.

"Can you find the judges?" she asked Nico. "Tell them we have a space for the contest."

With a nod, Nico sprinted off down the hall. Tucker shook her head, grinning, and followed at a slow jog. Mikey shot me a questioning look and I waved him off after them.

"Move or reschedule?" I asked Claire. My heart paused on the last word. I didn't want to go through these nerves again and I wanted to be married to Claire like yesterday.

She frowned at her dress, beautiful despite its dampness. "I don't want to reschedule. Though if we did, maybe my aunt could make it. But…Mom can watch the video years from now when we have a bunch of cute kids that she can't resist. I'm ready to do this now."

"Me too. There's got to be another place we can get married. This convention center is huge."

"Hey!" Claire yelled to the audience. "Hesse-Davis Wedding party, we are leaving this space to the cosplayers and going to find another place to get married. Let's move!"

We all gathered in the hallway, waiting for Mikey, Nico and Tucker to get back. Wedding nerves did not get better standing in a mass of people in a hallway instead of being on a stage.

I struggled to not send Mikey ten more angsty texts, when I heard his voice booming down the hallway, "Make way for Colossus!"

He held up half of a small tent awning, the kind that went over display tables, a back support pole in each hand. Nico and Tucker carried the front poles. And under the cover of the awning, protected from the sprinklers, walked Angel.

Angel's glowing, golden wings spread to the sides of the awning and rose as tall as Mikey's head. In the comic book, Angel's wings were made of light, so this cosplayer had created long sheets of thin plexiglass that looked like giant feathers and illuminated them.

I'd looked up a picture from the comic books while we waited and indeed that Angel was very blond and white and a smidge taller than the dark-haired, also white Laura Kinney. Our Angel was short and round with dark brown skin and the same earnest, good-natured look on their face as comic-book Angel.

At their side, holding their hand, walked a slender, dark-haired girl almost as tall as me. She looked pissed off enough to be the new Wolverine. She had that rope-thin, tense, defensive, curve-shouldered look that I remember from my first few years being out, especially when I still had to present as a guy sometimes.

Mikey and our friends put the awning down as the group entered the not-raining-indoors atrium. Behind them came more pairs of people in elaborate costumes and three wet, angry people who must've been the judges.

"What parts of the convention center aren't soaked?" I asked Nico, who also was soaked at that point.

"Only the south wing had the alarm. The center expo area and the north wing should be okay."

"That expo area is huge," Mikey said. "I saw it during the hockey expo. There's got to be space there."

We rallied our wedding party and headed outside. A straggling line of formally dressed people hugged the side of the building, trying to keep out of the rain. We came back inside through the grand entrance: a triple set of double doors.

Vast, high-ceilinged hallways stretched to the right and left, the alarm ringing down the left one. In front of us, a massive archway opened to a cavernous room filled with booths. Above the archway to the expo area hung a banner decorated with plant stalks and the words: *Welcome Minnesota Crop Production Retailers!*

I stopped, creating a traffic jam in the foyer.

"Holy wow," Claire remarked. "That's so not our demographic."

"You don't know that," my dad said. "South Dakota second cousins are all farmers. They demanded a video of this wedding."

Dad moved around me and approached the young men standing on either side of the archway with brochures. I followed, as did Claire and the others.

"Hoping you can help me out," Dad said. "My daughter's getting married today, to this beautiful girl, and we got rained out. You must have some space in here where we could hold a wedding, don't you?"

One of the guys winced, but the other nodded, gazing back along our formal, bedraggled group.

"You want the GeoDiscovery display. Head that way, you can't miss it."

Dubious, I followed Dad. We walked past two lines of smaller booths. Abruptly the room opened up and a field stretched away from us. It was bigger than the first floor of our house: starting with rows of tiny plastic plants just pushing through the soil, then knee-high, waist-high, shoulder-high.

Dad went to talk to the people standing under the GeoDiscovery sign.

I turned to Claire, "Do you want to get married in a fake cornfield inside a convention center?"

"I want to get married," she said. "And that fake corn is kind of pretty. Plus we have elves. They're going to make the fake corn thing work, I'm sure."

"We could slo-mo run through the plants toward each other."

"You don't think that's too corny?" she said with a smirk. I groaned at her.

Dad came back. "Next demo is in five minutes and it's the last of the day. They say we can have it as long as we want after that. Also they're wondering if it's okay if they stay for the wedding."

"Really?"

"Yeah, Jim over there's got a gay son, wants to see how it's done in case he gets a chance to stand up in his kid's wedding some day."

"Oh totally." I waved at the grinning guy who had to be Jim and he waved back.

Nico pushed to the front of our mass of guests and said, "Hey, the contest is wrapping up in a few minutes. Angel's texting me. Wants to know if they can come, and Laura, and a bunch of other people from the contest."

"We have a lot of space," Claire said. "And I'll never turn down costumes at my wedding. Did they place?"

"Second," Nico told her, beaming. "Five hundred bucks and, more importantly, the chance to tell the naysayers to get lost."

While the GeoDiscovery people ran their presentation in the field, most of our wedding party went into the booths to find extra chairs. They got enough for everyone who wanted to sit and a bit of surplus.

The minister picked a spot and worked out where Claire and I should each walk in from. There hadn't been a space in the Atrium for us to walk from and I liked this change. I wanted to get to walk down the aisle.

I thought that was going to be the best perk to moving the wedding, but it wasn't. When Angel and Laura and two dozen other people in costumes and a few who probably weren't in costume all showed up, they brought a familiar face with them.

"Aunt Debbie!" Claire yelped and ran to hug her.

"I got back in time!" Debbie announced. "But you weren't in the chapel, so I guess God sent us an angel to bring me to you. Am I too late to walk you down the aisle?"

"Perfectly on time," Claire told her.

Claire's Aunt Debbie walked her in and then my dad walked me in and already everybody was crying.

I only wanted to look at Claire in her intricate dress, her face shining up at me, but she tugged on my hand and made me take a half turn and gaze across the brilliantly lit corn field.

Amid the little green plants, and the knee-high ones, were superheroes, elves, more than one real-life angel, my family, Claire's and my chosen family, and her aunt. Behind them, a bunch of people had wandered up, many in ball caps, a few in overalls, some of them already wiping their eyes and trying to hide it.

"Beloved friends, we are gathered here today to celebrate love…" the minister began and I turned back to Claire.

AUTHOR'S NOTE

I've been wanting to revisit *Being Emily* for a few years now. Already when it was published in 2012, language in and around the trans community was changing at a rapid pace. In 2013, the DSM-5 changed the diagnosis many transgender people required for medical transition from "gender identity disorder" to "gender dysphoria." At the same time, the media was exploding with stories about trans people (though much too often not *by* trans people).

Being Emily is set in 2008 and this hasn't changed. But I decided, since this is fiction, that I can be somewhat anachronistic. In this new edition, you'll find language much closer to what's being used in 2017-18. In addition, the story references scientific studies done after 2008. The setting and pop culture references are still very much 2008-9.

I found in this edit and partial rewrite that I'd tried some things in the initial version that didn't work. Now I know how to do them better. This is the reason for the major changes to Claire's chapters later in the book.

Editing *Being Emily* has also been a personal revelation. Writing and stories are how I get the world to make sense to me—how I interpret my life and the actions of other people for myself. That has a lot of upsides, but the downside is that often I don't fully know how I feel about something until after I've written one or more books about it.

When I first drafted this novel, in late 2004, I told myself it was the product of having a very good imagination and spending a lot of time in the community of trans women. It was easy for me to identify as a cisgender woman ally when *Being Emily* was first published. I'd identified that way on and off for years because I thought the only choices I had as an assigned-female-at-birth person were to be a cis woman or trans man. Given those two, I'm closer to cis woman.

And I am a woman some of the time, just not all the time. Going back through *Being Emily*, I saw the places where I'd described gender dysphoria from my own experience of it. While we haven't had the same experiences, Emily and I are more alike than we are different.

I began writing about trans girls in part because during my twenties and thirties their experience was the closest I saw to my own. I hadn't found people just like me, but when I met Kate Bornstein, Debbie Davis, Rachel Pollack, and others, I was able to be more comfortable in my skin. They made a place for me in the world.

In her intro, Stephanie Burt says, "…we are inside a novel made so that trans girls can see ourselves." I knew how much trans girls needed to see themselves because I also needed to see myself.

I came out very young as a lesbian, starting when I was thirteen in the mid 1980s. By age sixteen, I was out in suburban Ohio, even though I did not know a single other lesbian. But I knew they existed. I knew I would find them.

At the same time, I was role-playing characters who blended male and female, or were aliens who shapeshifted (including changing sex), or were nongendered space dragons who could turn into humans. But I had no words to talk about my gender outside of these imagined worlds or outside of historical references—brief mentions of Native American two-spirit people and genderless beings in ancient Sumer that I've spent thirty years chasing down in academic literature.

I didn't know if there was a community of people who experienced gender the way I did, or what they might call themselves or how to find them. I didn't make a conscious choice, but because of where I grew up and how, it was safer and more effective for me to come out as lesbian. And once I did, I mostly stopped thinking about my gender. I just folded it into lesbian because that identity, to me, included gender diversity.

I'd been bullied a lot as a kid so finding a community that wanted me, welcomed me, and took care of me was lifesaving. Thank you, lesbians and bi women! (And, huge bonus, this community included all the people I wanted to date and still includes most of my favorite people.)

Turns out some of the bullying stemmed from me not doing social cues "right," including not performing "girl" properly. When I was seven, my family lived in Germany for a year. I came back, for third grade, to the same school and social group I'd been with in first grade. But everything had changed. Before I'd left, it seemed to me we were all kids playing together. Somehow, during the year I'd been gone, my friends had become boys and girls.

I didn't understand why these people I used to know so well were behaving so strangely and why they'd turned against me. Before going to Germany, I was a kid. In Germany, I was "the American." Now I was supposed to be a girl. But I didn't understand what that meant for me. No one had given me a copy of the girl handbook and the few pages I could figure out didn't really fit me.

I didn't feel like a girl or a boy:

- I hated dolls and loved blocks and stuffed animals.
- I loved nail polish and had no interest in trucks and cars.
- I loved Star Wars action figures and battles with friends, especially when we fought physically against each other.

- I hated playing house and instead played "college students" with my best friend.
- I loved numbers and analytical games and dragons and unicorns.
- I loved stories and words and letters more than just about anything.
- I did not love riding horses, but I loved a girl who did, so I learned to like it.
- I loved girls and women, even though I was told I wasn't supposed to.
- I loved superheroes and comic books and role-playing games.
- I loved God and each year that love is greater and more vast and I was always clear that God loved me.

What gender is that?

I'm still working on a succinct answer and suspect there may not be one. But these days I often say (and like): genderqueer, genderfluid, nonbinary lesbian and (thanks to my brother for this one) gender malleable. I like all the pronouns, but most commonly use she/her and they/them. Thanks to these words, I'm finding other people like me and there are a lot of us!

We're still crafting the public spaces and lenses required to see people in the full spectrum of gender diversity. I'm excited to see the stories that continue this work and I intend to write more of them.

I hope to see you there.

Rachel Gold
Minneapolis, MN
2018